Tell

HarperCollins Publishers Ltd

Tell

A Novel

FRANCES ITANI

Published by HarperCollins Publishers Ltd

First published by HarperCollins Publishers Ltd in a hardcover edition: 2014
This trade paperback edition: 2014

HarperCollins books may be purchased for educational, business,
or sales promotional use through our Special Markets Department.

HarperCollins Publishers Ltd
2 Bloor Street East, 20th Floor
Toronto, Ontario, Canada
M4W 1A8

www.harpercollins.ca

Library and Archives Canada Cataloguing in Publication
information is available upon request

ISBN 978-1-44344-244-2

Printed and bound in the United States of America
RRD 9 8 7 6 5 4 3 2 1

For Aileen Itani, Soprano,

and for my aunts Jean Stratton and Carrie Oliver,
and my uncle, Harvey Stoliker,

whose stories I've listened to all my life

*But isn't that why
we fall in love anyway, to be able to say the secret,
dangerous words that are in our heads? To name
each other with them in the dark?*
—FROM ANTHEM, BY HELEN HUMPHREYS

Tell

Toronto: November 1, 1920

Zel glances around the room: oak floor, oak desk, wooden cabinet, two windows that look down over city streets three storeys below. Shelves behind the desk are stuffed with black binders. These, she suspects, are guarding secrets stored for generations.

She is in this room with three other women, a man and a baby. The baby, six weeks old, sleeps while nestled against her mother's arm. Papers are arranged neatly before a woman who wears a tailored jacket over a grey dress. Zel sees compassion on her face; she senses it from her manner and her voice. A brooch in the shape of a miniature sleigh, with silver slats and curved gold runners, is pinned to the woman's jacket. A tiny gold chain droops from the crossbar to represent a rope attached to the front of the sleigh. It's as if the woman, who has introduced herself as Mrs. Davis, has a playful side, though not here, not as the official who will ensure that the documents on her desk are duly signed. In other circumstances, Zel would ask Mrs. Davis about the brooch, its origins, its maker.

A low rumble from the street railway outside seems far off, though sounds are muffled because the windows in the room are sealed. Tracks are being laid on nearby city streets, and in some areas it is difficult to cross from one side to the other. After a rain, the roads here must be a morass of mud, Zel thinks, and she looks down at her boots as if she will have to shake them later, dust them off. Earlier, from inside the cage of the ascending elevator, she glimpsed, as she passed the second floor, rows of women at sewing machines, whirring spools, strewn garments spread over long tables in a large, open room. She had already noticed the sign outside advertising LADIES' WHOLESALE LINENS, and her fingers itched to manipulate folds of material on her own work table at home. There had been no advertisement for the office used by adoption officials, only a number beside the door at street level, which matches the number of the room where everyone is now tensed, waiting for the proceedings to end.

The woman who holds the sleeping baby is thin, green-eyed, taut with nerves. Her arms have begun to tremble and she rearranges the baby's knitted blanket in an attempt to disguise the shaking left hand she can barely control as she leans forward to sign. Zel moves quickly to stand behind, to place her hands on the woman's shoulders. To help her through this moment, this day. The baby stretches. A small fist is raised to her plump cheek; there is a tiny indent like a star in her fist. She does not wake.

The young couple rise together and now, as parents, receive the baby. They cannot hide their joy, their happiness at leaving with this new and precious daughter. Each of them embraces the woman who has given up her child. The two do not linger; they are first to exit the room. The baby, still sleeping, has shown no sign that her life has been set, this very moment, on a new path.

Zel watches the young man tilt his cap over his forehead as he steps through the doorway, shadowing his face before he returns to street level. There are many such men on the streets below, now that everyone is back from the war.

The three women who remain sit in silence, their thoughts perhaps stretching back to earlier moments in each of their lives. A noon whistle pierces the air from somewhere inside the building. Footsteps can be heard in the sewing room on the second floor. Feet clatter down the stairs to the street below as workers take their midday break. Mrs. Davis pushes back her chair and rises to her feet. She nods to Zel and then extends her hand to the mother, who has already begun to feel the physical absence of her child as if it were a spectre that has insistently returned to fill out its former shape.

"You have a long journey ahead," says Mrs. Davis, "if you're to travel across the lake to Oswego today." She adds, as if she has said this too many times to too many women, "Try not to look back. It will be easier if you don't. Put your efforts into moving your life forward." She goes to the window and looks down. The sleigh's golden chain sways slightly with her movement. "Somehow," Mrs. Davis says, as if the words have been cut from the cloth of her own experience, "somehow, we manage to survive."

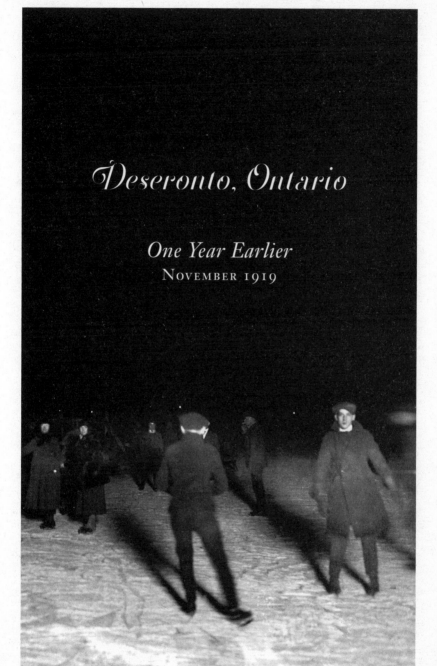

Deseronto, Ontario

One Year Earlier
NOVEMBER 1919

DESERONTO POST, November 1919

Local Items

The wind came howling down Main Street near midnight last night. Those who rose from their beds were rewarded with the spectacle of rain rolling along the road like a grand carpet unfurling. While looking out over the tempest, one could not help but think that a winter freeze would be a welcome sight.

We have received news at this office that plans are afoot to set up a scholarship to commemorate students of Deseronto High School and other young men of the vicinity who took part in the "World's Great Struggle" just brought to a close, and especially those who made the SUPREME SACRIFICE in said war. Further details are to be announced about a War Memorial Fund, also to be set up by the high school.

They did "their" bit for you. You do "your" bit for them.

Late stragglers: On the morning before the heavy rains, several of our citizens saw a small flock of wild geese flying in front of an airplane. The birds appeared to be frightened as they headed south, but they were keeping ahead of the machine.

A horse belonging to one gentleman by the name of O'Neill made a lively runaway up Mill Street Tuesday afternoon.

Windsor Salt is on sale in the local stores. Purest and best for table and dairy. No adulteration. Never cakes.

Chapter One

THERE WAS NO ESCAPING THE WIND. GUSTS blew in off the bay, gusts beat against shirts and trousers and linens pegged to the clothesline. Air pockets were trapped; sheets snapped out furiously. From inside the closed veranda at the rear of the house, Kenan Oak could not shut out the sound.

He closed the outdated newspaper he'd been reading and made an effort to align its edges. Once he'd folded it along the creases, he placed it on top of a neat and growing stack beside his chair. He had read about but had not attended the fall reception in town, nor had he attended the sports dinner or the grand ball—all of which had been held, as editor Calhoun, of the *Post*, had reported, "to thank Deseronto's red-blooded manhood for its sacrifices, its heroism and its gallantry on the far-flung battlefield."

The town had waited until late in the year for the big celebration. "DECORATE! DECORATE!" Calhoun had urged the town.

"Decorate your lawns, decorate your homes, decorate your places of business, decorate your streets, decorate your autos—but decorate."

And people had responded, at least from what Kenan could see from his parlour window. Yes, the town had decorated, and waited until everyone was home—those who were alive to come home. The nearby city of Belleville had sent a brass band for daytime events and an orchestra for evening. Kenan, who had lived in Deseronto all his life, felt far-flung indeed, having brought the battlefield home with him. Or so Tress, losing patience one day, had accused. Kenan had come back as a "walking wounded," but he had not walked out of the house since the day he'd returned and set foot in it.

Wind hurled itself at the outer walls. The veranda windows rattled and this caused him to stand suddenly, as if he'd been yanked from his chair. He turned his back to the bay and saw a small black spider disappear behind a calendar on the side wall. He ignored the spider and told himself to escape, leave the veranda, walk through the rooms of the house.

Stay calm, he commanded himself. Stay calm.

He closed his good eye, the right, and kept it closed. He imagined himself threading a route through darkness, the way a blind man might. Did a blind man move forward because of faith in the unseen? Faith had not helped the men at the Front when poisonous gas drifted across no man's land, dropped into the trenches, made its way between walls of dirt and clay as it sought its victims. Those men had been blinded, skin bubbling around their eyes, their lungs frothing as they choked and gasped for air. Kenan had witnessed such a group who had been brought back behind the lines. He'd rushed to help, just before the men were led away to a dressing station for evacuation—those who could walk. Others were lying on the ground. The walking soldiers, a dozen or more, had been formed up in a line. Each had a hand on the shoulder of the man in front; each had a field dressing covering his eyes, blistered skin showing on his hands and around the edges of his bandages. The soldier who led this piteous parade of afflicted men was unaffected by the gas; he'd been ordered to lead the others out. And then, just before they began to move, they tilted their heads down, all at the same time, as if each blind man had chosen that moment to stare into the same angle of darkness. Some still wore their helmets from up the line; others were bare-headed. None would be back for more fighting. The man at the front of the line suddenly shouted out and began to walk slowly, allowing his retinue to shuffle and stumble behind. From a nearby field hospital, the wounded soldiers would be sent on to Blighty and, much later, home.

Kenan, a witness to this, had the use of both eyes at the time. A few months later, he, too, became one of the wounded, but not from poison gas. His left arm was useless and bloodied; a field dressing covered the entire left side of his face. He'd been lifted onto a stretcher. His right eye had stared into a sky of protective, merciful darkness while the stretcher bearers cursed and bumped along, carrying him away from the battlefield in the night. Thunderous noises, whistling and sobbing, accompanied him as he was moved farther back from where he'd first stumbled into a trench, his hand holding the pieces of his face together.

He was in the parlour now, the soles of his shoes pacing a

thin carpet Tress had laid over the floor. He took no step for granted; each was slow and considered. Feet could be swallowed by bottomless holes. Had he not watched men his own age swallowed by sinkholes? He had. He carried on, reached out with right hand, right arm. He felt for familiar objects as he began to trace a known sequence through his narrow house.

He did this only when Tress was out, only when he was certain that she would be away for hours, working in the dining room of her parents' hotel at the other end of Main Street. If she were to witness the treks he made through the house with his good eye closed, she would think he was crazed by war. No, that was unfair. Tress wanted to bring him back from the darkness that held him down. She had not given up, nor was she likely to. Or so he told himself.

Now his fingertips brushed chairback, tabletop, circle of doily that slid under his hand. Upper edge of fire screen, pewter candlestick and curve of curly-birch chair. The knowledge of wine-coloured upholstery registered behind his closed eye. At the doorjamb, he dipped his knees and searched below waist level for a familiar indent. His fingers explored this smooth depression during every walk, as if acknowledging that a creature with a single tooth had dwelled here long ago. A creature who had stopped to take a bite from the wooden frame before ambling past.

He circled the kitchen, registered the aroma of bread rising in the dough box, soft butter on the countertop, an overripe apple. He smelled coal dust in the scuttle, lifted his foot over a slight ridge as he left the kitchen, never a step missed.

Kenan had lost the vision in his left eye when he'd been sent out on a trench raid for a second time. The locations blurred. The German dugouts were deep, he remembered his surprise at that. But going out two nights in a row, he'd been tempting fate. Or rather, the officer who sent him had. The night Kenan was wounded, shells had burst around him without warning, scattering shrapnel. One side of his body had been hit. As a consequence, the left side of his face was now sealed in rippled scars. He seldom looked in a mirror, knowing the damage without having to stare it down. His good side was the right side. His legs were fine. He had a good arm and a good hand. The war had left him with one seeing eye and one ear to hear. He'd escaped total blindness. Sometimes he thought of the lineup of gassed men and wondered why one of his own eyes had been spared, the events of the carnage having been so random, so finite. There was no explaining who walked away, who returned home, who vanished into a landscape of mud roiling with bodies, dead and alive.

He carried on, moved silently from room to room—expert at the silent part—continuing to honour the blind man's pact with himself. He kept the good eye closed. The hand of his dead arm was tucked into his trouser pocket to prevent the arm from banging into door frames or knocking over the remaining vase of a former pair—the same arm had destroyed the other— or to keep it from swinging into Tress. All of these mishaps had occurred more than a year ago, when Kenan had first come home. He did not go out into the town, because it was safer to stay indoors. That was his reasoning. He was safe when he did not have to make the decision to leave. In his home, he was not subject to interference. He did not have to look at people, and no one had to look at him. Family members came, and he tolerated their brief visits. Dr. Clark visited from time to time, and he, too, was tolerated. Kenan had not left the house since the day he arrived home, the final day that marked the end of *his* war, during the winter of 1918.

He finished his exploration of the ground floor. Unable to escape the continuous billowing and snapping of the wind, he decided to include the upper level in today's wanderings. He extended his right hand, touched the banister and allowed it to direct him up the stairs. On the landing, he took four sure steps to the left and entered the main bedroom. He ran his fingers along the metal bed frame and the solid mattress upon which, night after night, he and Tress slept. The place where he was certain of her warmth soaking into him. Where their love, their lovemaking—that, too, altered by war—had become resolute, intense. His intensity, perhaps. Or hers—possibly the other way round.

In the early months when he'd first come home, Tress had tucked into his good side at night, laughed and talked softly, evenly, pulling from the air, or so it seemed, the continued threads of story, sometimes their own.

Two children grew up in the same town, in houses on adjacent streets. They liked to run and play, lickety-split, along the boardwalk and in the schoolyard and on the paths around town. The boy did handstands in the schoolyard, so good was he at balancing. Occasionally, he was invited to the girl's house for Sunday supper. The meal wasn't actually served in her house; family meals were taken in the dining room of a hotel next to her house—the hotel owned by her father. When roast beef was served, the boy was asked if he would like the outside piece and he always said, "Yes, please," because the crispy part was his favourite. So the girl's father carved the roast and said, "Pass your plate along, young man."

More recently, Tress had become less talkative, settling, he thought, into some sort of grim resolve. She wanted a child. There was no child. She was trying to accept what Kenan had become. And what was that? She was adjusting to what she had become in response.

Barren, Kenan thought suddenly. We're barren, the two of us.

The word startled him. He had seen barren. Charred landscapes where nothing would grow. Trees without leaves, branches without birds. Razed earth that supported no life. Villages without people. Oh, yes, he had seen barren. He had known it intimately.

And Tress's behaviour had become confusing. Only a few nights earlier, they had made love, and afterward, instead of moving close against him, Tress had turned away and had begun to weep uncontrollably, sobbing for several minutes. Nothing he did or said would comfort her. When the weeping ceased, it was only to resume a few moments later, hiccups of sorrow escaping into the room. They'd both fallen asleep from exhaustion.

Barren, he thought again. There was no explaining why a child had not been conceived. He pushed the word aside. What of it? War changed everything. Including what went on in the bedroom.

He crossed the upstairs hall and walked into the room opposite their own. Empty, except for a made-up bed, an extra blanket folded against the foot rail. Back to the hall again, he reached for a door between the two bedrooms and stepped into a closet that had been lined with shelves below the peak of the house. His fingers traced towels, wool blankets—every inch of space used efficiently beneath the ceiling that sloped on both sides. On the floor beneath the shelves, a few cedar branches warded off moths. He pulled the door shut and stood inside the cramped space. He did not have to open his good eye to sense darkness. His hand began to shape words in the silent language he had learned from Tress's younger sister, who had been deaf since she was five. Grania had helped him to recover the language inside himself, the language of words he had not been able to utter after he had come home. He had heard people well enough. With his good ear he'd understood what they said. But his own words had stormed and tangled inside his head. He hadn't been able to separate them into patterns. In some strange way not fully understood, he'd had to relearn the language he already knew. The bridge between, while he was stuttering his way back to speech, was Grania's sign language. She had taught him signs he could make with his good hand, words he could spell, rhymes for his voice. He missed Grania. The entire family missed her. But she had moved away a few months after her own husband returned from the war.

Here in the dark closet, Kenan had not escaped the snapping sheets below, the invasion of blunt thuds. Tentacles of sound criss-crossed like maniacal weaving through his brain. His right hand made half the sign for "peace," for "quiet," one side of an X arcing down. He pressed his palm over his ear as if to slow a swelling that would not be contained. He left the closet and walked down the stairs. To keep the blindman's compact, he did not open his good eye until he reached the bottom.

He tried to remember what Tress had said when she left for work that morning. She'd opened the front door, and wind circled its way into the house. She'd called to him over the sound to say she'd be late coming home. Someone had the day off—the name had blown away with the wind. Usually, Tress was home Mondays. She'd done a wash and hung the clothes before she left. He had spent the morning alone, working at the table, completing the work found for him by the GWVA. He had joined the vets' association without leaving his house; the work they'd found for him could be done at home. For that, he was thankful.

The light outside was fading. Kenan returned to the veranda and stood beside the wicker chair. A one-eyed foreman, he inspected his intimate patch of backyard and bay. Shadows cast from the house next door transformed the clothesline tangles into menacing lumps. He considered the earlier snaps and thuds—benign compared to the way gusts were now battering at the windows of the veranda. He had a sudden flash of memory, an image of himself as a small boy leaving the house where he'd been raised by his uncle Oak. He saw wind puffing up the inside of his jacket. He saw himself trying to press air from his pockets, fastening the top toggle to prevent the jacket being ripped from his back and blown out over the waves. Whipped-up waves that now, almost twenty years later, distorted the surface of the bay.

He began, again, to pace. He walked to the small enclosed vestibule at the front of the house and reached up to the hook that held his new jacket. Tress had purchased the jacket several weeks earlier: a heavy mackinaw, navy blue, hooded and lined with tweed. She'd placed it on the hook and there it had remained, hanging limply, waiting for Kenan to slide the insensate hand and arm down into the pit of the left sleeve.

He wished Tress would return. He was sorry she was working late. He wanted to follow her up the stairs, watch her long, thick hair as she shifted it to one side. He wanted to hear her laugh again. He wanted to lie beside her, feel her skin next to his, listen to her voice as it was absorbed by the room's dim light. He wanted to listen while she spun stories until the two of them drifted off to sleep.

The boy was an orphan who lived with his uncle, a kind but silent sort of man. The boy had dark hair that was thick and curly, and he was a fast runner because he was long-legged. Like his uncle, he, too, was possessed of a kind nature. He and the girl had a favourite hideaway in a fort they created under an abandoned pier beside the bay. The fort was shadowy and damp and smelled of settled ashes from the Great Fire of 1896, but it was their secret place. The girl brought books, and sometimes read aloud. The two invented passwords; they spoke words of longing and belonging. The boy and girl vowed, under the old pier, that someday they would marry.

In winter, they skated, though the boy always had holes in the thumbs of his mittens. In summer, they walked beside the bay. Sometimes, the boy had candies in his pocket, a striped kind he liked. The candies were sticky with lint, so the girl said, "No, thank you," when she was offered one.

One afternoon—these two were much older then—they were walking in the woods at the edge of town and the young man's arm reached around the young woman's shoulder. They continued on like this for a while, but then his hand slid lower and brushed against her breast. Perhaps by accident, perhaps on purpose. Neither of them dared to breathe. Neither mentioned what had happened, but both knew that something had changed. When this happened again, the young man began to unbutton the top of the young woman's dress and slid his hand in behind those buttons.

And Tress would shake with laughter, teasing, and Kenan would reach with his good hand, this time for his wife.

But there hadn't been much laughter, he reminded himself. Not for a while.

He heard loud steps and was instantly aware of the boardwalk on the other side of the door, only a few feet away. He had not turned on a lamp. As he backed into the parlour, two or three lights came on in the town and cast a glow over the dusty street. Most business establishments lay to the west of his house. Thirty feet to the east, Main Street ended at the place where the boardwalk stopped. Kenan's heart raced as he thought of town and bay and wind. Bars of yellow light swung crazily across the stirred-up dirt. Lampposts swayed and tottered on both sides of the street.

For the second time, he walked to the vestibule and reached for his jacket, but once again he left it on its hook. He paced through the house and retreated to the back veranda. He imagined the cold beyond the door. Winter was moving in early. He stared into a sullen sky that had begun to lower itself over the shadows of the bay.

KENAN HAD NEVER SEEN THE INSIDE OF THIS HOUSE BEFORE departing for the war in 1914, though as a boy and a younger man, he'd walked past it often enough. Tress had returned to live in her parents' house beside the hotel while he was overseas. But the week she received the telegram from the War Office, she rented this narrow house on the bay from Jack Conlin, the postmaster. Not long after that, she moved in, readied the place with help from her sister, and waited. That was weeks before Kenan arrived home. He was able to walk in, his two legs holding him up, injured but alive. He'd had a lengthy stay in a hospital in England while recovering from the damage to his face and the wounds to his arm and hand. When he was finally sent home, the war, and all its killing, was still under way. Tress had met him at the station in the nearby city of Belleville and they'd travelled together to Deseronto. It was a harsh winter day when he first stepped through the front door. The wind had driven a ridge of snow along the bottom of the storm door and he'd had to clear the snow away with the side of his boot before he and Tress could enter. He'd removed his boots in the vestibule and walked into the parlour of what was to be their home. When he'd taken his first look at the unfamiliar rooms, he'd been ambushed by a sudden unravelling of memory.

Gates and doorways of countless billets in France had risen before him. Every French village he'd entered was swarming

with troops, water carts, guns, horses, wagons, autos. Debris
was piled high in the streets and along sunken roads; the ground
never stopped shaking. So many dwellings were taken over,
dwellings where soldiers slept like tinned smelt on rubber sheets
laid out over salvaged boards, or on sandbags layered together,
or on kitchen floors that were nothing more than hard-packed
earth. The men were used to sleeping as close to the source
of heat as they could manoeuvre their bodies. In winter, they
tried to grab a place nearest the stove or fireplace, and slept
under their overcoats in an arc-like formation around the heat.
He thought of his friend Hugh, whom he'd met on the ship
when they'd first set out after joining up. Somehow, they'd been
assigned to the same outfit while in England, and they ended up
in the same boxcar playing poker as they headed, weeks later,
to the Front. He had heard not a word from his friend since
returning to Canada. Hugh, who'd grown up in Prince Edward
Island on the East Coast, might be alive or dead, equal chances.
During the years they'd been overseas together, Hugh had a
peculiar way of sleeping: face down, palms on the floor below
shoulder level—on wood or stone, on earth or hay—as if making ready to pry himself up in his sleep.

Sometimes, Kenan and Hugh and the others in their unit
were ordered to take cover in the ruins of shelled buildings.
They waited in damaged attics or in dank enclosures, bodies
pressed against one another in cellars that lay beneath suffocat-
ing rubble. Kenan had found a corpse bent in jackknife position
in one of those cellars, the corpse of an elderly man who had
perhaps lived in the building and refused to leave. Or maybe the
inhabitants of the village had forgotten the old man when they'd

been evacuated. He might have starved to death; the family might have been killed. Perhaps no one had come looking. The stench had made it difficult to go down into the cellar, but men were to be billeted in that place, so Kenan descended and then went outside to dig a grave behind one of the outbuildings. It was winter. The roads were half-frozen; the earth was cold and hard; there wasn't enough time; he needed rest. Hugh came out to help and together they dragged the body away. They threw a covering of straw over the man and returned to the house and took turns shifting beside the woodstove in a half-collapsed room, always edging toward the source of heat.

In summer and fall when the air was warm, Kenan had preferred to sleep outside. Against orders, he'd frequently abandoned his billet—a hayloft above a shed, a row of cots in the dormitory of an abandoned convent, a classroom in a school with shattered windows, a destroyed factory. He felt safer under open sky but understood the contradiction, knowing that he was more exposed. Inside or out, he knew that safety was no more than an idea in his head. The building where the men slept could receive a direct hit and they'd all be killed anyway.

And now, in his Deseronto house, every inch of which he'd explored with his good eye open and his good eye closed, he wondered if he had invented the memories of more than three and a half years of war. Memories of staring up into night skies, expecting the stars to explode. Waking up with dew dampening his uniform, puttees tightening around his lower legs. Standing in wisps of fog that rolled low along the ground in the mornings, so that in every direction, only heads and torsos could be seen above the mist, while legless men called back and forth to one another as they shaved and laughed and groused and swore, and prepared to fill their mess tins for breakfast.

He might have invented those memories, but he had not invented the war. The newspapers Tress brought home from her father's hotel had been emphatically real, emphatically clear about the Armistice and its aftermath. Half a year after November 1918, the Treaty of Versailles had been signed. These days, the papers had less and less to say about the conflagration. People wanted to move on, and who could blame them? Earlier in the week, the past Tuesday morning, the nation had been asked to devote two whole minutes—as Calhoun had written in the *Post*—"to concentrated thought in reverence to the dead, and in appreciation of the sacrifices of the living." Tress's uncle Am had connected the bell in the clock tower over the post office on that single occasion, and at the end of the two-minute silence, eleven strikes against the bell had clanged out over the town. From behind a curtain in his living room, Kenan had seen a few people on the street pause to bow their heads, but after that they kept on with what they were doing. The bell had been disconnected again, the show of observance over.

And now, would everyone forget? Surely not. Surely the men who marched through Kenan's head by hundreds, hundreds of thousands, had not marched into oblivion, erased from collective memory.

How was he to know anything about the world as it was now, when he, himself, had dropped off its edge? Perhaps others like him had made similar choices. Reading the obituaries in a fall paper, he'd noticed the name of a Belleville soldier called Frank, whom he'd chanced to bunk beside on the hospital ship on the way home from England. The man had been gassed and was being sent home. He was a talker, and didn't mind Kenan's silence. When their ship docked, a band on the pier below was playing "The Boys Who Fight for Freedom," over and over, as if the musicians had learned only that one tune. The two men had been in different coaches on the train west to Ontario, but Frank had come to find him when they reached Belleville. He had shaken Kenan's good hand and said goodbye. He planned to go back to work for the railroad, he said. Before the war, he'd had a good job working at the Belleville coal chutes and he knew he'd be given his job back, no questions asked. But he hadn't lasted much more than a year, according to the date of the obituary. The coal dust had killed him and no wonder, given the damage already in his lungs. "The lungs of our boys who were gassed have turned into a spongy, decaying mess. We have to do something to help." That was what one Toronto paper reported. The sentiment had come too late to help Frank.

Kenan thought of Hugh again and wondered if his wartime friend was at this moment looking out over some segment of field or road or sea on the East Coast. He wished Hugh were here beside him. They'd shared a few laughs; they'd helped and relied on each other. Was it too much to believe that they might be able to laugh again? Hugh had always greeted Kenan by saying, "Hello, old stuff." Making fun of the Imperials.

Kenan hoped Hugh was alive. Hoped that unlike himself, his friend still had the use of both eyes. He wondered how to go about locating him. Wary of looking to the future in the midst of war, they'd never exchanged addresses. Friendship could take a turn over there and be snapped apart as soon as it had begun.

All of this was tiring to think about. Kenan looked through the windows of the back veranda again. The clothes on the line were so twisted in the shadows, their individual shapes were unrecognizable. He hated disorder. As if to punctuate his thoughts, a blast of wind shook the windowpanes. He retreated, and once more made his way across the house.

This time, he lifted the new jacket off its hook and pressed it to his chest. His right hand explored the inner lining while he estimated the warmth and weight of it. The jacket smelled of newness, though it had been hanging there for several weeks. Using his right arm to hold it in position, he slid his dead arm down into the left sleeve, the way he'd been taught by the nursing sisters in the English hospital. With that done, he pushed his right arm into place. He buttoned with one hand and pulled the toggles over a double strip of cloth that hid the buttons down the front. He reached back and pulled the hood up over his head. The hood was coarse and new to his fingertips, the weight of cloth evenly distributed over his shoulders. The jacket could not have been a better fit. He tugged at the hood in such a way that only half his face could be seen through the opening. The dead eye was covered.

He walked through the house again, but this time, for the first time, he opened the side door and stepped out. His heartbeat was erratic. He placed a foot on the outdoor step and understood that his exit had been rehearsed a thousand thousand times. He left the door unlocked behind him.

He thought he should stand on the stoop at the back and wheel in the line, one-handed, so that he could make an attempt at untangling the clothes. But he did not want to risk being

seen. Someone might look out an upper window of a neighbouring house, get a glimpse of the man who stayed inside, the
man crazed by war. Was that what the town thought of him? *He*
went a bit strange. He was a bit funny in the head after he came home.
Poor Tress, who has to put up with him.

He made his way toward the street, veered right and walked
away. The town map opened in his mind. Leaves scuttered at his
feet. He had once loved the sound; now it surprised and startled
him. At the end of the boardwalk, he stepped down into hardened ruts in the road. He kept his head lowered. He knew he
could turn back at any moment. He began to take long strides,
making up for the many months of short, repetitive steps in the
house. The worn path was there at the eastern edge of town,
just as he knew it would be. He followed the path, kept close to
the bay, wide of the old gasworks, sharply away from a rotting,
unused pier. There was no one around. Not in this wind.

He had not been seen.

Relief attached itself to the old danger. Relief and danger,
these were familiar edges he knew how to move between. He
sucked in air stirred by the wind to which he'd listened all day.
His lungs filled with cold. He registered the mix of scents: weeds
at the edge of the bay; still, deep water; brittle and fallen leaves;
damp and hardening earth. Portents of winter. Scents of such
pleasure, they knocked him back in surprise.

He was afraid that he would break down in some threatening way. Or that he might turn back. Everything was new-old,
in the way a person might stand in an open doorway at the turn
of season and raise his head and breathe deeply, knowing that in
this familiar place, change had come.

Because he was walking, Kenan instinctively allowed his good eye to close. He stumbled, recovered and swore to himself. This was not the meandering of a half-blind man through the rooms of his own house.

Cues entered his good eye and slid into body memory—a branch, a tree, a shape. The path dwindled. He'd come far enough to be out of the way of ordinary business conducted by the town. The path ended in a tangle of weeds at the edge of a wide inlet that slipped in from the bay. Kenan knew every rock, root and shrub. The small boy in him pushed on, deciding which way to turn. For an instant, he tried to understand where the boy and man had met and merged, but the thought was quickly gone. He circled the inlet and joined a second path, his body at one with the tilt and roll of the earth. He was no longer concerned that he might trip and go down. He entered the woods, which were heavy with dusk, and stayed in the shadow of thinning trees as long as he could. A gust of wind swayed the branches. He heard the sound of many small sticks tapping together. Light had drained from the sky.

When he saw that he would be forced to divert up a rise toward the road that led back to town, he took the opposite fork and kept the lights of town behind him. He left the bay and continued to walk until he neared the outbuildings of a farm. He did not want to be seen; he needed to be alone. He approached an abandoned barn that had a perilous tilt. The roof sagged in the middle like an old swayback. He found a place where he could squeeze between loose boards, and ducked into a half-upright room. The space was dark. It smelled of old manure, of dust, of stored apples and packed earth and sweet, rotting hay.

He was cold, safe, out of the wind. He stayed there with no sense of time passing. He looked toward the outline of the owner's farmhouse not far off. Someone lit a lamp while he was watching and he saw movement across a lower window, probably the kitchen. A woman. He tried to remember who had moved into this place after he'd left for the war. Someone who was a friend of Tress's aunt Maggie. He couldn't think of the woman's name at first. Tress had spoken about her. Something with a Z. Zeta or Zelda, something like that. Zel, an unusual name. Yes, that was it. He could hear Tress's voice.

Zel was a widow who moved here from the next county after her husband died. She started up a rooming house beyond the town's edge.

The lamp moved past the window again, and a flicker of memory reminded him of a time and place when it had not been safe to show a light. The widow's house was newly wired for electricity—he could see the wires—but clearly, lamps were used as well. There were occasional blackouts in his own house, and he and Tress kept a supply of candles and a few kerosene lamps. No one got rid of their lamps.

He tried to recall more of what Tress had said about Zel. Because of his own long silences since coming home, Tress had sometimes fallen into the habit of talking on and on, telling him about people, connecting him back to the daily activities of the town. At times, he heard every nuance of her voice and vividly pictured the scene or person she was describing. At other times, he heard her voice as if it were searching him out from far off, a voice without individual words.

The widow who moved into the place bought the house from a travelling salesman. The salesman never pretended to like farming, and he allowed the barn to fall into disrepair in the span of a few years. He built a smaller detached building beside the house, a workroom of sorts, where he stored his supplies. When the town began to shrink because of industries closing one after another, the salesman moved to Toronto.

From the sagging barn where he now stood, Kenan could see the outline of the separate workroom in the shadows. The house itself appeared to be in good shape. He did recall the man, though they'd never exchanged more than a "Good day" before the war. The man had spent weeks on the road, travelling from town to town, around the time Kenan and Tress married. What Kenan remembered most was the auto. The salesman had bought a Model T a year or two before the war, and Kenan would have given anything to get behind the wheel. He'd been shown by a friend how to drive when he was overseas, training in England. But he never forgot the Model T. The auto, of course, would have left town with the salesman.

According to Tress, Zel began to take in boarders shortly after the salesman moved out and she moved in. She needed the income and wanted the company. Boarders were allowed free use of the kitchen, because Zel provided only breakfast and an occasional Sunday supper. The house wasn't far from the centre of town, but Kenan knew that no woman would walk home through the woods and path the way he had just done. Women would stick to the road, where they'd pass other houses, another farm.

He stood for a long time, his face turned in the direction of the light in Zel's kitchen. A far-off but comforting light. A second light went on in one of the upstairs rooms, probably the room of a boarder. Tress had told him that an elderly couple now lived there, and a new schoolteacher. A handyman from town came out a couple of times a month to chop wood and look after the maintenance of the place. The wood had to be stacked behind the house under a lean-to; it wasn't in the half-rotted building Kenan stood in now. From here he couldn't see what was on the other side of the rooming house at all.

He relaxed, leaned against the boards of the old barn and closed his good eye. His right hand made a sign, a word. A finger to his lips and back to his chest. *Tell*, it seemed to be saying, but the word was directed at himself. It was his private communication: *Tell*.

WHEN HE LEFT THE BARN, HE WAS CAREFUL TO AVOID being seen, even in the dark. He had no trouble retracing his steps down the slope, through the thin woods, along both paths, close to the inlet and the bay, and finally back to the short strip of boardwalk in front of his house. He slipped around to the side door. The bulges were still on the line, which meant that Tress hadn't returned. She would untangle the clothes later, carry them inside. They would be cold and stiff; each would stand upright—another sign of winter—as if a spirit person dwelled inside. Kenan was sometimes spooked by this. He didn't like to be in the kitchen when Tress batted at the half-frozen clothes, laughing aloud when they slumped in front of her while their phantom shapes collapsed.

While Kenan had been out—he had no idea how long—the wind had lowered its edge. He sensed a new quiet when he entered from outside. He slipped into his house, flicked on a light and bolted the door behind him.

Chapter Two

AM HAD BEEN WATCHING. FROM THE CLOCK
tower above the third-floor apartment in the post
office building he had seen first the movement and then the
man. He recognized the figure from the moment young Kenan
rounded the narrow house and placed a foot on the boardwalk.
Am followed his progress, the ease with which he stepped down,
the lack of hesitation when he chose the dirt path. He saw him
stumble and recover, saw him fight the bitter wind. He watched
him disappear beyond the trees on the far side of the inlet, heading east toward the outskirts of town, where there was a low rise
and, after that, a few farms.

Am nodded. The figure was hooded, blurred from this far
off, but the long-legged stride could not be mistaken for anyone
else's. Am had watched the boy grow up in the town alongside
his own nieces and nephews. They'd played together, walked
to school together, built a fort under the old pier, which they
had believed to be their secret. During those early years, Am

had always thought of Kenan as the spindly orphan lad with the curly hair. Raised by the man known as Oak, who owned a welding shop and walked so slowly he might have been wading through water. Everyone addressed him by the single word, *Oak*, as if he possessed no Christian name. The man had adopted the boy as a baby, and assumed responsibility, but he didn't seem to know exactly what to do with him. And yet, he had surprised the town. He'd fed Kenan, kept him clean, sent him to school— he'd raised him.

So. The boy was finally out in the open. First time since he'd come home from the war. Am still thought of him as a boy. Kenan was in his mid-twenties compared to Am's fiftieth birthday coming up. Because Am was related—his niece Tress had married Kenan just before the war—he was one of the few permitted to visit after the boy had returned home.

Kenan had never objected to Am's presence. During the early months, Kenan hadn't spoken at all. The two men sat in the glassed-in back veranda, often on a Sunday afternoon, side by side in wicker chairs that were arranged to face the bay. The silence was not uncomfortable. When Am spoke, it was to talk about boats on the water, who owned which, who drifted over from Napanee, who was out for a Sunday excursion, who had caught the biggest walleye or bullhead that week, who was unlucky enough to be bailing water from a leaky flat-bottomed boat. One day he pointed out a father and son who fished for mudpout, skinned and sold the fish from door to door out the back of their tumbledown auto, and then drove to farms to barter there, too, if there were any fish left to sell after they'd been through the streets of town.

In response, Kenan nodded. Later, when he'd begun to speak again—haltingly, at first—he'd offered shorthand news of what he'd been reading from the orderly pile of papers and magazines stacked beside his veranda chair. Tress brought home the Toronto and Ottawa papers from her father's hotel, as well as magazines and the local paper, the *Deseronto Post*. Kenan still had a good eye, he told Am; he could read. He had a good arm and hand; he could write. With his good eye, he also read *The Veteran*. Men who'd returned from overseas were banding together in different parts of the country, and Kenan was interested in what they wanted from the politicians. In his opinion, there were too many organizations starting up. He had joined the Great War Veterans' Association because he believed they would help, now that just about all the boys were home. And hadn't they found work for him? Easy work he could do at home, but work nonetheless. Edwards Drugstore in town had been searching for someone to look after the account books, and Kenan was suggested for the job.

Am knew that the lad was good with figures, and that he could keep the books up to date, no problem. The owner of the drugstore, Hal Edwards, had told Am that Kenan's work was more than satisfactory. He'd also told Am that after the first time he looked into Kenan's scarred face, he no longer flinched when they were face to face. Edwards, never without a pencil tucked behind his ear, delivered the paperwork to Kenan at the end of every week, on a Saturday. Sometimes, if Tress was working on a Saturday, she picked up the ledgers on the way home and saved Edwards the trouble. Kenan worked at the books Monday and Tuesday, and got them back to Edwards on Wednesday—with Tress delivering.

Am had known the Edwards family for close to twenty years. He knew, too, that Kenan had worked for the drugstore after school when he was sixteen or seventeen, delivering necessities to people around town. After that, he'd begun to work at the bank, being trained as a teller, but the work had been cut short when he joined up and left for the war.

A few months earlier, Kenan had received a one-time payment for his war service: six months' gratuity. He also had a small pension, and now, he had the books from the drugstore to keep. The money earned would not support Kenan and Tress for the rest of their lives, but the work would do for the time being.

Kenan did not want pity and he did not speak about the war or his part in it. Nor did Am ever ask. When he visited the boy, they talked of the present but with some topics unmentioned. Neither spoke about Kenan's prospects for the future. Neither spoke about the fact that Kenan did not leave the house.

But this evening, everything had changed. Am was certain it was Kenan who had battled the wind at the end of the street as he emerged from the side of his house and walked away from the town with his quick stride.

Am nodded to himself again, and held a hand over his abdomen as he stepped away from the clock. Last Sunday afternoon, at the end of his visit with Kenan, he'd surprised himself and told the lad about the pain he'd been having in his gut. He'd blurted it out, the tale springing from his lips.

He had been suffering from pain since early fall. He had not told Mags that he'd gone to see the town doctor, or that Dr. Clark had examined him and said, "Am, you and I both know you're as strong as a bull. Are you certain there isn't something else bothering you? Have you told Maggie about this?"

Am said he planned to tell her soon.

But he had not, because he knew Mags would question him. She would want to make up one of her home remedies. No bottled goods from Edwards Drugstore for her. She would want Am to drink hot milk and pepper. Or something she'd mixed with turpentine or concocted from bitter apples, or melted lard mixed with camphor gum—something that would certainly make him want to throw up.

Everyone in town knew that Mags had a remedy for everything, even for growing back eyebrows that had fallen out. Problem was, she'd have to find someone who had no eyebrows so she could try out her concoction. She'd also been threatening to come up with something that would cause rapid growth of hair on the back of Am's head—where, once again, Grew the barber had chopped too much during the last haircut. But Am was loyal to Grew, whether the barber drank excessively or not. And if Grew did drink too much, he had good reason.

In the end, it was Kenan, not Mags, whom Am had told about the pain. After returning home from visiting that Sunday, Am wondered why he'd spilled out his concerns to the younger man. Not that Kenan would say anything, not at all. It was left to Am to tell Mags himself. He had decided that he would, the very next day. But after making the decision, he woke in the morning and lay quietly in his bed as if pain had never been part of his life. He'd slept so soundly, he was cheerfully surprised at being filled with his old energies. Cautious, he tested his strength at the edge of the bed. Made no sudden movement. Placed his feet on the floor and commanded his body to stand. The memory of pain settled into his past like a forgotten, used-up day. He dressed himself and began his routine, working on the floors below, caring for the building that housed him and Maggie on the third floor, the post office at ground level, the busy customs house in between.

Two days after that, the pain came back, and now he still hadn't told Mags. What would he say if he *were* to tell her? That he withstood the discomfort as he went about his work on the floors below and up in the clock tower, muttering all the while? In the end, he shared the knowledge only with Kenan, whom he told at the Sunday visit, moments before pushing himself up from the chair and saying goodbye.

Local Items

Farmers have been much incensed at the condition of the boundary road, and the heavy rainfall surely has not helped. Our friends from surrounding areas frequently have to make wide detours to get to our town at all to conduct their business.

It has been rumoured that a poet and songwriter who shall remain unnamed but who recently lived in our midst will return at the end of the year, for the sole purpose of giving a recitation of a new work as part of the New Year's Eve concert to be held at Naylor's Theatre.

Speaking of the upcoming concert, rehearsals taking place at Naylor's are becoming downright secretive. What is in store for us this year? Readers, be assured that I'll be present in my front-row seat, ready to report in the *Post* the delights that await, especially those under the direction of the talented Lukas Sebastian, the music director, who has recently moved here from faraway Europe, and who promises a splendid programme. Meanwhile, providing few clues to inform us, the singers, musicians and thespians in town quietly prepare.

Public Library
All residents of Deseronto over 12 years of age are entitled to the privileges of library and reading room, on complying with regulations.

Twin Torturers! Lumbago and Rheumatism Are Made Harmless by Dodd's Kidney Pills.

Chapter Three

MAGGIE O'NEILL STOOD INSIDE THE TOWER, where giant hands on the four surrounding clocks pointed to twelve minutes before six. She had been wakened early in the morning by a singing voice, she was certain. In the apartment below the clock tower, Am was still in bed, sleeping or not sleeping. At this moment, Maggie couldn't muster the effort to care.

She looked through the peering-out space scraped at eye level between IIII and V on the front-facing clock, and watched the moon drop from the sky. A flat-bottomed glow thinned to become a domed handle. The handle became a wisp. Finally, the last trace was swallowed by an ocean of darkness, though the nearest ocean was a thousand miles from this tiny Ontario town.

Light from the new day began to spread itself over shingles and chimneys, drifting through narrow alleys that wound in and out of a puddled Main Street below. Maggie glanced up at the hands of the clock and took a final look out. Dark woods, which only moments before had shrouded the edges of town, were separating into particular tree shapes. Black waters of the bay lay to the south, wharves and piers directly ahead. A ragged shoreline curved east and west. She sensed the grey-brown tempo of late fall.

She pulled back, away from the clock. "The sun will rise of its own accord with no help from me," she said to no one but herself. She gathered the folds of her dressing gown around her hips and realized that in her head, she'd been going through the lines of a gypsy song she would soon be singing to an audience larger than herself.

Who give their all, a simple note,
At peep of dawn or parting day
But fortunes here I come to tell.

Her solo. One of them. She could not think of her upcoming performance without wondering if she would freeze in front of the audience. Forget the lines, the notes. Or worse.

She made her way around the massive bell that hung from the central beam in the tower; she tugged at her dressing gown again to prevent it from tangling, and stepped onto the wooden platform. When she was steady, she lowered herself onto the rungs of a ladder that poked up through the opening in the tower floor and was flush to the back wall of her parlour below. She left the trap door open. Am would be going up later; this was the day he oiled cogs and gears and checked the horizontal rods that jutted into the centre of the tower and controlled the hands on the faces of each clock.

Maggie made no sound as she placed her fingers against the door of a tall cupboard that stretched from floor to ceiling in the back corner of the room. Knowing the weight of all that was above it, she thought of the mahogany cupboard as a repository of woes. Cleverly disguised behind its door were long pendulum cables that hung from the clock above. The cables extended through the tower floor and were suspended over a three-foot bed of sand that filled the bottom of the cupboard. From the parlour, no one could possibly know that sand lay behind and below the closed cupboard door. Maggie had had more than one nightmare about the cables crashing down, or the giant bell falling and bringing the tower with it. Now, despite her thoughts of calamity, the music for the gypsy song played in her head again, and she had to consider how remote from a gypsy's life was her own. She, who had been nowhere, had grown up on her parents' farm and then, along with Am, owned a farm after marriage. After selling the farm, she and Am had spent the past twenty years in this same small town. Any trips she took were to nearby Belleville and back, or to Toronto to shop once in a blue moon, or across the lake to Oswego, New York, for a visit to her sister, Nola. That was the extent of her wandering gypsy life. Safe, and not far at all.

She walked the long hall to the kitchen and filled the kettle for her tea.

Maggie and Am's apartment was the only one in the building. During the day, employees moved about the two floors below as if they were working the decks of a merchant ship. Before and after hours, and on weekends, those same offices were empty. Maggie was glad enough to have people in the building during the daytime, but she was grateful for the early-morning quiet. Grateful for afternoon light that spilled through the south-facing windows into the apartment, summer and winter. Grateful for the number of rooms and the privacy these afforded. Am, with the title of "caretaker," was employed by the town. Along with being responsible for the workings of the clock and the heavy clapper that hovered, ready to strike the bell—though he connected it only once a year, every New Year's Eve—he did maintenance work for the entire building. He was always downstairs doing something. Or in the basement, looking after the coal supply and the boiler.

As for the apartment itself, it was long and spacious and took up the entire third floor. A private entry was accessed by a side door at street level. An equally private oak staircase led up to the landing outside their door.

Despite the comfortable kitchen, Maggie missed the spacious farm kitchen she and Am had left behind a long time ago. She stood before the sink and pushed the memory aside and, instead, tried to call back the voice that had wakened her, the golden voice of Melba. As certainly as her left hand now lifted the kettle to the stove, Maggie knew that the great soprano Nellie Melba had been singing in pure, mellow tones while she, Melba's private audience, had lain quietly in bed in the early morning. As certain as a dreamer could be.

Maggie had not thought of the Australian diva for months. In her dream, she had fought wakefulness, knowing that if she opened her eyes, the voice would disappear. Reluctantly, she had given in. She had slipped out of bed, trying not to disturb Am, but he had shifted noisily when she'd shut the bedroom door.

Maggie could easily detect the occasions when Am was feigning sleep. Easily, because her own night patterns were similar: legs bent, legs straightened, restless turning, never a deep sleep. She wondered, not for the first time, if Am was concealing symptoms of an ailment that was worrying him. Sometimes he acted as if every movement pained him. Sometimes he lay still for hours and then got up to wander about in the dark. Occasionally, he helped himself to food from the baking cupboard. From their bed, she could picture his every move. Am standing in the dark before the cupboard, pulling open the door as quietly as he could—the squeaking hinge gave him away. Am eating the oat-and-raisin cookies she stored there—a trail of crumbs was present in the morning. More crumbs lay in the sink—she rinsed these down the drain. A few were scattered on the floor—she swept them up. And crumbs were often hardened beneath the icebox door, where he'd stood staring with an unsatisfied look—not difficult to imagine.

Maggie poured boiling water into the teapot and sat at the kitchen table on her high-backed chair. Am had made four of these, carved and ladder-backed, during the first year they were married. She did a rapid calculation: almost twenty-five years ago. The pine had come from trees on their own farm, and Am had made the chairs with love and care. Memories tried to crowd forward, but once more Maggie pushed them back. She was a town person now.

She thought of Melba again. Two years earlier, in 1917, she had met Nellie Melba face to face. That had not been a dream. She sat quietly now and turned over every astonishing detail.

MAGGIE HAD BEEN VISITING TORONTO DURING A GREY AND overcast weekend. The war was still in progress. Casualty lists were long and morale at a low ebb in the town and elsewhere across the country. Winter had begun to wane, but slush and a thin layer of muddied snow coated Toronto's streets. During the winter, she had learned that Nellie Melba would be in the city for a fundraising tour, travelling to several places across North America, singing in theatres and halls, raising money that would be donated to the Red Cross to help soldiers and their families.

From Deseronto, Maggie arranged to buy tickets in advance for a Friday evening concert: one for herself and one for her sister, who travelled across Lake Ontario from Oswego for the occasion. Maggie journeyed by train and met Nola in Toronto, where they shared a room in a downtown hotel.

At the concert, Melba disappointed no one. She had been sponsored by the Heliconian Club and sang on a narrow stage, her voice strong and true, the notes floating upward in the high-vaulted room. Her expression while singing was intense and composed. She sang "Je veux vivre" from Gounod's *Roméo et Juliette*, and Maggie felt the joy around her. She sang Gilda's "Caro nome" from Verdi's *Rigoletto*, and the undulations of her voice stilled the audience. After a full programme, her listeners begged for encores and Melba exhausted herself, trying to please. She even sang "Swing Low, Sweet Chariot" and "Comin' Thro the Rye" at the end. And finally, giving in to the crowd, she sang "Home, Sweet Home."

The morning after the concert, Nola announced that she was tired and wanted to stay in bed for an extra hour. Maggie pulled on her heavy coat, stuck a hat on her head—she hated having to wear a hat—left her sister in the room and went out to browse in the downtown shops. She enjoyed being a visitor in the city but was not prepared for sharp wind, or for ice beneath the slush in the streets. On a side street not far from the hotel, she lost her footing and went down. While struggling to get to her feet, she realized that a woman was standing before her, reaching out a hand. Maggie's reaction was first embarrassment, and then confusion. She was dazed from the fall, but from the ground looking up, she recognized the diva instantly. In the same instant, Melba knew she'd been recognized. The knowledge passed between them while Melba hauled her up from the sidewalk. Maggie brushed at her long coat, now smudged and soggy with slush and dirt.

"Never mind the coat," said Melba. "Are you all right? Broken bones? No? We'll deal with the coat inside. There are people after me. Lord knows who." She laughed lightly, as if she were a queen running from her retinue—though there was no one in pursuit. She pushed and steered Maggie through the doors of a large, half-empty diner that was near at hand, and the two slid into a booth in the farthest corner. Melba faced the rear wall, presenting her back to the door.

"Remove your coat," she said. She spoke rapidly, as if she was entirely accustomed to giving orders. "We'll sponge it with a table napkin. Someone will bring water. Have you eaten? We're going to have an adventure. Nothing fancy here, and who cares? I'm starving." She was laughing to herself. Maggie thought her speaking voice was what royalty must sound like. Commanding, certain. "Let them look for me," Melba added. "I need an hour to myself." She removed tan suede gloves that matched her woollen coat, slipped her arms out of the sleeves and pushed the coat behind her. She held out a hand and took Maggie's hands in her own.

"Melba," she said. "That's what people call me. I'm sorry you went down so hard on the street. I'm sorry for hurrying you in here. I'm not a madwoman, I promise, but I needed to escape. I hope the fall wasn't serious, even to your pride."

Maggie O'Neill, of the tiny town of Deseronto, had so far mumbled no more than two words. She was sitting across from a world-famous diva whose performance twelve hours earlier had, at times, brought her to tears and an audience to their feet. She had been yanked up from the sidewalk by Melba, and she had to push down her shyness and show the woman that she was grateful and that she could speak.

Now, from her kitchen table in the tower apartment, when Maggie thought about the encounter and the breakfast they had shared two years earlier in the booth of a Toronto diner, it wasn't food or the surrounds she first recalled. It was the dramatic, commanding presence of the soprano. And yet, almost instantly, Melba had put Maggie at ease.

Melba had a prominent nose, full cheeks, bow-shaped lips, thickly rolled hair. A violet scarf was twined around her throat. Up close, Maggie saw that the diva's eyebrows had been darkened artificially, as if in preparation for the next role. Her eyes, a mixture of intelligence and curiosity, revealed a woman of temperament, a woman who knew what she wanted and what was expected. At that moment, Nellie Melba was intent on being hidden. The size of her hat helped; her face was partly in shadow. Notices of her image—hatless—were posted around

the city; the two benefit concerts in Toronto had been well pub-
licized. Maggie was instructed to be on the lookout, as she was
facing the door to the street.

The miraculous part, she thought as she sat in her own
kitchen, was that we conversed as if we'd known each other all
our lives. I had the audacity to blurt out the news that I used
to sing. Not the way she did, of course—but I told her how
I had loved to sing when I was a child. I had the nerve to say
that without embarrassment, a kind of declaration. At the time
it didn't seem strange; I felt I was confiding in someone I'd
known all my life. I was forty-one then, and Melba was in her
fifties. I could have been a younger sister she hadn't seen for a
very long time.

Melba had made it clear that she needed to gather her forces
to face what she must always face: the press, interviews, critics,
the public and, that same evening, her second Toronto performance. Once assured that no one had pursued her, she ordered
breakfast for the two of them—sausages, eggs, baked apples,
toast, tea—and then, only then, she relaxed and turned her full
attention to Maggie. She listened carefully, but she was also a
woman with stories to tell. After full plates had been brought
to the table, she turned over a stubby sausage with her fork and
embarked on a story of herself and Caruso onstage singing *La
Bohème*. The time could have been any time; the stage could
have been Milan, London, Paris, Vienna. She did not explain.
Maggie understood that the moment was about story.

"Caruso was standing close, staring fiercely while he sang to
me—I was the shivering, weak and pitiful Mimì. *Your cold little
hand, let me warm it*—in Italian, of course. And then, furtive man

that he was, he reached into his pocket and pressed a warm sausage to my bare hand. Wicked, wicked. The two of us could hardly keep from roaring with laughter. I drew upon every acting talent I possessed so that I could maintain my composure." Melba held out a hand as if, at that moment, Caruso was bending forward at the edge of the booth, ready to press a second sausage to her palm. She wriggled her fingers, smiled, picked up her knife.

"Now," she said, "first tell me about your wonderful green eyes—from whom did you inherit those?"

"My mother," Maggie said. "Hers were greener, even darker than mine. I was always happy that I was the one born with the green eyes."

"And your singing? When did you begin?"

Maggie found herself launched into a tale of being ten years old, little Maggie Healy singing "O Holy Night," the highlight of the Christmas concert in her one-room country school. She told Melba about singing at year-end ceremonies and at June graduations for older students. She told about singing at her own graduation, when she finished school herself. How she had sung to the accompaniment of the teacher, Miss Miller, who played the only instrument in the school—a piano pushed to the edge of the platform that also held the teacher's desk. This was the same piano upon which Maggie had practised after school, for days, months, years. Miss Miller had provided lessons at no charge. She had offered because she believed in Maggie's ability to sing. She taught the scales and how to play with two hands and how to use the foot pedal. She taught until Maggie could sight-read sheet music and play almost anything that was put in front of her. All Maggie had to do to repay Miss Miller was tidy the classroom after school and provide a bottle of water for every two seats, along with a rag to clean the slates, though they both knew that some of the boys used spit instead of water. It became Maggie's job to empty the water bottles, fill them again, distribute the supply of freshly washed rags. A pump in the school porch supplied drinking water.

She stopped.

Melba had been listening carefully. "Many people in the music world had similar beginnings," she said. "You might be surprised. When I tried to get my first roles, your own Canadian, Madame Albani, was the reigning star. What was left over was what I was given to sing, and I dared not protest. In Brussels, I had no jewellery to wear when I performed. One of the directors gave me a set of paste so I wouldn't look so pathetic and plain when I sang. There were many kindnesses. But there were also weeks when I went hungry. Tell me, Maggie, what were some of the other songs you sang—besides 'O Holy Night'?"

"Whatever was popular at the time," said Maggie. "'I Knew a Pretty Maiden,' 'Molly! Do You Love Me?' 'Whispering Hope'—songs like that. Irish favourites, of course. And hymns."

Melba nodded. "'Little Brown Jug'? That was on everyone's list when I was asked to sing. Vernon and Irene Castle danced to the same tune. Well, they could dance to anything."

Maggie was surprised to hear Melba say that she had sung "Little Brown Jug." But what she didn't and couldn't say to Melba was what music meant to her, or rather, what singing had once meant. There had been times when she was so moved by what she was singing, she wept afterward. Music—she had known this as a child—was inside her. Songs played in her head.

She could not have stopped them if she'd wanted to, not from the moment she'd first heard her own mother sing. As a young child, countless times during country parties, she had concealed herself beneath the kitchen table, hidden by an overhanging tablecloth, a dark cloth, sewn and patterned with indigo and scarlet squares. Her mother knew she was there but allowed her presence. Maggie had grown up listening to men play the fiddle, the tin whistle, the flute. And always she had listened to voices joined in song, men's and women's voices, but especially the voice of her mother. It was possible that Maggie's own first songs had been sung from beneath the same kitchen table. She strained to grasp at those fragments of memory.

On every occasion, with friends crowded around, her mother had sung by herself, some Irish song. Hidden behind the overhanging cloth, picking at a scarlet patch whose threads had become loosened, picking at it until the same threads bled into her fingers, Maggie had thrilled to hear the familiar voice buoy up the room with its own distinctive strength, its own distinctive spirit. When her mother came to the end of the last line, it was always with a burst of laughter, as if the song had been a joyous kind of mistake. As if the song had leapt into the midst of the party by some caprice of its own.

When Maggie was older, she sang alongside her mother. But later, much later, Maggie stopped singing. Except for the church choir in town.

Facing Melba, she reached under the diner table to rub at her own knee. She would have a bruise the following day.

"You mustn't feel badly about your fall," said Melba. "I know the feeling only too well. Let me tell you the story of a time when I was beginning a tour in California. I was knocked hard on the head, hard enough to be rendered unconscious. I was in the home of old friends—I had just arrived—and sat on the edge of a settee that slid back and tilted as it slid. Later, I found out that a caster was missing from one of the legs. Well, the movement of the settee caused a bronze bust behind me to fall forward. The blow to my head knocked me out completely. I might have been killed. My hosts were horrified." She shrugged. "Happily, I survived and lived to sing another note. What I still find strange, however, is that I experienced a feeling of pure sorrow when I regained consciousness. Quite some time passed before I could absorb what had happened, but that was secondary to the feeling of sorrow I was not able to shake."

They shared the moment quietly until Melba laughed, an enveloping laugh that made Maggie join in. Melba glanced furtively around the back of the booth and put a warning finger to her lips. "Hush," she said. She shook her head as if to admonish herself. "We'll be discovered. How wonderful is freedom! How wonderful to sit in a diner eating warm sausages." And this set the two of them off and they laughed again.

When they sobered and began to talk once more, Melba surprised Maggie with her next comment. "You've experienced sorrow, Maggie. I see it in your face. Am I being forward? When one has had sorrow in one's own life, one sees it in another. One of my early sorrows was my marriage, which I knew immediately to be a disaster. I married young, without the slightest knowledge of where I was headed. I had no direction whatever. But I recovered from my mistake, and freed myself to make many more. Now, well, I don't care so much if I make mistakes.

Nor am I afraid to speak up. I have opinions about the music I sing and where I sing it. I have opinions about what goes on in the big wide world, even though we women are not expected to express our thoughts about worldly matters. This terrible war, for one." She paused for a breath. "Forgive me if I intruded on your privacy just now."

Maggie had not interpreted Melba's observation as intrusion. Nor had she permitted her own sorrow to surface.

Melba did not push. She looked down at a remnant of apple peel and a limp end of sausage that lay side by side on her plate. Once again, she took Maggie's hand in her own. This time she began to sing softly, music Maggie recognized at once as lines from the end of "Donde lieta uscì," one of Mimì's arias from *Bohème*. Noises inside the diner fell away. Or did they? The room quieted. Or did it? Was everything shut out by the moment between them? In this distilled and indelible moment, Maggie received the gift of a private, almost whispered concert, until Melba allowed her voice its freedom, until the radiant sound suddenly swelled, soaring up to the tin ceiling and filling the room:

Se vuoi serbarla a ricordo d'amor!
Addio, senza rancor.

People turned to look. A man stood and applauded. Melba called for the waiter and paid him handsomely. The two women slid out of the booth. Melba bundled herself into her coat, kissed Maggie soundly on both cheeks and swept away. Maggie never saw her again.

Perhaps the encounter had never taken place. No, Maggie was certain it had. All in a brief morning. A singular moment in her life. She had told Melba about her love of singing when she was a child. Nellie Melba had talked to her about love, and told her how important it was that they continue to make beautiful and meaningful music with their voices. And then she had sung "Donde lieta uscì" privately, to Maggie, in the booth of a diner on a grey winter's day.

Now, with the war over, with the onset of winter and the end of 1919 in sight, the New Year's Eve concert in which Maggie herself was to take part was not far off. She wondered what she had allowed herself to be manoeuvred into. She had been singing in the church choir of St. Mark's for years. But in the early fall, her friend Zel had persuaded her to audition for the new choral society and the end-of-year concert that would be held in the theatre. *Partly* persuaded. Maggie had to take responsibility for her own actions. Why had she so quickly agreed to audition? Because of Lukas. She had gone because she was curious. Not expecting that the man responsible for choosing the music would also choose her to sing solo.

Rehearsals at the theatre had begun in early October and were becoming more intense. Maggie found herself immersed in those, along with her usual choir practice at the church. No time to think of anything else. Christmas would come and go, as it did every year. She and Am would have dinner with his brother, Dermot, and his wife, Agnes, at the hotel across from the wharf at the other end of Main Street. Dermot and Agnes lived in the house joined by a passageway to the hotel, but they took their meals in the hotel dining room, where they had their own family table. Agnes did most of the cooking, and the hotel was known for its good food.

Other family members would also be present at Christmas: Dermot's youngest son, Patrick; his oldest son, Bernard, who along with his wife, Kay, helped manage the hotel—they would be there. Probably Am and Dermot's father, too, would be brought in from the farm in the country. And then, one week after the end of Christmas celebrations, Maggie was committed to taking part in the New Year's concert.

At that instant, as if responding to her thoughts of family, Am walked into the kitchen. He pulled at the icebox door and peered in. Maggie had not heard him come out of the bedroom. Her reverie ended. She waited for him to look across the room and say, "Have you made the tea, Mags? Hot enough to burn a hole in my throat?" He'd leave the tea in the cup for ten minutes anyway, before drinking. Or dump in so much milk the tea would be ruined.

"Have you made the tea, Mags? Hot enough to burn a hole in my throat?"

Maggie, refusing to answer the worn-out question, filled his cup.

He turned to look out over the slopes and angles of rooftop that were visible from their kitchen window. A fragment of bunting he'd hung outside in the fall to celebrate the returning soldiers had snagged on one corner of the roof and was caught there still.

"We'll soon have snow," said Am. "This week. I've been predicting an early winter, and now look at the dull sky. All the signs of a storm are there."

Watching Am sideways now, Maggie was once more reminded that half his head was missing. The back half. She wanted to roar in rage. Grew had cut his hair several evenings before, even though she'd asked Am to go to a different barber. Grew's need for drink was out of control since he'd lost his only son in the war. Now Maggie couldn't look at her own husband because of the way Grew had snipped the hair on the back of his head. Removed it. Totally. Yes, half of Am's head was definitely missing. She didn't know whether to laugh or cry.

Chapter Four

KENAN WAS GRATEFUL THAT HIS BACKYARD sloped down to the rocky shore of the bay. Grateful that Tress had chosen this house to rent. He had not told her as much, but there seemed no need to voice what she already knew: that his chief pleasure since returning from the war was to sit and face the waters of the bay. If it weren't for occasional pains shooting through his dead hand, if it weren't for the fact that he had stayed so long indoors—others no doubt thought him eccentric, even pathetic—he might consider himself, in some strange and empty way, whole.

With winter arriving, the veranda floor was cooling, but a cool floor was no deterrent. Kenan remained in the wicker chair and allowed his gaze to fall between the newly filled coal shed on his left and a leafless maple tree on the right. Snow was falling heavily, wetly, settling in clumps on the branches and on the clothesline, which gave the appearance of a mooring rope tethered to a ship. Along shore, he could see the ice house, which, in another month, would be filled with squared blocks of ice. Farther along, an edge of the broom-handle factory was visible. Between the two were remnants of a ramshackle wharf.

During the past year, Kenan's body had been forced to adjust to a narrower visual field. He turned his head and looked left toward the railway tracks that curved north and out of town. He knew that, out of sight, machine shops and warehouses were standing empty. He knew, too, that a couple of tugs and a steamboat or two would now be in winter layup at the main wharf.

He turned his attention to the horizon and the bay. Despite his blinkered view, he had been entertained through the changing seasons by considerable activity on the water. Fishermen out for a day's catch of walleye; pleasure craft—plentiful during summer and fall; flat-bottomed boats, narrow rowboats, canoes. By now, and partly because Tress's uncle Am had pointed out various shapes and markings, Kenan was able to recognize vessels that returned like old habits to the same shadowy inlets and coves. He knew which steamers headed south toward Long Reach and the open waters of Lake Ontario, and which ones chugged westward, staying close to shore, stopping at local docks and piers to discharge passengers and take on more. Water traffic had decreased with the beginning of cold weather. The last steamer had sailed more than a week ago.

This week, his interest was aroused by a new activity that inserted itself directly into the centre of the area under his watch. Stacks of lumber, poles and fencing had been dropped off no more than two hundred feet down the slope. At once, he'd understood that this year's rink would be at his end of town. Last winter, it had been below Mill Street, near his in-laws' hotel. Now, the entire construction seemed to be planned for his personal entertainment. After a good freeze, the boards for the skaters' shack would be carried closer to shore. It was Kenan's good fortune that the rink would be located in a line directly south of his own backyard.

He was surprised by the stirring of the old excitement, the anticipation of winter. He thought of the bay freezing, the testing of the ice, men and boys from town shovelling and clearing and pushing back snow until the banks enclosed a surface shaped in a near-perfect oval. After that, tall poles would be hoisted and secured, one at each end of the rink. Sometimes, a hockey net would be set up on a cleared space outside the oval. All of this construction was forthcoming, an annual event for the town.

Around the outer circumference of the rink, a walkway would be tramped into the snow, and this would be kept clear so that skaters could manoeuvre along the outer edge of the rink as they approached. The oval walkway would also provide a place from which non-skaters could watch the activities on the ice. On either side of the path from shore, long sticks or posts would be stuck into the snow at regular intervals, and loose fencing strung between. To enter the rink, skaters would be able to choose from one of two openings in the snowbanks so that they could step from the walkway onto the ice.

Kenan thought of the day he stood in the doorway of the shed of the Mill Street house when he was a boy, watching Uncle Oak bend forward in the bibbed overalls he wore in his welding shop. His uncle sorted through a heap of harnesses and old reins, and finally disentangled a pair of skates. He held them up so that Kenan could see the smoothly carved pieces of wood into which long steel blades had been inserted, one in each.

"Fasten these to your boots," Uncle Oak had told him. "Tighten the straps until they're firm and snug. And don't ask for anything better. They were good enough for me when I was a boy and I guess they'll be good enough for you."

Kenan did not want anything better. He loved the skates from the beginning, loved the way the straps attached through side slits, front and back, permitting him to tighten the grips when he fitted his boots to the wood of the skates. He loved the long strips of steel, curled at the toes and blunted at the heels, perhaps by a blacksmith from some earlier time when his uncle had been a youth, or maybe even before that.

On those same sharpened blades, Kenan had learned to dart around couples who swayed as they strained to hear music from the horn of the Victrola. *The Skaters' Waltz* alternated with "We Will Meet at the Rink To-Night." These were repeated over and over, but no one complained, no one seemed to mind. The skating couples cruised round and round, tracing patterns on the ice, laughing and intent at the same time.

Kenan found himself hoping that under the thin layer of white, everything would freeze quickly so that the rink could be resurrected. A few energetic souls used to skate across the part of the bay he could see; probably a few still did. He'd been one of those who'd skated the distance to Napanee, but he had done so only once. He was eleven years old when he and one of his boyhood friends, Orryn, had skated across.

He remembered the sensation of striking out, pushing off with a quick jump, pumping his arms—left arm crossing his chest with the thrust of the right skate, right arm with the left. He'd allowed himself to glide when the strongest gusts were at his back, but he'd loved the speed, the freedom, the cold against his face, the exhilaration, the conquest, the sensation of carving his own path across the ice.

By the time he and Orryn reached the far shore on the Napanee side, it was late afternoon and darkness was dropping quickly over the bay. His long legs fatigued without warning; he collapsed onto his back in a snowbank and told Orryn he needed to rest. The snow cradled his head like a pillow. He might have gone to sleep against its warmth, but his friend yanked him up. Orryn needled and joked and teased that Kenan couldn't make it back, and that was enough for both boys to get a grip of themselves, to force themselves to turn and face the wind. They hadn't given a moment's thought to the return journey when they'd started out; they'd been thinking only of the adventure of crossing the bay.

During the trip back, they did not try to speak. They had to keep moving. They had to concentrate: one breath, another breath; one skate, the other skate; backs low, bodies doubled over, pushing into the wind. They had to focus on the lights of Deseronto in the distance, lights that hovered above the ice to form a shifting mirage of hope, beckoning and promising safety and warmth.

Uncle Oak was neither surprised nor impressed by the boys' adventure. He had taught Kenan from early childhood that "life is treacherous." If he was grateful or relieved that Kenan had made it back to Deseronto's shore, he had not expressed his thoughts aloud.

Where was Orryn now? As boys, he and Kenan had been inseparable. They'd left Canada the same year, but ended up fighting in different areas of France. After an assignment in Berlin at the end of the war, Orryn had gone on to England. He might have been demobilized there. There had been talk of an aunt and uncle and several cousins in Dorset. Maybe he had married in England. Maybe he had stayed there and begun to raise a family of little Tommies.

Kenan focused on the bay again. At one point during his childhood—he couldn't remember the exact year—electric lights had been attached to the crossbars that were nailed up near the tips of the poles at each end of the rink. Skaters and onlookers came out at night to marvel at the miraculous cones of yellow light that pooled down onto the ice and blazed over its surface. Kenan was one of those who'd marvelled. He had raced in and out of the cones of light, never allowing fatigue— not until the last skaters were shooed off the rink at ten o'clock at night. Only then did his feet turn to unfeeling stumps; only then did his ankles give out. He was still able to call up the sensation of unstrapping the skates from his boots and dragging himself, his feet in pain, back to his uncle's house and to bed.

Closer to the onset of war, when he was older, Kenan had skated with Tress, whirling around to the same waltzes they'd listened to when they were children. In January 1914, they had dressed for the carnival, too, for the masquerade, held every year on open ice. They had been a gypsy couple—Tress wearing a long skirt and curtain hoops for earrings. They'd been surrounded by the usual inventive array of costumes, the result of people rummaging in closets, piecing together relics and props, some of which were hauled out for use year after year.

Now, an entire war later, the makings of the rink itself appeared to be unchanged. Boards for the shack were stacked in readiness a short distance from Kenan's veranda—boards he was able to recognize by their size and shape. Was it possible that something familiar had not been altered by war?

He imagined the inside of the skaters' shack, soon to assume its own shape. Workmen would nail boards together to make a floor that would be blade-scarred soon enough. There would be a hammering together of three rough timber benches, where the skaters would sit to lace up and unlace; a stovepipe would reach up and out of the pot-belly stove and through an opening in the roof. A sizzle and spit would be heard as hardened pellets of ice and snow were plucked from the folds of mittens and brittle socks, and tossed onto the hot surface of the stove.

Skating came to a halt every year at the time of breakup, usually in early March but sometimes as late as April. Depending on the severity of winter, breakup occurred within a predictable range of a few weeks. Some of the town men laid bets about the exact day this would happen, but it was Tress's uncle Am who was most accurate in his predictions. He swore by a formula he'd created from records he'd been keeping for decades, scratching *ice out* dates into one of the corner beams of the clock tower up over the post office. Kenan had been taken up there several times by Tress and her sister when they were schoolmates. Maggie and Am were childless, but had always welcomed young people to their tower apartment.

Kenan stood now, and left his chair. All of those memories were far removed from his present state. He might have been imagining the details of the skating shack—which, at the moment, was nothing more than a stack of boards in a heap on the ground—in the same way he had begun to imagine his memories of war.

He had been a child when he'd joined up. Or might as well have been. If anyone had asked, he'd have said that he considered himself a gentle person, not someone who shouldered a rifle and marched off to war. No one had asked, and he had done both. Tress, concerned about his decision, had nonetheless given her support. She wasn't happy about moving back to her parents' home while he was away, but both she and her sister, Grania, had done exactly that.

Kenan had been one of the first in town to enlist in 1914. He'd felt the excitement, the urgency to rush to the aid of Mother Britain. Thousands of young men across the country had signed up and were being transported toward the East Coast as they trained and boarded ships to cross the ocean. But in the same way that objects now fell off the visual horizon of Kenan's left eye and vanished, so had all of those young men fallen from the peripheries of his life.

Chapter Five

SUNDAY MORNING, MAGGIE WAS LOSING HER FOCUS. She opened her hymn book and looked at the singers who stood facing her. She watched familiar heads tilted at a slant one way, the other way, rounded backs, slumped backs, tall backs, chins raised, chins tucked, heads burrowed into collars as if about to disappear. Flora, the alto next to her, gobbled at the air as she began the first verse. The movement startled, though Maggie always tried to be ready. Andrew, across the aisle, made a sudden dip forward as if his pointed chin would dig the notes right off the page. One of Andrew's eyes was set slightly lower in his face than the other, and Maggie sometimes felt she was being looked at from two levels. Andrew glanced up at that moment and Maggie was certain that his upper eye winked. She grinned. Andrew, who had a fine tenor voice, had also joined the choral society and he, too, had been asked by Lukas to perform solo at the New Year's concert. Maggie looked at the singers on either side of him. She knew every face in the church, had known most members of the choir almost two decades. They sang as one, sat as one, and now leaned back into their seats as one. Her hymnary slid out of her hands and she caught it before it hit the floor. She stared down at the wide plank of polished pine beneath her feet. How could one tree have provided such perfect wood? She fidgeted, tucked the hymn book away and looked up at the arch of a window, where a single ray of light was bending in at a hard angle.

The minister stepped up to the pulpit and announced details of events leading to Advent. The sermon began. Maggie could not pay attention. She cast her memory back to a Sunday shortly after the end of the war, when a senior chaplain from Napanee had come to conduct the service. The church had been packed for the occasion. She was introduced to the visiting chaplain, and as he shook hands with her, one of his eyes looked off to the side, corrected and fixed straight ahead again. She wondered if he'd been wounded, or was suffering from the disease everyone was calling neurasthenia. The chaplain had spoken about his years at the Front. She was certain that everyone in the congregation had heard enough of the war, but not all of the men had returned home at the time and people were at the edge of their seats, hungry to hear any detail at all.

Maggie looked down at her lap now and saw that her hands were curved, palms up, as if in expectation of something dropping from the ceiling. She couldn't help glancing upward to ensure that no object was making a rapid descent. She glanced over at the minister, who was finishing his sermon, and finally, finally, the service was over.

SHE WALKED ALONG THE ROAD WITH ZEL, OUT PAST THE
edge of town. They'd made a plan to go directly to Zel's house
to have something to eat and then practise their parts for the
concert, maybe even sew a bit on their skating costumes for
the January masquerade. Maggie had told Am she'd be at
Zel's for the afternoon. Am no longer attended church ser-
vices. He'd stopped years before, after he and Maggie first
moved to town. No one had been successful in persuading
him to change his mind—not the minister at the time, or the
present one. Am did what he wished to do. Maggie knew that
he'd soon be heading over to Kenan and Tress's home for his
Sunday afternoon visit.

"What did Am do to the back of his head?" Zel wanted to
know. "I saw him in the post office a couple of days ago." She
took Maggie's coat and hung it from a hook on the back of her
kitchen door. They stomped clumps of snow from their boots
and set the boots on a mat to dry.

"What do you think? He went to Grew for a haircut again.
Even after I asked him to go to one of the other barbers in
town." Maggie sat herself down at Zel's long kitchen table. "I
could have done a better job myself."

"Grew does have to earn a living," said Zel. "There's that to
consider. And Am's hair will grow back—hopefully."

"He should be wearing a hat to cover the deed," said Maggie.
"But you know Am. No one tells him what to do."

"Well, no one tells you what to do, either," said Zel. "By the
way, did you see Cora's hat in the back pew this morning? All
those feathers and wings. It looked as if it would fly up to the
belfry at any moment."

Maggie waved her off with laughter. "I didn't see Cora's hat," she said. "I was having enough trouble staying with the music. Could you tell from where you were?"

"I saw that you were preoccupied," said Zel, "and not by the notes on the page."

"I lost focus. If *you* noticed, so did others. Well, maybe they did, maybe they didn't. I don't know what was wrong with me." She looked past her friend and through the window, where a small bird, one she couldn't identify, was flitting from branch to branch in a leafless tree. It settled and puffed out its throat as if rehearsing for a larger adventure. "What a beauty," she said. "I don't see many birds from the rooftop of our apartment. Anyway, most of the birds headed south weeks ago."

"The almanac says we're in for a long freeze," said Zel. "Mrs. Leary made her declaration weeks ago."

"Your tenant?"

"The same. When she isn't reading her Bible, she has her nose in almanacs, past and present. She keeps a pencil on the sill in the parlour so she can mark passages in the Bible—and in the current almanac. I confess that I'm curious about what's worthy of her attention, but so far I've resisted looking."

"I wonder," said Maggie. She tried to recall the kind of books Mrs. Leary and her husband borrowed from the library over the fire hall, where Maggie worked two afternoons a week. She thought of the titles she had entered in the register on their behalf: Sir Walter Scott novels, *Persuasive Peggy*, books about the Antipodes. Mr. Leary had requested *Tess of the d'Urbervilles* but it had been deemed too controversial for Deseronto's citizens and had been removed years before. He'd requested, instead, something about circus clowns. She had nothing to give him about clowns, but he'd borrowed one of two copies the library owned of *The Life of P.T. Barnum*. That had satisfied him at the time, though he'd returned the book with stains on its cover. She had wanted to ask, "Tea? Moonshine?" but she'd held her tongue.

"Most days," Zel went on, "the two of them stay in the parlour with the double doors closed. Except when they're having meals. In the evening, Mrs. Leary putters in the kitchen, though she doesn't cook anything fancy. A pity there isn't more for them to see out the parlour windows—except the road and the old barn that's falling down. They do like to watch the birds. I keep that room heated in winter just for the two of them. When I'm home, I'm always in the kitchen. Anyway, they love to sit in there during the daytime. Mrs. Leary reads by window light. She brought her rocker with her when she moved in. Her husband plays solitaire, but never on Sundays."

Does he slap down the cards? Maggie wanted to ask. Am had installed a shelf up in the tower—two shelves angled between beams. He kept a pack of cards on one of the shelves and sometimes played solitaire for hours at a time. From below she could hear every card as it snapped hard against the wood. Each time she heard *snap slap* she wanted to shout up to him: *Don't you have work to do somewhere in the building?*

She stopped herself. She hadn't discussed Am's behaviour with Zel. Except for the haircuts.

Zel went on. "In good weather, Mr. Leary goes for walks. I swear he keeps a bottle of something stashed somewhere, because I sometimes smell liquor when he returns. When he's out, Mrs. Leary stays in the parlour and talks to herself. If he's away for a long time, sometimes she'll ask me to help her wash her hair."

"Is that part of your agreement?"

"Not really. But there's something wrong with her collarbone, something not quite in alignment. She has trouble raising her arm to scrub her scalp. I guess she doesn't like to ask him for help. And she does need help. There are times when I think her mind is off with the fairies. One day, after her husband went out for a walk, she came into the kitchen and said, 'This is what happens when we get old, Harold. You should have stuck around.' The two of us laughed out loud as if we were part of a conspiracy. Another time, she told me, with no reference point except what was going on in her mind, 'People don't die, Zel, not really. We think of them just as often *after* they die, and just as happily.' I had no answer to that. Nor do I believe the *just as happily* part."

"Is she in the parlour now? Shall I go in and say hello? I haven't seen either of them for a while." Maggie was thinking of Zel scrubbing Mrs. Leary's head at the sink, the fragile wisps of hair criss-crossed over the older woman's scalp.

"They're away for a couple of months. Didn't I tell you? They boarded the last steamer and went to New York to stay with Mrs. Leary's sister in Rochester. You can't blame them for wanting to be with family. And they pay rent for their room while they're away. Although I do give them a special rate over this period."

"Maybe her sister will persuade her to move to New York permanently," said Maggie. "I met the sister, you know. She used to come across the lake to visit the couple when they lived in the centre of town."

"I don't know. The Learys are in their eighties, and I don't think they'd move now. It's easier for them to board here than to keep a house in town. Although there might come a time when they won't be able to manage the back stairs to get up to their bedroom. I guess we'll all face that when we have to."

"They sold their house in town. That couldn't have been easy for them."

"They feel safe here," said Zel. "Having others living in the same house."

"And the teacher?"

"She's still around, though she's often out with friends on the weekends. She'll be here until the school term ends in December, and then she'll go home to her parents in Belleville for the Christmas holiday. I'll be busy, because I still have a couple of rooms to work on so I can attract more boarders. I also want to cut some cedar boughs to strew throughout the closets. And I've promised the workroom out there to Lukas. Now that there's heating—I had a stove put in—he can cook his meals and be completely independent of the main house. Eventually, we'll move the piano out, too. He and the handyman will have to manage that with whatever help they can bring from town."

"Lukas is moving here? Our music director?" Did Zel detect her reaction, her surprise?

"He came to see me about taking over the smaller building when the warm weather comes again. The space suits him better than the rooming house where he lives now. He's already moved in some extra furniture, including a new dresser and bed. He and the handyman did the lugging and carrying. They managed to get everything straightened around and presentable. They've quite converted the space. But don't worry, you and I can still use the work table for our skating costumes. Lukas won't move in until spring. Don't forget, Maggie, he needs to have a piano wherever he lives. Mine isn't used much except when I practise hymns for church, so here it sits, pushed against the dining-room wall. When he moves into the other building, he'll be able to play whenever he wants. When Lukas was here to help straighten around the workroom, the teacher asked if he would play something for us, so he came into the house and sat at the piano and played Liszt—an étude. We sat in our chairs, transported. Sometimes he practises at Naylor's when no one's around. There are pianos in town, plenty of them, but not at his rooming house. He seemed pleased to know he could use the one here." Zel stopped to remember. "No one has ever played my piano the way he did that day."

"The boarders at his rooming house are going to miss him," said Maggie.

"I suppose they might. Though from what I hear, he doesn't talk much about himself."

"It's the same at rehearsals."

"That's true, but there are people who speculate," said Zel.

"I'm not sure what you mean," said Maggie.

"About where he's from."

"What difference does that make? He's from Europe. And he's creating something new in the town. People who care about music are glad he's here. I'm glad."

Zel went over to the oven to slide in a cookie sheet that was covered with bite-sized potato logs. She had prepared them before leaving for church, and now they had only to be heated and browned. The tiny logs, along with slices of cold beef and tea, would be their midday meal before they got down to work.

While Zel went upstairs to change out of her church clothes, Maggie thought about Lukas, who was responsible for the upcoming concert: her solos, three choral works, the tenor's solo—everything on the programme that was musical, including his own performances. She thought of his hands, the way his long fingers became one with the keys when he broke into the silence. She thought of *Clair de lune*, the beginning notes that invited the listener to be attentive, expectant. She thought of the way he paused and then continued, seamlessly. When she heard his music during practice, she wanted to drift outside herself and into some parallel world. A world unbruised and filled with healing. She wanted to lie on the floor during those moments, and rest her head against someone's arm. She wanted to close her eyes and imagine a world that held endless possibilities.

The previous week at Naylor's, Lukas had returned to the piano after rehearsal was over. He knew that Maggie and Zel were staying behind to tidy up. Everyone else had left. Lukas played for the two women, and Maggie was in no hurry to leave while he was bent over the keyboard. At the end of the piece, he stayed at the piano for several moments, looking down at the keys.

Maggie and Zel did not move. They exchanged glances, waiting.

"He died only last year," Lukas said, finally, his voice low so that the women had to strain to hear. "Debussy. He died early, in his fifties. He might have created so much more."

He closed the cover over the keyboard then, and reached for his thin winter coat. The three, Lukas, Zel and Maggie, left the theatre together through the side exit, and said their goodbyes in the street.

Until five months ago, Lukas had been living somewhere in Europe. So far away, Maggie could not imagine his part of the world. Her impressions of Europe were second-hand: images from books, photos in magazines, newspaper accounts—everything coloured by war. Ypres, the Somme, areas flattened, wiped out; areas in which injured soldiers readied for evacuation lay on stretchers lined up along the ground; photos of soldiers moving single file between trench walls; streets with rows of military ambulances ready to leap into service; wheelbarrows heaped with blankets and bedding; horses and carts dragging away sparse belongings when their owners were forced to move out of villages and towns. That was what Maggie imagined. That, and some sort of unfathomable darkness into which young men had disappeared.

There had to be other, undamaged parts of Europe. She knew there must be places that remained as they had been before the war. She had seen photos of celebrating crowds in London; photos of Wilson, Clemenceau and Lloyd George strutting along a Paris street in their top hats, bearing sticks and canes. She'd seen contrasting photos of chauffeurs playing cards outside on the street while, inside, their masters decided the fates and boundaries of nations. It was impossible to keep up. New books about the war had already begun to arrive on the library shelves, the ink barely dry on the Treaty of Versailles. How could Europe be imagined after what its people had been through?

Maggie had never had the opportunity to travel to England, Ireland, Scotland, the Continent. Few people in Deseronto had crossed the ocean except for the Scots and Irish who had settled in the town and on surrounding farms, and the young men who'd been transported on ships in the opposite direction— men who'd fought and died, and men who'd lived to come home. Some of her nephews had taken part in the war—including Kenan, who'd never spoken to her of what he had been through, and probably never would.

And then, after the war was over, Lukas, who had no connection whatever to the town, had made his own journey to Canada. Arriving in, of all places, Deseronto. Lukas had turned his back on his homeland, though Maggie did not know exactly where that homeland was. A wanderer, people in town were saying. Which meant: a wanderer without a home. What was astonishing, Maggie thought, was that Lukas had come to the town at all.

She wasn't sure of his age, though she wondered. Late forties, maybe. He might be about the same age as Am, who would be fifty in the new year. The few facts she was certain of were these: Lukas had boarded a ship that sailed to Canada, docking after some undetermined time at the port of Saint John. From there he made the long journey by train—probably one train after another—arriving in Deseronto during the summer of 1919. After finding lodgings on the ground floor of a rooming house on Fourth Street, he wasted no time before placing hand-printed notices in store windows around town. The first of his purple-inked signs had been fastened to the news board at the entrance to the library where Maggie worked.

Unaccompanied when he arrived, he had stayed on at the rooming house. Word around town was that he was a man who revealed nothing of his past. And yet, in a quiet way, he seemed to be fitting in. Or was he? No one was asking questions. Even the first sign he posted had contained minimal information. An identical notice had been placed in the *Deseronto Post*:

MUSIC DIRECTOR LUKAS SEBASTIAN
STUDIED IN PARIS, BUDAPEST, LONDON
ACCEPTING STUDENTS FOR LESSONS IN
PIANO AND VOICE

That was all. That, and the telephone number of his rooming house. "Music Director" was how he referred to himself. In September he'd placed additional notices announcing his intention to form a choral society. When Maggie auditioned—in no way could she account for her audacity in doing so—Lukas had chosen her not only to sing with the group, but to perform several solos at the New Year's concert. Now it was late November, and despite the man's quiet encouragement, the prospect of singing by herself humbled and terrified her. Lukas believed she was able to perform. He did not make a fuss about this. His attitude was that it was up to her to believe in herself.

She pushed the thought away and tried to add up what she knew of the man. He was unlike anyone she knew. He could speak four languages—she'd learned about the languages not from Lukas but from Zel. That was notoriety enough for any small town. He was beardless, had greying hair, was taller than Am by three or four inches. He had hands she thought of as *fluid*, and wore a brown jacket that was loose on his frame and had elbow-shine. Occasionally at rehearsal, instead of the brown jacket, he wore a button-up grey sweater over a white shirt. The collar of his shirt needed fixing. The button-up sweater was store-bought, easy to tell. He was soft-spoken. His expression held expectation; he listened with concentration and was able to discern the smallest nuance of sound. His passion for music could not be denied. Yes, she thought, Lukas is a man of quiet passion.

But something inside him had yielded. She sensed sadness. Some hidden part of him had given up. His shoulders were sunken, as if the bony structure that supported them was about to pull the soul of him deeper inside, if it could. He seemed unaware of this. He offered no extra information. He did not talk about Paris, Budapest, London during rehearsals. The singers had no knowledge of what he had done there. What he spoke about was the immediate moment, the notes that spilled from the throats of the singers. He responded to the sounds created by her, by Zel, by Andrew the tenor, by Corby Black the bass—all of whom would be singing the music of Elgar and Leslie and Ralph Vaughan Williams. Lukas cared about music that came from the voices of every one of the men and women who sang for him, those who gathered onstage at Naylor's for weekly rehearsals—twice weekly now that the concert date was closing in. That was what he was passionate about.

He had never once addressed her as Maggie. When he pronounced her name it came out as "Magreet." The first time he spoke directly to her during rehearsal, she'd looked down at her feet as if noticing for the first time that her shoes were outrageously shabby. Wondering, not so disconnectedly perhaps, if *she* were shabby. She was used to being called Mags by Am and Maggie by her friends, but never "Magreet." Not by anyone. She'd been aware of two red spots burning in her cheeks.

"You must not lose pitch, Magreet. Support the note there—and there."

And later. "This passage will work only if there is a little drama, Magreet."

"Forget the note you just sang. It's not there. Ah yes. Better. Very nice. Keep your mouth in the same position, shape the note, the next, then—a little break. Exciting, yes. Exciting, Magreet."

Maggie had never been bold enough to believe there would be a day when she would share her voice with an audience. Never an audience of men and women who had purchased tickets to listen. Bold. She was bold. Part of her believed that she must have made a mistake. Singing when she was a child in a one-room schoolhouse—that was one thing. Singing hymns or psalms in the church choir alongside six women and four men, switching from soprano to alto and back to soprano when substituting for someone who had a sore throat—that was expected. But alone on Naylor's stage, preparing for a performance with a choral society in a real theatre with forty other singers? The stage upon which the famous Vernon Castle had danced with his wife, Irene, when he'd lived in Deseronto and had trained pilots during the war? Yes, the same Vernon Castle who had starred in moving pictures and who'd died so tragically in a plane crash in Texas the previous year. The very man, the very stage. Little wonder that after evening rehearsals, Maggie had begun to drag herself home, worried and exhausted. Little wonder that she was having trouble sleeping.

And there was something else. At the end of the last rehearsal, Lukas had asked her, matter-of-factly—though no one else was close enough to hear—to call him Luc. He said this without embarrassment, looking directly at her for a quick moment and then away. Privately, Maggie had shaped the new shortened syllable, allowing it to hover over her tongue.

ZEL RETURNED TO THE KITCHEN AND PLUNKED TWO plates onto the table. She slipped on an oven mitt and served the potato logs. There was a down-to-earth quality about Zel that Maggie loved. She had never quite believed her good fortune when Zel became her friend after moving here during the war and setting up a rooming house at the edge of town. At my age, Maggie thought, a new friend is a gift sent by the gods. And Maggie loved to listen to Zel's voice, whether she was speaking or singing. Especially while she was laughing. A dusky alto voice with a softness to its edges. And comforting. A distinct, strong voice that Maggie had learned to love.

The first time Maggie had seen Zel—they'd met in Meagher's clothing store—Zel's head was tipped back and she was laughing with abandon, her mouth open wide. Two ladies of the town, at the other end of the store, looked over, disapproving. But Maggie had gone up to her, held out a hand and introduced herself. It was as if she'd been tugged across the room by the spell of Zel's personality. It was as if Zel had been gathering all the colour of the room into herself.

Zel also gave the impression that there was no time to lose. That life was here and now, in the moment. Maggie wondered, not for the first time, what Am thought of her friend. He'd met her, many times, but had not commented. Had he, too, fallen under her spell? Maggie wasn't certain.

She got up now, to help. She was almost as comfortable in Zel's kitchen as she was in her own. The two sat across from each other.

"What shall we work on today?" said Zel. "We have the entire afternoon. Music? Our parts for the concert? Costumes for the carnival? Are you still planning to dress as the Angel of Peace? If so, we'll have to make wings. I have muslin here, some wire. And I could be the Joker, standing at your side. What do you think of pantaloons for me, a tunic overtop? I could make a jester's hat, attach bells to the tip of the extensions. We could carry a banner between us and print the word PEACE across it."

"So no one will mistake the message."

"Exactly. The Angel of Peace and the Joker, side by side."

They sat for a moment.

"Of course," Zel added, "we could relax here over tea, and just talk."

"Let's start with music," said Maggie. "We can work on our costumes later. Right now, I need to practise."

She had a sudden memory of Nellie Melba taking her hand, looking at her across the table in the Toronto diner, singing softly, with confidence and with joy. Where was joy when Maggie sang? It must have been there at one time.

"I don't know why I'm so worried about the solos, Zel. But I am. I'm terrified."

Chapter Six

AM LEANED INTO THE SIDE OF THE VAULT AND pressed his palm over his right eye. He was surprised by a visual swirl of brilliant red. He lightened the pressure and the red was replaced by deep blue, studded with closely packed but distant stars. He pressed again and this time a distinct pattern emerged, branches of a fir tree, a latticework of needles, vivid green observed from deep inside a forest.

Was it memory that provided this rush of imagery, this show of colour behind closed eyes? He regained his balance and breathed deeply. His body straightened and he pulled into his full height. The moment passed.

He'd been working inside the walk-in vault on the second floor of the building when a dizzy spell had caused him to reel. Now he inspected the work he'd been asked to do—repairs on an oak shelving unit at the rear of the vault. He appraised the alignment of angled boards, the efficiency of his own efforts.

Ben, the customs officer, walked into the vault to inspect the work.

"Better than when it was brand new, Am. Those shelves have been in the vault since the building opened. They've had their share of wear and tear."

"They won't break now," said Am. "Not before the building itself falls down."

He gathered up his tools, knew that dizziness was about to rock him again, but didn't let it show. He and Ben walked out of the vault, and the heavy door was pushed shut and sealed.

"The fixtures in here gave a good shake when you hooked up the bell to the clock, Am, on the eleventh. Everyone here felt the vibrations. No wonder we keep it disconnected except to ring in the new year."

"I felt the shudders in the tower well enough. I was standing right beside it," said Am. "Mags said the rooms below were quaking, too."

"Imagine, the whole town stopping its business for two minutes. It's good that we did that, to let the soldiers know we appreciate them. And speaking of soldiers, how's that nephew of yours doing? Young Kenan." Ben's face showed genuine concern.

"He's all right. Just likes to be alone most of the time. Won't be forever. I visit him most Sunday afternoons."

"Some of the boys get back on their feet quicker than others," said Ben. He shook his head. One of his own nephews had not come back at all.

Am went down to ground level, to the post office, and checked behind the counter to see if anything else needed fixing while he had his tools handy. He knew everyone in the building:

Jack Conlin, the postmaster; the clerks; just about every man, woman and child who walked in off the street.

A few people stood waiting at the postal counter, including old Clarence at the end of the line. Clarence, who had once practised law, had snow-white hair and carried a scroll around with him whenever he was out on the streets. He'd gone mad years before. The most important object in his life was his scroll. He was always attending to it, rolling, unrolling, peering as if to read the fine print, rolling it up again. When Am greeted him, Clarence smiled and then looked down quickly and busied himself with his scroll.

Another man entered the building and took his place behind Clarence. Am nodded. Had to be the new music director, though they'd never formally met. The man nodded back and then looked straight ahead. His neck was bare, his coat thin, given the weather outside. He looked as if he'd come straight in from the war.

He keeps to himself, Am was thinking. That's not the way we do things here. The town likes to know what its citizens are about. Though what do I do but stay up in the tower most of the time?

Was that true? He supposed it was. He hadn't given the matter a lot of thought, but now that he considered, he realized he'd been spending much of his time alone. Mags was often out, here and there about town. She spent time with her friend Zel when she wasn't working at the library or practising at the theatre for the upcoming concert. She hadn't said much about the music director, except that his name was Lukas. That he was doing good work with the new choral society.

Am continued on down to the basement and checked the coal supply and the boiler. All part of his job to keep the building running. The three floors—including his own apartment—would have to be heated for the next six months. Nothing he couldn't handle. People relied on him. In extremely cold weather, half the town, it seemed, wandered into the post office to keep warm. Stood around and gossiped near the hot-water radiators. In warmer weather, they headed over to Calhoun's and gossiped in the newspaper office. But Calhoun didn't keep his office as warm as the post office in winter, nor was his office as big.

Now that snow had fallen, Am had the outside steps leading up to the stone arches to clear, along with the boardwalk and the walkway at the side of the building. He didn't want any of the town residents slipping and falling on his watch. And no one had. Nor had a soul ever complained about his work.

He thought of the layout of the town and rhymed off the cross streets in his mind: First, Second, Third running south of Main, Fourth, Prince, Centre, George, Mill—his brother's hotel at the corner. Am's part was smack in the centre. He knew the town and the town knew him. He had a role to play in keeping the whole place going. He was the caretaker. He took care of things. And he knew very well that the work also took care of him.

DESERONTO POST, November 1919

Local Items

Dermot O'Neill's New Arlington Hotel: Best $2.00 a day House in Deseronto. This hotel is convenient for travellers, being opposite the Railway Station on the corner of Main and Mill Streets. Telephone communication.

Your editor has read recently that the British Empire now covers about one fifth, or 21%, of the earth's surface.

We have learned that our own Deseronto-born Sgt. Teddy Freeman of the 2nd Battalion, CEF, headed a search party to look for bodies of fellow soldiers while in France. His older brother, James Freeman (Jim), began his pilot training here in Deseronto, and served with the RFC. Teddy was wounded, but the two brothers are now safely returned to the town.

By the grace of God, a glorious victory was granted us over a formidable and unscrupulous enemy. Let us now strive to prove ourselves worthy of the great boon which has been vouchsafed us in the freedom of the world, and the priceless heritage of freedom of speech, thought and action: by applying ourselves thoughtfully, faithfully, steadfastly and thankfully to that which "thy hand findeth to do." Aid is still desperately needed by repatriated French in the devastated areas of northern France. Money donations can be sent. Details obtained from the office of the *Post*.

PERRIN'S PINE TAR CORDIAL: *Don't neglect the cough.*

Chapter Seven

"Turn around," said Maggie. "Other way." She and Tress were standing by the parlour window, where they could watch over the comings and goings of the town. Across and beyond Main Street, despite the biting cold, sun dazzled the whitening surface of the bay. An industrial chimney spewed smoke that hovered over the waterfront in a puffed mass, its frozen shape pressed to the sky as if by a thumb. From a clothesline beside a house across the street, a skirt and pillowcase hung stiffly, the latter indicating undergarments hidden inside.

"Mrs. McClelland," said Tress. "She washes every day. A small load like that isn't worth the waste of soap."

"She believes in being extra clean," said Maggie. "And she launders six days a week, not seven. I know, because I get to look at her clothesline. She also uses my recipe for soap. *Castile, ammonia, sulphur ether, glycerine, alcohol,*" she chanted, as if she were standing there with a wooden spoon and basin in hand. "Look at that skirt," she added. "Must be her daughter being hopeful."

"Her daughter probably sewed it herself," said Tress. "It isn't as long as the ones we wear now. Isn't it shocking how for years we've swept the town streets with every step? Maybe she knows something we don't."

"Won't I be the first to cheer when hemlines are up to our knees and we're no longer required to wear hats," said Maggie. "Women should rebel, every one of us together. Now, turn again."

Tress felt her aunt's hands ladder up her spine, finger thumb, finger thumb. She reached back to shift her long hair. On her days off, she loved wearing her hair down, loose and free. When she worked in the hotel dining room, her mother insisted that it be pinned up severely.

Maggie counted aloud while she tracked rows on the knitted garment Tress had thrown over her shoulders. The laddering stopped at Tress's neck.

"Arms wide. Stretch."

Her niece assumed a scarecrow pose.

Maggie's lips moved silently this time. She counted the rows crosswise, shoulder to shoulder and down one sleeve.

"This won't be difficult," she said. "I don't have a pattern, but your Mamo—may her soul rest—designed so many of the clothes she knitted, a pattern won't exist. I want to knit one for myself, but mine will be a different colour, green, to match my eyes. Let me write down the numbers before I forget."

Tress slipped her arms out from under and watched her aunt write quickly before she ran her fingers along the inside of the garment, identifying the shape and life of it so that she could put wool to needles and replicate the design. Maggie was the busiest person Tress knew. She had recently finished a striped scarf for Am in contrasting browns. When she sewed, she did beautiful fancy-work: cuffs, collars, piping, buttonholes. She did needlework, too, using Berlin wool, though no one called it that anymore.

"Mamo described this as a shrug," said Tress, trying to be helpful. "It isn't exactly a shawl. She made it with sleeves and cuffs so it can't slip . . ."

She did not go on, and Maggie didn't try to fill the gap. The year before, Tress's grandmother had died of the terrible flu that swept through the town and the country just as the war was ending. Mamo's grave was on a hill that overlooked the bay. Although Tress had never voiced this aloud, she couldn't bear the thought of Mamo's body lying in the cemetery under cold earth.

She looked away from her aunt and felt a cold stab of anger. Kenan's life might have ended under the earth in France— beneath a ton of mud. France had kept part of him buried anyway, a living part. She wanted to believe that she and Kenan were as close as they'd been before he joined up, but he never spoke about the war. That part of him was unreachable.

Stop, she told herself. He came home alive, didn't he? Hasn't he walked out of the house for the first time since he returned? She knew, because his new jacket had been worn. She'd found a brittle leaf attached to one sleeve. The jacket had been replaced on the hook by the front door, and the leaf had crumbled in her hand when she'd plucked it from the fabric. She had smiled to herself, even though she'd felt like shouting, like weeping.

How many times had Kenan been out? They hadn't spoken

of this, either. The act, the knowledge, was too raw, too new. The best she could do was to keep believing that walking outside was an ordinary act. For someone like Kenan.

Reading her thoughts, Maggie spoke softly. "Do you think you can persuade Kenan to skate on the bay this winter, now that he's been out? You know how he loved to skate when he was a boy. He had to be chased off the rink at closing every night."

"You knew he left the house?"

"Am saw him from the tower. Not that Am says much. But he told me that."

Maggie could not tell Tress the rest. Could not say that by telling her about Kenan, Am had broken one of the silences that stretched for hours, sometimes days, between them.

"Kenan wore the jacket I bought for him," said Tress. "But he isn't talking. Well, he's talking, but not about leaving the house. And who's to know about skating? Should I be asking for a miracle?"

"He's taken a step forward," said Maggie. "A long stride. According to Am, he went out just as it was getting dark. He probably waited until then so he wouldn't be seen. Better not say too much, for the moment."

"I was working," said Tress. "He chose a time when I was away from the house."

"Maybe the time chose him," said Maggie. "He might not have had a deliberate plan. But he faced this alone, it's important to remember that."

"One way or another, knowing for certain makes me feel as if the earth has moved," said Tress. She pushed at her hair, shoved it back behind her ears.

"The earth does shift underfoot on occasion," said her aunt. She thought of Luc. His world must also have shifted during the war, though she knew no details of that.

"Grania told me months ago that Kenan would walk out of the house when he was ready—then and only then," said Tress, thinking of her sister's prediction. "Everything he does has to have order—some internal pattern I don't understand. He was never like that before he left for the war. Now he gets upset easily if his sense of routine is disrupted or altered. I never touch his stack of papers, magazines—anything of his, really. If I do, he's thrown into confusion. He wants everything to be stable, predictable."

"You have to be patient, Tress, and you are. More than the rest of us, because you live under the same roof as a man who has been through a terrible war. He's had experiences you and I can only attempt to imagine. Maybe he isn't able to imagine being completely better . . . not yet. But he will." Maggie wondered if she sounded convincing.

Tress was thinking to herself but did not tell her aunt that she was not so patient after all. A few weeks ago, she had lost her temper completely. Several mornings in a row, Kenan had refused to come downstairs. He seemed to be losing ground. He stayed in their room until late in the day and came down only after dark. After a few days of this, she had gone upstairs and stood in the doorway and shouted at him to come down. To stop. Stop what he was doing, stop the isolation, stop and join the world because he was driving her crazy. To her surprise, he came down immediately. He went to his chair in the veranda—his safe place—and picked up a paper and began to read.

That was the end of him staying in the bedroom during the daytime. Later, she felt badly, ashamed of the scene she'd created. He could have been pushed to do something unspeakable, something terrible, though she had no idea what that might be. There was anger beneath the surface of him; she had sensed it from the day he'd returned. She had smelled it on his skin.

She could have made things worse.

"If Kenan does get out onto the rink," Maggie went on, "I think he'd be happy to be on skates again. I can't help but remember him as a boy racing around the ice. One time, he skated all the way to Napanee—late in the afternoon, as it turned out. He might have frozen to death. He and Orryn, his friend—well, your friend, too—didn't get back until after dark."

"Neither of them showed up for supper in the evening. Uncle Oak came to our place looking for Kenan, and so did Orryn's father. Everything turned out to be all right, thankfully."

"Well," said Maggie, "I'll never skate as far as Napanee, but I intend to take part in the masquerade in January. Zel has persuaded me to work on a costume. Something we can skate in without tripping. Don't ask what we're planning. We're working on an idea to go as a pair."

"A secret. I don't mind secrets. I won't pry."

"We work at Zel's place whenever we have a chance. Once a week, sometimes twice. Zel is good company and we do laugh together. We use the workroom for sewing, the small building next to the house. You know the one I mean. Zel will be taking in another boarder next spring, she tells me. The second building has only one room but it's big and wide, plenty of space."

Maggie did not mention that it was Luc who would be moving into the workroom when winter was over. Zel's new boarder. That was private information. Though the whole town would know soon enough.

"I want to skate in the carnival," said Tress, "but I haven't decided on a costume." She was thinking that she, too, would like to be with someone with whom she could laugh. Laughter was becoming rare in her own home. There were times when she came through the front door and felt that a curtain of darkness had been drawn, a curtain that could suffocate.

"There will be women on the rink in furs and muffs," said Maggie. "The muffs are shaped like melons this year."

"I've seen them on guests at the hotel. And the men in town will dig out their buffalo mitts and their mouldy beaver hats so they can go as old-timers."

"Someone is sure to dress up as Charlie Chaplin. Last year there were four Charlies. Calhoun, from the town paper, will be a magician. We can count on that. He hauls out his black cape every year."

"There'll be a nun and a bride," said Tress.

"But not the two together." Maggie allowed a wry smile, acknowledging that she and Tress were of different faiths, attended different churches. Though each attended her separate church without the company of her husband.

"I'd like to wear something different," said Tress. "Something that hasn't been thought of before. Maybe I'll borrow my brother's old hockey uniform from school and go as 'Canadian winter sports.' Though that's nothing new. Anyway, I still have plenty of time; the rink isn't ready yet."

"It will be soon," said Maggie. "This part of the bay should be frozen by the end of the year. Am helped, one afternoon, to carry lumber to shore for the skaters' shack. According to him, the weather has been so cold, the men are prepared to build. One more freeze-up is all they need. People are already coming into the post office to stand around downstairs to gossip and stay warm."

"Do you remember the year Kenan and I dressed as gypsies for the carnival? That was just before the war started."

"I do. The two of you danced around the ice like dervishes. I remember how happy you both were."

"Kenan won't be with me this year. Will Uncle Am dress up?"

"I don't know," said Maggie. And she didn't. Am had said not a word about the carnival.

"You two used to skate, didn't you? Together, I mean."

Maggie nodded, though she wanted to stop there. Her niece knew nothing of that time in her life.

"There was no rink at our farm. Who would have made such a thing in the country? We skated on ponds or the creek— it was known as *the crick*. The crick meandered through fields and woods and joined one pond to another. The ice was lumpy and rippled from the wind, but we skated just the same, even in moonlight. That was my favourite time to skate, nighttime. If there was no moon, Am carried a small lantern, a brass one we still have. He was the best man I knew on blades, and then some. If I tired, he was strong enough to pull me along behind. One winter he made snowshoes from birch, with leather straps, and we tramped over the snow around the woods on our farm. He was a man of imagination."

She frowned when she realized she had used the past tense, and wondered if Tress had noticed. But while bringing up the past, she had also called up for herself Am's younger, firmer face, the life and sparkle of his eyes, his wide, strong shoulders, even his narrower hips. None of this, she told herself, has anything to do with my life now.

"Uncle Am can do anything," said Tress. "But he says the same about you. The last time he was at our place to visit Kenan, he told me that when you were in your teens, you were the only girl on the Ninth Concession who worked in the hayfields alongside the men. He said he had to wait for you to grow up so he could marry you."

"He said that? Well, he did have to wait, because he's six years older. And it was my father who got me working in the fields. He taught me to drive the team because he knew I loved the horses. I was skinny and didn't weigh much, so he wrapped the reins around my body and fastened me to the crossboards at the front of the wagon so the horses wouldn't yank me off. He bragged to his friends that I could turn a load of hay on a dime. When I drove the horses, that freed up a man to pitch hay. I *was* good then, though I'd never do it now. I wouldn't be able to."

Maggie laughed softly inside the memory: the raising and lowering of the horses' heads, dust stirred by their hooves, the clanking of harnesses and reins, the scent of new-cut hay, the odour of sweating men around her, an occasional word echoing through the silence that encompassed and made them a single unit with a single purpose. Am had often been part of the crew, keeping an eye out for her, always.

"At the end of the day, it was Father who drove the team through the fields and back to the barn. He sat me on top of the load of hay, and I perched there like a banty rooster." She laughed again because she remembered her father's pride. He had worked hard on the farm because of his love for her, for Nola, for their mother.

"Whatever I did to help," she said, "was a long way off from working two days a week in the town library—and I'm thankful for the job. I've always loved a good book, and now I can put my hands on any one I want."

"You sing. Don't forget that."

"If I talk about the concert, Tress, my nerves will undo me."

"It's almost sold out, you know. There won't be a ticket left by the beginning of December. That means more than five hundred people."

"Which worries me even more," said Maggie. "I've never performed on a stage. Not in a real theatre."

"You sing at your church every week. Can't you think of the concert as a different sort of choir?"

"I can't think of it like that at all."

"Will Uncle Am be there to offer support?"

"He will. I've already bought his ticket."

Maggie looked down at the street below, where two school-children were heading home. They were laughing together, hand in hand, slipping and sliding along the boardwalk in their boots. She glanced down again, but they had vanished.

"If I'm not allowed to ask about your singing, tell me about the farm," said Tress. "I've lived in town all my life and the only farm I ever get to visit is my grandfather's."

"There's nothing to tell. After Am and I married, we bought our own small place. We had a bit of land, a few animals, a few rows of apple trees."

"Did you sell the land when you moved to town?"

"We did. And I don't miss it, not one bit."

What she did not say was that during the weeks and months before they moved to town, she had begun to dream of small hands combing through her long hair. Even now, thinking about the dreams, she remembered the sensation of her hair being sifted through fingers. The dreams stopped when she and Am moved to the apartment. She'd have gone mad if she'd stayed there, on the farm. She'd have gone mad if the dreams had continued.

She passed the knitted shrug back to Tress. Over the bay, a new chain of clouds was about to snare the sun. One cloud broke free and skittered along the horizon, a beetle looking for cover. She shuddered.

Tress understood that Aunt Maggie wanted no more questions today.

Chapter Eight

KENAN HELD A PHOTO IN HIS GOOD HAND. THREE soldiers in uniform in France. Hugh on the right, Kenan on the left, the third soldier between. Out of the depths, grappling for a name. *Bill*, the soldier in the middle, killed only days after the photo was taken. No body found, presumed dead, *was* dead. Kenan dropped the photo to the floor as if it were in flames. He bent forward and picked it up again. Details surfaced quickly, too quickly, firing into his brain from unknown directions.

Bill. A lean, hard-muscled man whose words rattled out of him like rapid-fire bursts from a machine gun. He'd always cursed a blue streak. Told the others that his two biggest fears were being gassed and being buried alive. After the war he planned to work with the Great Farini so he could be shot out of a cannon. As a human cannonball he'd be able to withstand the noise, he said. If he ever got out of the trenches alive, he'd be deaf by then anyway.

But Bill had become a different kind of cannon fodder and had disappeared. A short time after that, Kenan had been wounded and sent to England. Bill's disappearance was one of the gaps in Kenan's memory. Maybe Bill—or his body—had been found while Kenan was in hospital in Blighty.

Now it was Hugh who had tracked Kenan down. Hugh remembered the name of the hometown Kenan had spoken about, and acted on the impulse to write. Kenan could not help wondering what contact would be like if he and Hugh were in the same room. He hadn't seen any of the boys he'd served with since the night he'd been carried off on a stretcher. Nor had Hugh seen Kenan and his half-face of scars. All this time, neither had made a move to find out if the other was alive.

Tress's brother-in-law, Jim, had stopped in at the house to visit several times after he came home from the war in April 1919, and before he left Deseronto. For a time, Kenan had relied on Jim to bring in news of the larger world. Their shared experience allowed a comfort between them, though they'd been to different areas of the Front. Except for Vimy Ridge— they'd been there at the same time. Jim had served as a stretcher bearer, and they had compared notes. How the roads leading to the place had been lined with dead horses. How a pint of hot tea could mean so much to cold and thirsty men. How they'd eaten beans underground—two men to a can—and cheese and jam and biscuits and stew. How, at one stretch, Jim hadn't taken his boots off for thirteen days, and when he was finally able to do so, he had a swelling on his heel so large it had to be lanced.

And sound, the two men had talked about that. About the whumps that felt like the smothering of dynamite. About coming up out of crowded, sweat-soaked rooms and tunnels beneath the earth on Easter Monday, 1917, and emerging into what they instantly understood to be the noises of hell.

Jim had applied to the Soldier Settlement Board and was hoping to farm with the help of the board to give him a start-up. He had the background—he'd grown up on his grandparents' farm in Prince Edward Island—but hadn't yet purchased land. He and Grania had gone to the island to see what properties might be available, and they'd been there since summer. Before making a decision, Jim wanted to spend part of the year in the province where he'd grown up. And now, here was Hugh, from the same island, reappearing in Kenan's life.

Until now, Kenan had received no personal letters since coming home. Only documents about his discharge from the army, messages from the veterans' association, pension applications, letters concerning his injuries. Loss of an eye rated forty percent disability pension; one finger, less than twenty. There had been official suggestions of paying out fifty dollars for each finger lost. But what about an arm, a palm, a wrist, an entire hand? One commission after another was supposed to be working this out.

While he was overseas, Tress had written every week the entire time he'd been away. Uncle Oak had also written and sent news about his bulldog, Jowls; news about who brought what to the welding shop for repairs. He'd even sent Kenan a package containing a rat trap, hoping that would help reduce the misery. But since returning home and until this moment, Kenan had had no word from or about Hugh—who, it was now apparent, had survived after all.

Knowing that Kenan was always at home, Jack Conlin, the postmaster, had dropped the letter off at the house. There were two mail deliveries a day, and occasionally, if something special arrived, Jack would walk along the street and deliver it personally instead of putting it in the box to be collected later. Jack knew how rare was the receipt of personal mail addressed to Kenan. He also owned the house Kenan and Tress were renting, and he knew enough to knock on the front door, leave the envelope and depart.

Kenan sat in his wicker chair in the back veranda to read Hugh's letter. Three pages of letter. He wanted to take his time. He wanted to weigh every word.

Hello Old Stuff

Is this missive finally in your hands? I've thought of you so often, it's a wonder my words didn't spill into the air and reach you in flight. They probably did anyway if this envelope travelled in a mailbag in one of the new flying machines—and not one of the wood-and-canvas contraptions that flew over the lines. One way or another, I hope I've correctly remembered the name of your town.

You would not guess where I am as I write this. In a TB sanatorium, built on the highest point of land on our island, a whopping five hundred feet above sea level. Well, not quite five hundred. Don't laugh, it's a low-lying land.

Yes, that's right, I came down with the white plague, the wasting disease, after I returned home, though I was probably infected when we were "over there." Now, after being "over here" the past eleven months, I've been told that another few months should have me healthy again. If I get to leave this place, I won't be sorry. The staff takes good care of me, but I'm hopeful that I'll be free to pick up my life again by March or April, if I pass muster.

The place isn't exactly a hospital because we live here, though some of us wander about in pyjama suits or bath robes. As you'd expect, only consumptive cases are treated here. And as I've lived in the confines of one building for a very long time, the only news I have to tell is how I spend my days. So here goes.

Everything happens at the slowest possible pace. The passwords are rest and more rest. Sleep all night, up at six-thirty, temperature taken and tray brought for breakfast. Imagine, Old Stuff, how soft we'd be if breakfast had been carried to us on a tray over there. I had no trouble adjusting to the service.

After breakfast, into bed again. Along with pyjamas, this means wearing (in this cold weather) toque, gloves, scarf to cover my throat, a heap of heavy blankets, and then I'm pushed out—or rather, my metal bed is wheeled out by orderlies—to the open-air pavilion for fresh-air treatment. Real air, sea air, salt air. The verandas in the pavilion are wide enough to hold two rows of beds. That's where we—every one of us—spend the next couple of hours. The beds are lined up side by side, and back to sleep we go.

After "the cure"—that's what it's called—our beds are wheeled indoors. We have dinner at noon and the food is good, better than army, I don't complain.

The routine is the same in the afternoon: into bed, toque

pulled over the ears, gloves, scarf, a weight of blankets, and we're wheeled back out. No movement, no talking. We're told not to stretch or reach or cough, if we can help it.

The best part for me is being outside. Don't imagine that we freeze in our beds. Truth is, we're so bundled up, we manage to stay warm. The clear air here beats the fresh-air routine we were subjected to in the trenches, and here there are no lice. I guess the part that bothers me most is that I've been idle. Idle is worse than . . . I don't want to say what it's worse than. After what we've been through, I won't try to compare.

Back to the routine. At the end of the afternoon cure, we're wheeled inside. The nursing sisters wear gowns and keep everything disinfected as much as they can, cards, games, the dishes we use. There's no hand shaking, no smoking. Anything that leaves the place has to be fumigated, including this letter. I'm not allowed to lick the stamp or the envelope, so you don't have to worry. Don't drop the letter where you're standing.

The sun helps clean the bedding, and in good weather, mattresses and pillows are laid out on the grass on the hill to soak up the rays. Much of the year, cows are in the nearby fields. It's all dairy around here, milk and butter and cream. The cream is sent to the cheese and butter factory nearby. The cows are so placid on the slopes, they look as if they'll slide right down to the bottom if the wind blows the wrong way. And wind blows pretty much all the time.

There are two young boys on a farm over on the next hillside. I can't see the farm buildings but I can see fencelines and the top of the hill. Some days, the boys take a kite outside, and sure enough, herring gulls soar in and dive at the kite and screech and flap until the boys tire of the interference and haul their toy out of the sky. Sometimes, I imagine that I can catch a glimpse of sea. A grey sea with the same rumpled look as the quilts on my bed.

We have early supper at five, and another "cure" from six to seven. At bedtime, we're given warm milk to drink. If I have trouble getting to sleep, I listen for far-off waves, especially if there are heavy seas. In the morning, our routine starts again, identical in every way.

The doctor tells me the sounds from my lungs are improving. Some of the men have been coughing blood. I'm free of that now, though others haven't been so lucky. I was plenty scared when I brought up blood last year, and I thought I was done for. It's an awful feeling, as if the inside of the body is about to drown, or smother. But as I said, I am luckier than most. Some who are in worse shape than I am don't get out of their beds at all. Quite a few have had the collapse therapy—a lung collapsed as part of their treatment. And sandbags— think of it! sandbags!—are leaned against their chests while they lie in bed. If the hospital runs short, there'd be a surplus of sandbags, you'd think, from overseas. Shiploads.

Many of the boys here complain of boredom, but I try not to fill my hours with gloom. I manage to keep some of the others in good spirits, but to tell the truth none of us has any energy to spare.

How about you, Old Stuff? I don't know what your injuries amounted to, but I was told that you'd taken shrapnel to the face and one side of your body. One of the boys said your leg, another said your arm. You're the one who'll have *to give it to me straight. However you were hit, I hope you have the least amount of damage, and that you're up and around and faring well. I look forward to a letter from you, and when I get out of here and I'm free of the plague, I have every intention of travelling to Ontario to find you. You'll be forced to introduce me to your wife—you went on and on about her so much, I feel as if I know her. Here, except for nursing sisters, I see only other men.*

Yours, having survived hell and expecting you to have done the same. Keep your head down, mate.

Hugh

P.S. Do you remember when this photo was taken? Not long after, that's when Bill caught it. There was a terrible barrage. We were all in it together. I wasn't more than thirty feet away from the two of you, but there was so much confusion in the dark, I lost contact. I never understood how Bill just disappeared. His body was never found, and of course we had to leave the area immediately. More unfinished business. He might as well have been shot from one of our big guns over to Fritz on the other side. Remember what a fast talker he was? He always said he was going to track down the Great Farini after the war because he wanted to be shot out of a cannon.

Kenan examined the photo again. Stared into it with his one eye. Stared at himself, or rather, the person disguised as his former self. There he was in sepia tones inside a younger, whole body. Two hands to move, two arms to stretch, two ears that listened, two eyes that could see. He looked at Hugh in the photo and wondered if his friend would be recognizable now. By the time Kenan had been taken out of the war, not one of the boys in his unit looked like his earlier self, wounded or not.

In the photo, he and Bill and Hugh were standing side by side. They were holding half-filled mess tins—meat in one, mounded-up potatoes plopped into the other. The tins were dented and battered, as if they'd been flung about when empty. Thrown up into their packs, thrown down onto the ground. Bread, a third of a loaf being his ration, was visible and spilling out of one of his tunic pockets.

Kenan remembered exactly where and when the photo was taken. He could have drawn the scene in detail with pencil and paper. They were behind the lines at the edge of a French village of low hills, with a black stream running through. A few spindly trees remained near the stream, though most had been chopped for firewood. A mess tent had been erected on a flat stretch of ground. He and Bill and Hugh had been ordered to dig pits for burying tin cans. The photo was taken when they stopped to eat.

Kenan had shoved his cap back crookedly, and here was the proof. One ear appeared to be larger than the other because it was pressed forward by the crooked cap. His head had been itchy. Like everyone else, he was full of bites. He was wearing a change of underwear and new socks, neither of which showed in the picture. Like his two friends, he was grinning at the camera as if war did not exist. Except for the uniforms, war might not have been part of the photo at all. He and Hugh and Bill had been marched out of the front lines one day earlier, Bill swearing all the way. All of them knew that the way to benefit from their time behind the lines was to push war away until they had to face it again when they were marched back up. Why not grin at the camera? They were alive in that moment, weren't they?

"Don't let the war smother you, Old Stuff," Hugh used to tell him. "I plan to survive this madness and come out laughing, and you will too. Even if it's the laughter of madmen."

Hugh had survived, and now Kenan had a letter to prove it. Bill had not survived.

In the moment captured by the photo, the expressions on the three faces said nothing more than: *Fill our tins with food and let us wash our socks. Hand over a few cigarettes and we won't think of what we've just been through or what we're heading into when we're sent back up. Let us get rid of the lice and wash and be clean for a few days, let us find a quiet corner where we can read our mail. Mail is what we want. And please don't ask us to think or talk of war.*

They were kept busy. No time to think when they were out of the line. They'd finished their assigned duty; they'd buried hundreds of empty cans. They'd been hosed off with cold water; they'd immersed their bodies in a vat in the bathhouse. After mail call, there'd been training, more training, route marches, gas drill, weapons training, stops for tea or hot Oxo. And occasional sports, if they were lucky. One memorable day, a day of warmth and sunshine, they got to watch a ball game. There was a pitcher named Herb, a wiry man, a youngster from Ontario, but a wonder on the mound. Everyone knew about him. A captain from the YMCA, a giant of a man, a full head taller than anyone on either team, took on the role of umpire. The players removed their tunics and stripped down to their shirt sleeves, braces hitching up their trousers. They all wore puttees, and changed from boots to canvas shoes. More than a few bases were stolen that day because some of the players could run like the wind. Hundreds of men on the sidelines around the makeshift diamond showed their appreciation with whistles and cheers.

Kenan heard Tress coming in through the front door. He took a last look and slid the photo into its envelope, along with Hugh's letter. His hand was shaking.

Bill, he said to himself. *Bill*. And he saw a man's face, unrecognizable, the man's lips shaping the words: *Help me*.

Tress called out while she was removing her boots, and he answered from the veranda. He shoved the envelope deep into his pocket, knowing he'd pull it out later. He'd tell Tress about it soon enough. But until he had a chance to read it over a few times, he wasn't ready to share.

Chapter Nine

BREATHE. BREATHE. WE BREATHE TO SING."
Maggie took a breath and let it out slowly. She listened to Luc's voice as if it were meant for her alone. Did every other singer do the same? She looked around and thought, *Probably*.

Back to the music. They continued on and on, facing him from a double arc of chairs, though they stood to sing. Maggie watched the familiar movement as Luc's hand pivoted at the wrist, created a circle, flicked upward. Every voice responded to the signal, stopped in unison.

Luc was looking around the room, taking in the faces of forty men and women. "Find the expression here. The phrase begins too slowly. Give it new life. Remember, this is a celebration. The audience will be spilling out into the street, ready to face the new year as they leave the theatre. Sing together, sing joyously."

They were working on music for the second half of the concert. Maggie, Zel, Andrew and Corby were to sing solo parts in Elgar's "Peace, Gentle Peace," which immediately preceded the finale, "Land of Hope and Glory." Before intermission, the entire group would be singing two pieces: Henry Leslie's "Annabelle Lee," adapted from the poem by Poe. Andrew, as tenor, would sing solo for that. The other piece was the last of Ralph Vaughan Williams's *Five Mystical Songs*, based on the poetry of George Herbert. Everyone loved singing that one.

As expected, "Auld Lang Syne" was added at the end of the second half. The audience would join in for that, as well as for the closing, "God Save the King."

Luc resumed. "From where we left off. Shape the vowel correctly here. Every one of you has to shape the vowel in the same way. Please."

They sang another few minutes and he stopped them again.

"Approach the last note from above. Try again? Good, good. No, that's not quite what I'm looking for. Make a single statement, stay in tempo. Emphasis on the third beat, yes, yes. We must be together at this point or not at all."

Two hours of this, and everyone was fatiguing. But Luc was not giving up. Not yet. "We need more emphasis on the strong syllables, not *all* syllables. Throw that note away, please. Throw it away completely so I won't have to hear it again."

A ripple of laughter. He thanked everyone, allowed a smile. Told them they'd done well and that was enough for the evening.

After rehearsal, Maggie walked the short distance home. It was past ten o'clock. She and Zel had stayed behind again to tidy up while Andrew stacked chairs at one side of the stage. Luc had asked Maggie to go through one of her solos again. Not only was she to sing Beethoven's arrangement of "A Wand'ring

Gypsy," she would also be performing "The Sun Whose Rays Are All Ablaze" from *The Mikado*. The latter was technically more difficult, but Luc had assured her she could do both. He would work with her later on the Gilbert and Sullivan. This evening, Zel had accompanied her on piano for "A Wand'ring Gypsy" while Luc listened.

"Forget that you're singing Beethoven," Luc told her. "The song has a pleasing natural melody. It is completely in your range. Your challenge is to make it meaningful, give to it your emotion, vary the verses so that each is different from the last. Do not overthink the piece, Magreet. This is a folksong."

Maggie was doing her best to sing with spirit. To stay focused. But it was neither Beethoven's arrangement nor the gypsy song that disturbed her. It was the text from "Peace, Gentle Peace." She was certain she'd sung one of the lines backwards during the earlier part of rehearsal. Mixed up the words. The father to the children's arms? The children to the father's? Had she? No one had said anything. No one seemed to have heard. Her voice must have blended with the voices of the others.

Later, when she and Zel parted in the street, Zel raised an eyebrow.

"What?" Maggie said. "Why are you giving me that look?"

Zel reached out, put her hand on Maggie's arm. "I think you know. I'll see you tomorrow, Maggie. I'll try to stop in at the library for a quick visit."

Maggie climbed the stairs to the apartment, all the while thinking about what her friend had said. There was an air of drama about Zel, a sense of urgency. Perhaps I'm drawn to her because of that, Maggie thought. When things happen in Zel's world, no matter what's going on, she's certain to maximize the drama.

This evening, for instance, she had worn a hackle-feather ruff to rehearsal. A trailing black ruff her late mother had worn around her neck thirty years earlier. The ruff stretched down past Zel's hips. She didn't give a whit for what people in town said about her sense of style. She set her own standards. Sometimes she walked hatless along Main Street, with pink and black ribbons woven through her greying hair. That was enough to keep people talking. And she created her own fashions. A cape when a cape wasn't exactly called for; nonetheless, it was thrown over her shoulders with drama. A bright bow added to a shoe . . . well, who could predict what Zel would wear next? But despite her eccentricities, she was likeable and attractive. Nor could anyone deny her kindness.

Maggie knew that Zel was a strong woman. She had to be to survive on her own. She was capable of making half-turns away from situations that might otherwise contrive to pull her down. She was capable of helping others turn away from hardship and sorrow. She had a head for business. She'd set up a rooming house by herself. She had much to give, so much life to live. It seemed unfair that she was alone in her early fifties. She had married late, and she had loved her husband as she'd loved no one before or since. She told Maggie as much one day when Maggie was visiting.

"I felt responsible," Zel had said. "Responsible for his death, even though my rational self knew that it wasn't my fault. He died of consumption. I kept thinking that if I'd had access to different remedies, or special foods, or more advanced knowledge, I'd have been able to keep him alive. At one time, he was so close to death, I hauled out the sad-irons and ironed my black dress for the funeral. He didn't die until five weeks later, and I felt guilty because I'd ironed my dress too soon. Well, at least it was ready the day he was taken around the farm on the hay wagon. In his coffin."

Maggie understood. The wake for her own father had been held in the parlour of her parents' farmhouse, the single window at the end of the room wide open, the sheer curtains sucked out gently while the breeze wafted in. After the wake, her father was given the last tour of his land in the same manner Zel had described. Every farmer in the area received his final salute this way. A salute from the hard, rocky soil he'd worked throughout his lifetime. Maggie was present when the team was hitched up that October day. Her father's body, in its coffin, was hoisted up to the very wagon upon which he had fastened Maggie to the crossboards with the reins when she'd been a skinny teenager, so she wouldn't be yanked off by the horses.

She and Nola were already married when their father died. The two of them, along with their mother and their husbands, were joined by relatives and friends from neighbouring farms as they walked behind the wagon in October sun. The quiet, deliberate procession made its way around the boundaries of the fields, the horses staying close to the fenceline. The slow and solemn walk was still vivid in Maggie's memory.

When they reached the field farthest from the house, Maggie's mother began to sing. She sang alone, her gaze never leaving her husband's coffin, her voice rising like a bold banner unfurling. She sang "The Bantry Girls' Lament," a song passed down to her from her own family, who had come from County Cork. Maggie had never heard her mother sing so purely, or with so much heartbreak.

> *Who will plow the field now, and who will sow the corn?*
> *Who will wash the sheep now, and keep them neatly shorn?*

The procession passed cairns of stones Maggie's father had heaped at the ends of the fields every spring. Picking stone had not been his favourite work. "The stones," he always told his daughters, "multiply under the earth when we're not looking. They wait until winter, when they're under the snow and have nothing better to do."

Maggie's father had long ago dug the grave for his own father and mother, a grim task. And now, both he and Maggie's mother were buried in the same country cemetery, in a plot beside the one he had dug for his parents.

Maggie had never sung the Irish lament. She vowed she never would. On the day she heard the lament, after her father had been buried and after everyone had gone home, her mother said to her and Nola, the three of them bowed by grief: "I wish eight children had been born to me instead of two, so that when sadness falls we could spread the pain more thinly among us."

Zel had come up out of her own silence after talking about her husband's death. "Isn't it amazing," she said, "how you think you can't survive without someone in your life, and then you find out—you're forced to find out—that you can, after all. Though a part of you goes on loving that person forever."

Maggie had not replied. It was a rare private admission from Zel, who turned away after speaking, and refused to allow Maggie to see her face.

But Zel could also laugh. Loved to laugh her deep, dusky laugh. Laughter was an invitation, as if her life's mission was to engage others in lightheartedness. Maggie could not imagine her own life without her friend's laughter, though she and Zel had known each other only a few years.

MAGGIE OPENED THE DOOR TO THE APARTMENT AND KNEW instantly that Am was out. Even so, she went to the parlour and looked up the ladder. The hatch was open but she'd have sensed his presence whether it was open or closed.

One evening when she'd come home after rehearsal and found the hatch closed, she had quietly pulled back the door of the mahogany cupboard in the parlour. She'd ignored the pendulum cables that hung over the sand, and God forgive her, she had stood there and eavesdropped. Am had been up there with young Kenan, who had ably, it appeared, climbed the ladder. She'd imagined him making his way up to the tower. There was nothing wrong with his legs or feet; one of his arms was perfectly healthy.

The two men were talking and she had spied on them. She had spied, she now told herself, because she was concerned that Am was letting out the old sorrow. Breaking the pact of silence. A surge of anger flared as she thought of this.

It was Kenan's voice she'd heard when she'd first opened the mahogany door. He was saying the word *egg*. And then he cursed. She had recoiled, listening. Kenan never swore in her presence.

"Why did Uncle Oak never give me a goddamn egg to eat? He raised hens—*we* raised hens. I did as much work as he did when I was a boy. One egg a year, that's what I was allowed."

"Don't be harsh on Oak," said Am. "He did his best by you."

"He rarely comes to the house anymore. Well, actually, he does visit, but I never know when to expect him. Weeks go by before he'll stop in."

"He doesn't know what to do. He brought you up, a healthy and spirited boy. When you came home from the war, he didn't—still doesn't—know what he should say. If he did, he'd try to make you better."

There was a long silence and then Am added, "The hurting. He'd want to make the hurting better."

"I shouldn't have lashed out just then," Kenan said. "I eat all the eggs I want now."

"Do you remember how many letters you sent to Oak from overseas?" That was Am.

"I wrote to Tress as often as I could, just about every week."

"But to your uncle?"

"Four times, maybe. At Christmas. One for each year I was in the war. The last was from the hospital in England. Just a few lines. A nursing sister supplied the words and I nodded while she wrote them down. Before that, I figured Tress would pass on any news."

"Five," said Am. "That's how many times you wrote to Oak. He kept the five letters in the pocket of his overalls. The bib pocket. Through the entire war, until you came home. The letters were taken out of the pocket when the overalls were washed, and were tucked back in when the overalls were dry."

There was silence then, as if Am had sensed that Maggie was eavesdropping below. She imagined him pointing to the hatch, letting Kenan know she was there. She had crept away, ashamed because she'd listened, ashamed at being caught.

Now she wondered if Am had ever spied on *her*. Wondered, for that matter, what they really knew of each other after twenty-five years of marriage. Maybe there would be surprises, if ever they tried to put this into words.

But they didn't try. And wouldn't, not after all this time. Instead, they blundered forward day by day.

She would know if he was up there brooding now, wouldn't she? And he *had* been brooding. For weeks, he'd been climbing up to the tower and staying there for long periods. Sometimes he sat on a stool he had dragged behind him up the ladder. He told her he'd taken the stool up so he could reach to clean the cobwebs from the top rafters, but he hadn't bothered to bring it back down.

The only thing she liked about Am staying up there was that Kenan was coming out of his house more to visit, if only after dark. She wondered if Tress knew where his wanderings led him. Kenan had a liking for Am, that was plain to see. When he joined Am in the tower, his visits were good for both men. In Maggie's estimation.

She stood beside the closed cupboard now, wondering about the two chipping away at each other's silence when she was out. She had to smile to herself.

She turned her thoughts to Luc. When he had stood before

the forty singers in the choral group this evening, he'd told them, "I want you to fill your own space. Don't rely on the person next to you. Be aware of the singer beside you, but don't rely. Take charge of your own space and fill it."

Maybe when Am went up to the tower by himself, he was filling his own space. On his terms.

To Maggie, Luc had said, "When you sing, Magreet, watch me. Watch me and trust." His eyebrows went up, his forehead wrinkled. He didn't expect an answer. He wanted the singers to trust what each of them could do.

Maggie wondered if Luc ever dreamed about upcoming performances. She would like to ask. She had begun to dream about hers, and every dream ended the same way. She was onstage at Naylor's, facing the audience, a full house. A disorderly sheaf of papers was propped on a music stand in front of her. She knew what she was supposed to sing, but as soon as she began, her tongue thickened. After a few phrases, her tongue flattened against her lower palate. Panicking, she looked down at the papers, only to realize that the wrong music had been placed there. She shouldn't need the music at all, but she was unable to recall the text. Not a word, not a note. She began to have a heightened awareness of her own breathing. Her heart was beating too rapidly. She was afraid she would stumble, fall over. She was afraid she would cough uncontrollably. Her tongue and her throat were dry.

The audience became restless while she fumbled and leafed through the music. At the same time, her anxiety increased. And then, one person in the audience stood, and another and another, and whole rows of people began to shuffle into the aisles. They turned their backs on her and filed out through the exits. No one looked in her direction.

The emptying of the theatre occurred at a slow tempo— what Luc might describe as *pesante*. It was only when she faced the room of emptied seats that she realized the correct music had been in front of her all along.

Too late.

"A panic dream," she told Zel after the first of the dreams. "Which makes me wonder if I'll be able to perform in the actual concert."

But there was something she hadn't told Zel. A part she had held back. She wasn't even certain this was part of the same dream. It might have been sensed, or added later.

After the exodus by the audience, two figures remained. They were crouched in the back row, side by side, looking up toward the stage. Maggie, her curiosity aroused, began to make her way toward them, down the centre aisle. She needed to know why these two remained when everyone else had left. As she walked, she found that she was unable to increase her pace, and was forced to maintain the same tempo set by the departed crowd. Because she was unable to move quickly, the two figures had vanished by the time she reached the back row of the theatre.

She wondered if Nellie Melba had ever experienced panic dreams in advance of a performance. She wished she had asked when she'd had the chance. And what would Luc say if he knew about Maggie's dreams, or even about her encounter with Melba during the war? What would he say if he knew that she'd met the diva by chance, face to face? That they had talked and laughed like schoolgirls while hiding behind the walls of a booth in a Toronto diner. That Melba had sung softly to Maggie, "Donde lieta uscì," from *La Bohème*.

Maggie had told no one. She had kept the memory of her adventure close and private. She hadn't even told Nola that day, though she'd considered doing so at the time. She knew it was foolish of her, but she was afraid that if she shared the details, she would render the encounter less meaningful. She wouldn't know how to describe what the meeting meant to her. And who would believe, anyway, that she and Melba had spoken to each other, not only as one woman to another, but as one singer to another?

She had never told Am, the man to whom she was married, so how could she now tell Luc, whom she'd known less than half a year? There was even a possibility that prior to the war, Luc had also met Melba, had watched her perform onstage in London or Paris or elsewhere. Still, she kept her memories of Melba to herself.

Maggie was under no illusions about her singing voice. She was forty-three years old. She was not ashamed of her background; she held no pretences. When she was growing up on the farm, she had known that her real gift was not her work in the fields alongside the men but her voice. She had been in demand for house parties and kitchen dances as she'd grown older. She had the gift; everyone said so. She had the wondrous soprano voice that made people stop what they were doing, circle round and listen.

What did one do with such a gift? There was no thought of studying singing. There were no voice lessons to be had. With no piano at home, Maggie had no place to practise except the schoolroom. Now, all these years later, she wished that she had insisted. But insisted what and to whom? She wouldn't have known the possibilities that existed even if she *had* persevered.

Maybe she could have studied somewhere, travelled, found a good teacher. But there was never a suggestion or a single thought of becoming a singer or taking voice lessons. Not for the slender young woman whose schooling came to an end when she graduated from high school. Not for the young woman who could turn a load of hay on a dime, and who, during one January thaw in 1894, married Am from the next farm over, when he was not quite twenty-four and she was barely eighteen.

Chapter Ten

Deseronto: November 27, 1919

Dear Hugh

Your letter found me at home in the town where I grew up. I've wondered for a long time if you were alive or dead, and I'm glad to know it is not the latter. I'm glad, too, to have the photo, and I know precisely where we were when it was taken—though I don't remember the name of the village. Nor do I have any recall of the person who held the camera. What I do remember is that Bill kept us going many a day and night with his never-ending banter.

He was writing too formally. He couldn't relax. He began to take rapid breaths, in-out, in-out. The photo was beside him on the table. He got up from his chair, paced quickly through the house, returned to the table, sat again, picked up the pen, dipped nib to inkwell.

I'm sorry you've been confined to bed in a san all this time, but it sounds as if you have almost recovered. I was sorry enough, too, to hear of the earlier problems you have now overcome.

He didn't have to ask what Hugh had meant when he'd described the coughing up of blood, the sensation of smothering or drowning, the threat of life being taken away. Every boy Kenan had seen die *over there* had hung on to his last breath. He couldn't put a name to even one who'd wanted to die.

But they had. Died. The waste, the terrible, terrible waste of life.

And he was wrong: there was at least one who'd wanted to die. If there was one, there were more. A junior officer had once told Kenan that he'd held a wounded soldier in his arms and the man was so horribly injured, he'd begged the officer to shoot him.

I don't have much to report, except that I spend much of my time sitting in my chair in our back veranda, which looks over the bay. I read for hours and days. No flapping kite to look at, as you describe, no cows sliding down the slope of the backyard. But there is plenty of fresh water, and ice has begun to form. The bay opens out into Lake Ontario—the largest body of water in our area, but never as big as the sea beyond the hills where you are undergoing the cure. Do you recall how we sailed and sailed on the Atlantic and never

*seemed to get anywhere after we set out from Canada? I
looked out over that cold, dark blanket of sameness and could
not help asking myself: What lies beyond? What lies beyond?
The same question, I suppose, that sailors have always asked.
I knew what was behind, but never what was ahead. Who
did? We went off to war like children who'd been blindfolded
for the occasion.*

*Here's what I can tell you. Since stepping out of uniform,
I have a job of sorts, keeping books for the local drugstore. The
job started this year, not last. I account for items sold, items
ordered, stock replacements, profits in, payments out, balances
due and overdue. All of this, I manage from our dining-room
table at home. You'll probably remember me telling you that
I had begun training at the local bank as a teller in 1913.
War broke out before I'd had a chance to work a full year.
I've always had a fascination with numbers, from my earliest
years at school.*

Kenan paused, pen over paper. He experienced a quiet
rejoicing while thinking about the orderly range of items he
listed in the books brought to him every week by Mr. Edwards.
After half a year, he was familiar with, had even become fond
of the sound of, each item listed neatly on the page of its pur-
chaser, line by line in the ledgers. When he was alone in the
house, he spoke aloud as he worked, the words rolling off his
tongue as the letters formed up to create pictures in his mind:
Arnica flowers, Beeswax, Bugleweed, Balsam of Canada, Ginger
lozenges, Rochelle salts, Creolin, Fenugreek, Lysol, Queen of
the Meadow, Medicated pelts, Menthol plasters, Cod-liver oil,

Tan and freckle lotion, Oil of tar, McCrimmon's Deodorant, Petroleum oil, Pitcher's Castoria, Rheumatic capsules, Horse balls, Hair vigour, Smelling salts, Evaporated prunes, Orange sticks, Tooth powders, Horehound drops, Elastic trusses, Gold Label perfumes. And more.

I write page after page of columns. I line up the names of people in town who use poultices for treating boils in unseemly places, or plasters for congestion, or Sunlight soap to control itching. I'm allowed in on the secrets of ailments. I am learning a new language. I know who suffers from gout and arthritis, who has chronic constipation or a disease of indiscretion, whose hand was mangled by heavy machinery and who was kicked by his horse. Item by item, the entries line up beside the buyers in perfect order on the page.

He stopped and decided to add:

Keeping track gives me satisfaction.
Two ledgers are delivered to my home every Saturday, along with a fat envelope filled with copies of sales slips. These are most often in a mess when I receive them. My job is to restore order. I can accomplish this in two days' work every week. Tress takes the ledgers back to the drugstore on Wednesdays.
I do not leave the house.

He pondered whether to remove this last sentence, and decided to leave it as it stood. After being through the war, Hugh would not think anything strange. Kenan's blind walks through the house with his good eye closed. The fingers of his good hand so sensitive—he'd trained them to be that way—he could feel his way through darkness.

> *Actually, I've left the house seven times, but only at night. That many, you say, and over so long a period! Tress has an aunt and uncle who live in town and I've begun to visit the uncle in his tower that overlooks Main Street. Sounds peculiar, I know, but it really is a tower, up over the post office and customs house. The uncle is caretaker of the building, and he and the aunt live in the only apartment, up top. He's a kind man. I've known him since I was a boy, and the aunt, too. They had no children of their own but were generous enough to everyone else's. Am, that's the uncle, says he'll show me how to look after the clockwork and the clock faces in the tower. He says that with a bit of practice, even with my injuries, I'd have no problem taking over his job.*

Kenan wondered if he should also mention his walks out of town, the walks that led him away from Main Street and into the woods in two directions, east and west. How he sought out places after dark. How he had returned to the widow's barn. The falling-down barn where he knew he was safe. He'd found a half-bottle of whisky there on a shelf and had taken a swig or two. If Hugh were here, laughing beside him, he'd say to Kenan, "Take me there, Old Stuff." And Kenan would. And Hugh would stand with him in that dark room that smelled of apples and rotting hay, and he would understand how, in that place, Kenan understood survival.

None of this was the kind of thing to explain in a letter.

You said you might be in the san another few months. Maybe when you are well and after winter is over, you can get yourself on a train and travel to Deseronto. We have an extra room and you can stay with us for a while. Tress would be glad to have a visit from any friend of mine.

Would she? Would she welcome a soldier in the empty room upstairs, across the hall from their bedroom? Kenan didn't know the answer to that. Nor did he know if their lovemaking would be stifled if Tress was aware of someone's presence in the bed across the hall. Everything might become more intense than it already was.

For the moment, none of this mattered. He had no intention of saying a word about a visit from Hugh. He'd wait until his friend wrote to say he was healthy and had been discharged from the sanatorium.

He tried to imagine Hugh sleeping in the extra bedroom, face down, palms pressed to the mattress at shoulder level, ready to pry himself up at a moment's notice. He wondered if Hugh shouted out in his sleep, as Tress told him that *he* sometimes did.

Since you've asked, I'll tell you that my two legs are fit. One arm is dead, my left, but it wasn't taken off. The right arm is good. Right hand is good. Half my face is a mess of scars. I have no vision in the left eye but can see with the right. I can walk through the house with my good eye closed. I've become expert at getting around in the dark. Strange, I know. But you and I have witnessed worlds stranger than mine. I manage. Except for walls.

What was that? He looked at the word the ink had formed. *Walls.* The pen dropped from his hand. His arm stretched out with a will of its own and his palm sliced through air. Was that a sign? A sign that Grania had once taught him in the language of hands? *Walls.*

He flattened a blotter against the word. Tried to organize his thoughts.

If he were capable of doing so, he would tell Hugh that he relived scenes in his head, terrible scenes, imaginings in dreams. There was one dream he could never get into focus. The one that caused him to shout into the room. The one that filled him with anger because he and his friends were close to danger and no one was doing anything about it, no one was giving the order to move them out of reach of that danger.

Those imaginings—what he saw in his mind, what he dreamed and felt and tasted and smelled—were not imaginings at all. They were real, *had* been real the entire time he was overseas. He had never put any of this into words and did not want memories to start tumbling out now. Better to hold the lid on what was behind his eyes. Memory saw with two eyes, no matter if one eye was blind or not. If half the memories had disappeared with the sight in his left eye, he'd be the better for it.

His heart was beginning to pound. He needed to get up and walk. End the letter here, he told himself.

Write again and let me know when you are ready to visit. Get the fresh sea air into your lungs. I'm glad to know that you are alive. I'm glad we made it out. There were times when we could not have believed that. Do you know that men—women, too—have begun to line up to sail the Atlantic now that war is over? They want to travel to Belgium and France; they want to visit graves or places that might be graves. They can't believe that their loved ones will never have a known resting place. They want to see for themselves. They want to ask why and why and why. God help them if they believe they will find an answer.

Kenan

Chapter Eleven

TRESS COLLECTED HER MAIL, WENT AROUND TO the side entrance and walked up to her aunt's apartment. She tore open the envelope, slowed while she read the letter, finished by the time she reached the top stair. She turned around and went back down, stepping into the street while she absorbed the news. She began to walk.

Her sister was expecting a child. The baby would be born the following June. Grania was more than two months into the pregnancy, and she and Jim had decided to return to Deseronto next spring in advance of the birth, because she wanted to be close to family. The next part of the news was that, after returning, they planned to stay on in Ontario. Jim had received a letter with promising news of a farm that was coming up for sale, land and buildings, between Deseronto and Napanee. In the meantime, they were content to remain on the island, and had no plans to travel during the winter months. They had moved to the north shore; they had made friends, Jim had looked up some of his old schoolmates as well as neighbours of his late grandparents. They were renting a small house near Malpeque Bay and Jim had found work, once again helping a local doctor. Some days, when extra workers were needed, he went along to the nearby mill to put in a shift. He was well satisfied with his temporary work.

Every woman I meet, Grania wrote, *hooks rugs or knits or quilts, or all three. The quilting stitches have to be even and tiny, and the lines of the pattern perfectly spaced. I have no problem with sewing tiny stitches after all the fancy-work I did at school, but what I am learning here is to use patterns effectively. I have my own basket of pieced wool and old skirts that I've cut up to work on. The women around have donated another heap for my basket. I've also begun to knit for the baby and will make a serious effort during the winter months. That's what I keep telling myself.*

Jim and I attended the fall fair, which was held nearby, and there were wonderful samples of knitting and quilting and needlework on display. There is a store here where we can buy most things we need, and a community hall where moving pictures are shown. There is a beautiful church at the crossroads, and another at nearby Indian River, though we might have difficulty getting there in the thick of winter— that's the one we attend. One family in the parish is so large, they take up an entire pew on Sundays.

I'm assured that there will be a rink nearby in winter, and hockey matches for the young people. I might get out on skates, as long as I feel well. I've been told, too, that a horse and sleigh can cut across the ice of the Baltic River, so we might try an adventure of that sort.

On hot, sunny days, before and even after the school year started, the neighbouring children begged to be taken to Darnley Shore and, once, farther along to Sea View. On special "outing" days, the children were granted their wishes, and Jim and I were invited along. We went by horse and buggy, though we've also made excursions on foot. We took part in the final fall picnic, bringing sandwiches, building a fire on the beach, making our own tea. The shore picnics are a great treat for everyone, and if there are fishermen around, they are kind about giving us fish, usually cod and mackerel. I'm told that in spring, late May or early June, the gaspereau come in on the tide and go up the streams to spawn. The men go to the run with a lantern and even catch them with their hands, but they have to be careful of the underside, which can cut like a knife—so sharp, the fish are known as sawbellies. I would like to see such a sight.

Just before dawn, gulls gather in the fields, swooping in and, as Jim says, "strutting large." The wind blows here for days on end and at this moment I can see, in the distance, white tips rolling over the surface of the water. Sometimes, a dark line of seaweed is twisted in a continuous thick cord that loops for miles along the sand. On the edge of shore, just before sunset, sandpipers skim close to the waves, lift in formation, swing out over the Gulf, then veer and come back to shore. They land as one, which I find astonishing, as each seems to keep the same position within the formation. During warm weather, anytime I was out walking on the beach, I never tired of watching the sandpipers. I would like to think I have seen all faces of the sea now, but how does one ever know?

Jim has wanted to show me his island for a long time and I've been happy here the past five months. We live in a place of shadow and light, and no matter which way I turn, I am startled by beauty. Sometimes I am saddened at the thought of leaving next spring, but of course I miss everyone and want to come home, too.

I recently met another deaf woman. She attended the School for the Deaf in Halifax, although she spent her early childhood on the island. Her husband is also deaf. They were at school together, and both are a few years older than I. We have begun to visit back and forth, and we share the same sign language. The rest of the time, which is most of the time, I lip-read. Everyone I know is hard at work, but we meet at the store or sometimes at the community hall in the evenings. Most people oblige by facing me when they speak, especially if I am in a group. If they did not, I would have no way of knowing what is going on—unless Jim is with me.

Before I end this letter, I want to tell you about an event that took place in a farmhouse farther along our road. The house is owned by Jim's friend Mac, who lives there with his wife and two children and his father, who is sixty-four. The house has been passed down through generations. You may have trouble believing the story, but it is the talk of the neighbourhood, and I have seen the results with my own eyes.

Ten days ago, there was an immense storm in the late afternoon. At once, I felt thunder in my body. The storm was more destructive than any I ever witnessed along our bay at home. Jim was home and we took refuge, as did anyone who was in the storm's path. Mac's family had gathered in their kitchen to wait out the weather. Mac's father was sitting nearest the stove and had rested his arm along the edge of it, over the water reservoir, when lightning struck the roof of their house. It passed down the chimney and into the stove, and now there is a scorched line running down the wallpaper behind, to prove that this was in no way invented by anyone's imagination. The floor beneath the woodbox splintered, so that will tell you the force of the lightning. The terrible part is that Mac's father was badly injured because of his arm touching the edge of the stove, and now he is paralyzed on one side. From outward appearances, he looks as if he has suffered a violent stroke.

The entire episode has had a grave effect on Mac's family, especially when all felt quite safe indoors. People say that this storm will be talked about fifty years from now, and I believe them. It is amazing how lives can be altered by a calamity of a single moment.

I must close now. I know you will be happy to hear our news—the baby, the move back. I have sent a letter to Mother and Father so that I can tell them myself. They should receive theirs the same day as you receive this. I will put the two in the post together.

With love to you and Kenan. I miss you both, as always,

Grania

After circling the block twice, Tress returned to the tower apartment. She greeted her aunt and handed her the letter.

Maggie sat down to read the news. When she looked up from the letter, she understood immediately her niece's mood.

"When you aren't thinking about becoming pregnant," she said, but her voice faltered when she saw the tears, "that's when you'll find out you are. You and Kenan will have children. It's sure to happen."

"I'm happy for Grania and Jim," said Tress. "I am." She wiped her eyes, drew a breath. "And I'm relieved that they're coming back."

"We all miss them," said Maggie. "But Jim needed to return to the place where he grew up. And they're together now, after years of being apart. As you and Kenan are. You know all about separation, you and Kenan."

"I know more than I care to."

"The war is over, Tress. Jim and Kenan have survived, and every one of us is thankful for that. I'm sure there are things to be worked out between you and Kenan, but you've known each other since childhood. It isn't as if you married a stranger before the war broke out."

"I thought I knew him—at the time. Well, I did. It's hard to explain."

"Of course you knew him. But no one was expecting war to sweep up the young men in its path. No one expected young people's lives to be changed so suddenly, so drastically." She paused. "Think of how much Kenan has improved. That's something we can be sure of."

"He has improved, and I try to remember those early days after he came home. He wasn't speaking then, and didn't, for months."

"That was resolved, thankfully. Now he just needs more time. You need time."

"I try to be realistic, Aunt Maggie. I try to tell myself that the man who wakes up beside me every morning and who walks through the house is the same man who left for the war. He is and he isn't. I don't want to fool myself. I don't want to live a lie. But I do want to live my life and move forward. Being in the middle of things, well . . ." Tress gave up trying to explain.

"There's some level of comfort that comes from knowing each other since childhood, is there not?"

"Yes, but consider how you would feel if this were happening in your marriage. How well did you know Uncle Am before you decided to marry?"

"Oh, I'd known Am and his ways all my life. I knew your father, too, although he and Am were older than Nola and me. Am and I grew up on side-by-side farms, but country life is different in almost every way from town life. On the farm, we were forced to depend on the land. We were bound to it. There was a sense of that, a quiet sense, all along the line. Families knew one another, helped one another."

"Did you and Nola like the same things?"

"We were as different as you and Grania are from each other," said Maggie. "You never knew my parents; I don't know if you're aware that Mother was forty when I was born. At the time of Nola's birth, she was forty-two. I assure you, no one was more surprised than she at our late arrivals.

"When Nola and I were growing up, we were expected to help out on the farm. Gardening, weeding, row after row of lettuce, carrot, radish, beet. Mother never trusted a woman who cut up beets for canning; hers were left whole in the pot. And Nola milked our few Jerseys without complaint, but she hated the milking while she was at it. I don't know how she deceived the cows, because those animals are quick to sense anyone who isn't comfortable around them."

Maggie recalled, while she was speaking, ragged edges around the garden where she had pulled at wildflowers that sprouted there: butter-and-eggs, brown-eyed Susans, campion, blue chicory that left a mark like rope burn down her palm when she tried to snap the stalks. She gathered the chicory anyway, and put her fistful of flowers in water in a jam jar on the dresser she shared with Nola.

"There was no ice in summer, so we couldn't keep perishables for long, but we had plenty of eggs. Father would come in and say, 'What's for supper?' and Mother would laugh and say, 'Let's have eggs.' We ate the hens, too. Nola didn't mind sneaking into the henhouse after dark and reaching up from below to pick a hen clean off its roost. I didn't care for the hens, but I did like being outside with Father, while Nola preferred to help Mother in the kitchen. During haying, when Father and I and the crew stopped to eat in the shade at the side of the wagon, it was Nola who carried our dinner out to us in the fields. A five-pound pail of honey, rounds of cheese that Mother had soaked in vinegar, a loaf of bread for each man. I can hardly believe, now, that I ate half a loaf, myself.

"When we were older, we went to dances and parties at the homes of neighbouring families. Card nights, too. Sometimes, parties were held at our place. There were plenty of dances, especially during winter months. Neighbours arrived by horse and cutter or in big sleighs. My mother sang if there were musicians around. And Am was always in the background, somewhere. He did pay me attention."

Maggie thought of a sudden storm, the sky blackening, wind whipping her hair, Am grabbing her by the hand and running with her to safety. The laughter and exhilaration. The force of the wind around them. They stood in the doorway of the barn and watched the storm, and Maggie turned and saw a wisp, a shape of something . . . a man, a movement, a ghost. The shape disappeared. When she told her mother later, her mother shivered and whispered, "Forerunner," between her teeth. After that, she always said that Maggie had the second sight.

"When did Nola move to Oswego?"

"She swore she'd get away from farm work and made a plan to study at the Ontario Business College in Toronto. She left, all right, when she was eighteen, but it was to move across Lake Ontario. By then, Am and I were married. Nola's husband, Dan, worked at the docks when steam barges used to criss-cross the lake with loads of barley. The barges left from Lazier's Dock right here in town. It was Dan who enticed my sister to move with him across the lake to the state of New York.

"Father didn't want her to marry Dan, and he was blunt about his reasons why. He had once been delayed in town here, on tax business, and had to stay over. Rather than taking a room at a hotel, he accepted an invitation to stay at the home of Dan's parents—Dan was a young boy at the time. At suppertime, Father looked on while Dan and his brothers and sisters heaped their plates with food and disappeared to their bedrooms or to different rooms of the house. He could hear bursts of laughter and conversation coming from here, there and everywhere. Dan's parents were unconcerned. Years later, when Nola declared that she would marry Dan, Father said he didn't want his daughter marrying into a family of people who wandered around at mealtime, setting their plates down in any room of the house. None of that worried Nola. I think Father was more concerned about her being far from home than he was about supper plates in the bedrooms. And he was right. We didn't see her often. Of course, she and Dan returned for Father's funeral."

Maggie stopped, as if her family stories were escaping from someone else's lips. "That was a long time ago," she said abruptly.

But Tress wanted more. "Why did you and Uncle Am move to town? No one in the family ever says a word about that."

Maggie was quiet for a moment. "Probably because we moved here when you were too young to remember. That's old news now. Your father had already bought the hotel. He's the one who heard about the job of looking after this building. He sent word to Am at the farm and told him to come to town quickly so he could apply. Told him the job included this apartment—the only one in the building. When I first saw it, the place appealed to me. Even in the middle of town. I like the daytime activity—I feel as if I'm connected to life that goes on below. And then, after five o'clock, the building becomes so peaceful there's scarcely a noise to be heard. Unless Am is wandering around, doing his work."

"I wish I could say we have peace at our place," said Tress. "Everything, every part of our lives, has changed. I've tried to talk to Kenan—about us, I mean—but my words sound thin and false, even to me. I know the problems have to do with the war. Sometimes I think it's easier to bury whatever happened over there and let it stay buried. Kenan doesn't exactly say that, but I think he feels the same. He says nothing of the war, nor do I ask." She pushed her hair behind her ears. "Other things have changed, too."

"What things?"

Tress tried to keep the bitterness out of her voice. "Kenan spends much of his time in the veranda and stares out at the bay. He likes to sit by himself in the dark. I don't think he notices when the lights are on or when they're off. He forgets some events completely and remembers others in astonishing detail. He takes long, slow breaths before he talks. There are times when he speaks with extreme care. At other times, he becomes silent unexpectedly, as if he's listening not only to me but to the room itself. That's when I think he doesn't hear me at all. I might tell him something important, and later, he'll swear that he didn't hear me speak. And yet, I have the feeling he's storing everything away, every word. I tell him stories . . . well, I did. I made an effort to help him believe that's he's still a part of town life."

Tress did not add that Kenan did talk about matters unrelated to war. That he blurted out memories of his childhood, of growing up in Uncle Oak's house. Memories unrelated to anything she could point to—except what was unseen and turning over in his mind. Nor did she say that he sometimes woke up in the night, shouting, reaching for her. Frantic.

"He never used to be like this. He loved being around people; he was carefree, happy to discuss anything. Don't you remember him dancing on the veranda of Father's hotel? Singing while he kicked up his heels? Now he behaves as if danger will come flying around a corner of the kitchen if he takes a step toward the doorway without checking first."

They were both silent, and then Tress added, "We've had some good moments, but our old laughter together is what I miss the most." She put her hands to her face. "So I turn away. I go out by myself or with friends because Kenan and I no longer go out together. I visit my brother Bernard. Sometimes Kay and I go to the moving pictures. Or we play cards. Or I stay and visit with Mother after meal shifts are over at the hotel."

Maggie was alarmed. Tress had never before gone into detail about life behind the walls of her narrow house. Now she was unable to stop.

"Did you know that when Kenan was overseas, he had two of his uniform buttons made into earrings for me? He sent them to me during his first leave in England. I can't bring myself to wear them, Aunt Maggie. I couldn't wear them while he was at the Front, not knowing if he was safe, and then, after he was wounded, I still couldn't wear them. What I want to do is throw them into the bay. They're one more reminder of the war."

"He probably doesn't think about them at all," said Maggie. "He has enough to deal with."

"He'd like to work outside the house. I know he would. But he doesn't want the stares or the pity."

"He's been visiting Am," said Maggie. "That's a good sign, maybe even a sign of healing. Am also tries to connect him back. Kenan has been coming out more and more now, even if it's only after dark. You and I both know that many of his wounds are inside and can't be seen." She experienced momentary confusion, wondering if she'd referred to her husband or Tress's.

Tress hadn't noticed. "Kenan reads about soldiers with shell shock all the time," she told her aunt. "I wish he wouldn't. What good will that do? Magazines, pamphlets, newspapers, he never stops reading. He joined the vets' association, and that group has plenty to say. There is always a stack of papers and magazines on the floor beside his chair."

"Have things changed since he started keeping the books for the drugstore?"

"He likes the job. It satisfies his sense of order, and we're glad to have the money coming in. He's already received the soldiers' gratuity. That helped, though it was a one-time payout—six hundred dollars. I put it straight into the bank. We have the small pension because of his injuries, and the income I bring in from my parents at the hotel. Eventually, he'll have to find something else. 'One-armed work,' he'd say if he were here. And then he'd add, sarcastically, 'One-eyed, too.' I hate listening to the sarcasm he sometimes aims at himself. At least he doesn't aim it at me. But I hate to see him like this. No matter how I try to help. Sometimes I think I *am* living with a stranger."

"I don't know what else to say, Tress. Am and I are twice your age and there have been times when we've reached a blind or a standstill in our marriage, and wondered how we got there. You two are young, you're obliged to—you *have* to—fix the problem. You owe that to each other."

Maggie wanted to add, *For me. Do it for me. Show that it can be done. That whatever is wrong can be healed. So you won't end up where Am and I are now. Too late to turn back.*

There is no intimacy, she wanted to add, bluntly. But she did not, and could not, speak this aloud.

She remembered, suddenly, something Nellie Melba had said to her in the diner when they'd met by accident during the war. "Love can distort behaviour, Maggie. Mine, yours, anyone's. Love can be used as an excuse for the way we act."

What had she meant by 'used as an excuse'? By whom? Love given? Love wasted? Love for whom? What Tress was describing was only partly about love. Behaviour was distorted, but that was because of war. Kenan was damaged, and maybe all he could think of right now was being more damaged. But he *was* speaking, he *was* leaving the house. Progress had been made, however slowly.

Maggie didn't know how to comfort Tress. Her twenty-five-year-old niece, whom she had loved since she was a baby and who should never have such cares, had worry lines in her forehead at a time when she might have been glowing with happiness.

How do we proceed? Maggie thought. How does any of us proceed when we are struck down?

And what about her own behaviour? How long had it been since *she* had loved and been loved in return? She thought of herself and Am, side by side in their bed, never touching. Not for a long time. Months? A year? Surely not that long. She did not want to remember.

Deseronto, Ontario

DECEMBER 1919

DESERONTO POST, December 1919

Local Items

The Bay Is Frozen

Take note, all you townsfolk. Pull your skates out of your cellars and sheds, and get sharpening the blades. We've heard rumours from reliable sources that the rink on the bay will be open before Christmas. And with Christmas fast approaching, boys and girls who are not yet in possession of their own skates can no better be pleased than by a pair waiting for them under the yule tree. Support our local merchants as we move forward into the season of whiteness and cold and winter fun.

Flying Trips to Europe

A local flier predicts that we shall within a few years fly across the Atlantic in the forenoon and return in the afternoon. We shall return in the afternoon, no doubt, because after paying the fare for flying so high, we shall have nothing left upon which to "do" lands beyond the Atlantic.

St. Mark's Church (Anglican)

First and third Sundays in the month, Holy Communion 11 a.m.
Sunday School 3 p.m. and Evening Prayer 7 p.m.

$65 buys Gable Square Piano. This would make a first-class practice piano. It is yours for $50 cash, $5 per month. E. A. Houle, Deseronto.

If you like our paper, tell your neighbours; if not, tell us.

Chapter Twelve

THE COLD SNAP LASTED MORE THAN TWO WEEKS. Boats had arrived at the wharf well before freeze-up, dropping off hundred-pound sacks of sugar and flour for the town hotels, bakers and grocers. Snow and more snow had fallen. The landscape was white, the ice on the bay the colour of unpolished silver. The skaters' shack had been constructed. On Wednesday morning, Kenan carried his tea to the veranda and sat in his chair.

Outside, men were slogging their way through newly drifted snow and onto the bay. Once they were offshore, they bored holes at several sites to test the depth of the ice. Now and then, some of the men paused to stomp their feet, expelling white clouds from their lungs as they worked. Even from a few hundred feet, Kenan recognized some of the faces.

An hour later, several men began the more difficult work of clearing snow. By eleven in the morning they had shaped a near-perfect oval. Holes were made at each end, and into each, a tall pole with a high crossbar was lowered. Water was poured around the base to freeze each pole in place. Several men began to work on the wiring for the electric lights that would be attached to the crossbars.

Kenan nodded. The oval was becoming, recognizably, a rink. From the veranda, the cleared ice gave the appearance of being smooth, but Kenan knew better. Up close, there would be wind ripples and bumps and cracks that could trip the skaters. A few men began to work at levelling hard tufts of snow that were stuck to the surface.

Some of the cleared snow was left as a perimeter around part of the oval, and some was pushed back and tossed up to form a bit of a wall along the far side of the rink. This served as a backdrop to the rink itself and gave warning, letting people know they shouldn't wander too much farther out onto the bay, at least not during the early days of winter.

Men had been going in and out of the skaters' shack all morning. Smoke was rising from the chimney. Two men with shovels and scrapers now began to clear a wide path that led from rink to shore. Another crew turned its attention to fencing. Lengths of wire were unrolled and attached to short posts driven into the snow on either side of the path. The posts would serve to signal the path's location, especially after any new snowfall. On the shore side of the rink, a walkway was cleared so that spectators could look over the waist-high snowbanks and watch the skating when they weren't on blades themselves.

By afternoon the rink was ready. The men appeared to be satisfied with their day's work, and Kenan, unseen inside the shadows of his veranda, could not hold back a slight grin. In heavy clothing, the men's bodies were stumpy and rotund. One man pulled off thick gloves and held them between his thighs while he massaged his fingers. He pulled a pipe from an inner pocket, lit it and jammed it between his teeth. He slid the gloves back on. A wisp of smoke floated in front of his face and disappeared.

Kenan looked beyond the men and off to the right. Later in the season, when conditions improved, a portion of the bay would be used for horse races that took place on the ice every year, usually during the latter part of the winter carnival, at the end of January. If the early freeze continued, some people from town would soon be crossing the bay by horse and sleigh, taking the shortcut to Napanee.

Kenan looked back toward the rink, the shack, the wire fencing, and realized that while he'd been daydreaming, the men had finished the job and left. As if from nowhere, a dozen waiting skaters, maybe more, swarmed onto the new rink. Most of them were young boys wearing jackets and caps, wooden skates and lace-ups, all of them in motion at the same time.

IN THE EVENING AFTER SUPPER, TRESS SAID SHE WAS GOING to the moving pictures at Naylor's. She'd be late coming home. She was going out more and more on her own now, with her sister-in-law, Kay, or with other friends. Out to the pictures, to the ice cream parlour, to visit Aunt Maggie, to play euchre, to this, to that. Kenan was losing track.

Before leaving the house, she'd propped a pair of men's skates against the coal scuttle near the side door. She said not a word about the new skates. She propped them there and left.

As soon as she walked away from the house, Kenan went to the side door and examined the skates. These were far more elaborate than his old blocks of wood with steel blades and straps that fastened at heel and toe. These were brown leather lace-ups with finely polished blades. He lifted a skate, held it between his knees and drew his index finger lightly along the steel. Such a blade would not snap like some he had seen during his childhood. He knew one boy from an outlying farm who'd come to town to skate on the rink and wore pieces of bone strapped to his ankleboots—shinbones from a horse or cow, smoothed and polished to a fine edge. The boy's grandfather had brought the bone skates with him when he'd come to Canada from someplace in northern Europe—Kenan couldn't remember exactly which country. Holland, maybe.

What Kenan did know was that every night at exactly ten by the tower clock, the lights on the poles at the ends of the rink went dark. The routine hadn't altered since electricity was installed in the town.

He paced through the house, upstairs and down, sat in his chair, read the newspapers, paced some more. At ten, dressed in outdoor clothes, he stood in his own dark veranda and watched the lights over the rink and in the skaters' shack go out. He waited another twenty minutes, until he was certain that the last of the lingering skaters had departed. He carried his skates out the side door and down the slope of his yard. The rink lay directly ahead. The wall of snow reared up on its far side and caught his attention. A sound roared inside his head and he turned quickly, to face the yard again. His heart was hammering in his chest. He had to will himself to stay calm, alert. He remained motionless for several moments. He turned to face the bay once more but looked down this time, toward the foot-path, and continued on to the rink.

He glanced off to the side. To the west, the frozen surface of the bay was hard and taut, stretching for miles beneath a char-coal sky. The moon, frozen in space, was a half-open eye that offered meagre light. Kenan continued along the path until he reached the shack. His boots crunched against snow, and the boards creaked as he entered. He left the door ajar and, in partial darkness, sat on the bench that was nearest the pot-belly stove. He tugged off his boots with his right hand and yanked up his socks so there would be no folds or wrinkles along the soles of his feet. He slipped his left foot down and into the new skate and felt the snug thud, the perfect fit of the heel. He slid his right foot in, flexed his knees one at a time and pushed his feet through air as if there were pedals beneath them. With effort, he managed to tighten and knot the laces, pressing one ankle against the other, using his dead hand to steady the lace, wrapping the extra length around each ankle before tucking in the ends. He teetered as he stood, but the skates held him upright on the plank floor. Solid.

He walked out into the night, his blades slicing through packed snow. He gasped in the cold air, left the path and stepped onto the ice. His torso shifted left. He shouted as his right arm whirled and he went down, left hip and shoulder slamming hard. He swore, and manoeuvred himself onto his knees. His forehead was resting against the ice. He waited, levered himself up, cursed the dead arm that dangled from his shoulder like an anvil.

The narrow strips of steel upon which his full weight rested were now threatening to tilt him into the surrounding snowbank. He moved forward awkwardly, walking rather than skating toward the centre of the rink. He held his body rigid, could not relax his muscles. He could not get the feel of what he was supposed to do. He wondered if he could count on his legs and feet to remember for him. *Let the body remember.*

Now that he was still, he became aware of the life and tremble of the bay beneath his feet. The colour of the sky had turned from charcoal to unrelenting black, and clouds were drifting across the thin face of the moon. The blackness flattened and spread itself horizontally. This was the same darkness, same horizon, same shore he had witnessed month after month from his chair. What he had not foreseen was how different the bay would be with him standing on its surface. It continued out and out, an unnatural frozen plain, pulled and stretched toward some unimagined vanishing point. He saw how insignificant and contained he had been during the long period he'd remained inside.

He tried to understand the darkness consciously now, not only above but below and all around. He imagined depth and danger. He shirked from neither. He was alone with the night. He had not forgotten the hard lessons about how to stay alive under protection of the dark.

His shins were stiff. He was cold and had scarcely done anything but fall hard and, after that, shuffle about on the new skates. Tomorrow, he'd have a bruise on his hip, probably on his shoulder, too. Once more, he pushed his right foot forward to see what would happen. He stumbled and thought he'd go down again, but saved himself by pulling back and righting his upper body. He knew he should drop his weight, bend his knees slightly, find the core of gravity he could trust. As long as he continued to skate with his shoulders held high, his sense of balance would be scattered. He had a sudden vision of his limbs on short wires flung out from the sides of a tin noisemaker a child might flail from side to side.

His head drooped as he lowered his shoulders, and he began to talk to himself. Face your feet if you have to. Drop your centre if you want to stay upright. Let your weight sink. Relax your knees.

He felt the hint of a large shudder then, a surprising snap that spread beneath his feet. He remembered the sound, the old sensation, the ice reminding him of its presence, the bay alive beneath him.

He propelled himself forward and experienced a moment of freedom, a free-flowing movement. But this, too, was short-lived. His taut body kept him from leaning forward and letting himself glide. The tension kept his head down instead of up, kept his good arm from swinging purposefully, crossing back and forth in front of his chest, doing the work of two arms while he struggled with the balancing act of staying upright.

His voice told him that he would fall again if he stayed on the ice.

He grated his left blade against ice and stopped.

He headed for the shack and removed his skates.

He did not look back, not once. He did not want to see the wall of snow on the far side of the rink, though he was aware of it behind him as he made his way along the path and toward his own white-blanketed yard. Though the distance was short, his legs were numb by the time he stumbled through the side door.

The house was quiet. He wanted to curse against its silence. He wanted to shout out the dangerous words that were in his head. He wanted to set things right. But what he knew and what he had done and what he had witnessed would never be set right.

He removed his heavy mittens, sat on a kitchen chair and peeled off his socks. He hung them, rigid and cold, over the sectional heat shield that stood behind the stove. As he stared at the socks he had another flash of memory, images darting. A quiet moment one evening in France. He'd been sitting in a trench on a low stack of sandbags. Bill, nearby, was perched on a bit of a ledge he had made for himself. They had just finished a meal of stew, cheese and jam. They'd turned over a bully-beef tin and Kenan had melted a bit of wax and stuck a candle on top. Behind the ledge was an opening Bill had dug into the dirt wall, a shabby attempt at a funk hole. Enough space where he could recline if he wanted to grab some sleep, his legs and feet sticking out. There were a few boards, reinforcements, strips of metal sheeting farther along.

Bill, with jam stuck to the side of his face, held up a worn sock that had a giant hole in its heel. He had rubbed his feet with whale oil and now he was showing Kenan his sock. He was grousing non-stop, chattering, laughing, swearing, wiping his cheek with the back of his hand. The never-ending banter continuing, as always.

A few minutes earlier, the two men had been given new socks, homemade socks sent up the line by the Red Cross. Kenan's hands were still functioning as a pair then. He couldn't remember exactly what Bill was saying, but he remembered pulling on his own new socks, registering as he did that they'd been knitted by some unnamed woman in Canada. Someone who had dutifully, perhaps even lovingly, followed instructions: no ridge under the heel, no ridge at the end of the toe, no lump or bump that would cause a blister to form on the foot of a soldier. On his foot.

Tugging that pair of knitted socks up over his heels and ankles was a simple act that soothed during a lull in the war. He couldn't help saying to himself, *A bless'ed pair of socks, a bless'ed pair of socks.* The socks had travelled far. He took a moment to think about each part of the journey they must have had until they'd reached their destination and were fitted snugly to his feet. Thinking about all of this had created comfort and longing. Yes, longing. To be home. To be in a warm bed. To be between sheets, clean sheets, any sheets. To be with Tress. To lie beside her. To reach for her.

But nothing had come out quite as he had imagined. He possessed every one of those yearned-for desires now that he was home again, but his life was . . . he could not put a name to what his life was now.

He walked up the stairs, barefoot, and got into bed. He was chilled through, could hear his own breathing. He got up again and hauled another blanket out of the closet. He threw it over the bed and slid back in again. When he was in France, the collection of an issued blanket was a sign that the unit would soon be on the move. The memory of the blanket, the socks, the memory of Bill disturbed. He did not want to stay awake; he would not wait up for Tress. She would crawl in beside him when she returned home, bringing warmth that might or might not wake him. At the moment, he wanted only sleep.

DESERONTO POST, December 1919

Local Items

This is a reminder that the choral society meets twice weekly, Tuesday and Thursday evenings. Watch for news and details of the New Year's Eve concert, to be held at Naylor's Theatre. There are few tickets remaining, so act quickly. The grand occasion is sure to provide exceptional entertainment.

The following poem was sent to us at the *Post* by a student from the high school:

> *War and Love are strange compeers*
> *War sheds blood, but Love sheds tears;*
> *War has spears, but Love has darts;*
> *War breaks heads, but Love breaks hearts.*

Your editor has read recently that during the late war, carrier pigeons were used by the thousands to bear official army dispatches. France alone had 15,000 at one time. Some pigeons were in use as photographers. A very small camera was strapped to the breast, and as the bird flew, the camera operated.

Think of this! What a marvel!

The ice on the bay holds strong. A few adventurous souls have already taken the shortcut to Napanee with horse and sleigh.

"Salada" Try It—*A teapot test is better than a volume of arguments.*

Chapter Thirteen

W HY DO YOU HAVE TO SPEND SO MUCH TIME up there? During work hours, too."

"In the tower?"

"Yes, the tower." She didn't mean to sound irritated, but her words had come out that way.

"I like it up there. I can see what's going on in the town." He thought of the peering-out space, the people he'd watched trek up and down Main Street through an entire generation: the leaders, the followers, the slackers, the workers, the timid, the brave. The adventurous comings and goings of children.

"You see out, but no one sees in."

"Something like that." She could tell that Am had not considered this in quite the same way.

She wanted to shout. She wanted to scream: *There has to be something better to do than slap cards against a board one after another, hour by hour. The shelf will be scarred from the beating it's taking. There has to be something more instructive, more vital, more interesting to do than peer out through a space between numerals on a clock. Think of your life, ticking away in that confined space.*

And then she thought of her own life and wondered why she should consider it to be any better. With remarkable self-control, she said, "Agnes and Dermot have invited us for Christmas dinner again. They plan to close the hotel dining room after breakfast Christmas morning, and take it over for the family the rest of the day. Bernard and Kay will be there. Young Patrick will be coming home for a few days. Your father, too. Dermot will go to the farm to get him the week before, and he'll stay on awhile at the hotel, as he did last year."

"I knew my brother would want us to join the family. Dermot likes to eat his goose at noon, you know. Twelve o'clock on the nose. Our father, too. That's how it was done on the farm."

"We can eat early. We've done it before. We'll have a light breakfast Christmas morning."

"What about Zel? Weren't you thinking of inviting her here for supper in the evening?"

"Zel will be in Belleville. I've told you before that she has an older brother, nieces and nephews, too. She wants to spend a few days with them, but she'll be back in time for the dress rehearsal. She's been busy making gifts. Sewing non-stop. Buying a few gifts. I've seen her in the shops several times."

"If we eat at my brother's, we'll have to be on time," said Am. "Dermot sticks to his own schedule. Always has. If we don't have a foot in the doorway by twelve o'clock sharp, he'll tell Agnes to go ahead and serve."

"Why would we not be on time?"

Am ignored the question and then considered, or reconsidered.

"Aren't you singing in the choir Christmas morning?"

"I am, but there's an early service, nine o'clock. I'll sing at that. And I'll be singing at the carol service on Christmas Eve."

She thought but did not add, If you'd bother to come to church, you'd know these things. But that discussion had ended long ago. There were times, she admitted, but only to herself, when she wondered why *she* bothered to attend. If she tried to think through the beliefs she'd been taught since childhood, her thoughts tangled in confusion. She prayed the same prayers by rote, sang the same hymns. But some part of her basic beliefs had altered. If this had happened gradually, she wasn't aware. A silent earthquake might have shaken every part of her, but she hadn't felt the ripples at the time. All she knew was that, some of the time, she came away from church with emptiness inside her.

"Will Tress and Kenan be at Dermot's for Christmas dinner?" said Am. "Has young Kenan been out during the daytime?"

"You'd be the one to know that," said Maggie. "You're the one he talks to."

"I know he goes out after dark. Sometimes he comes here, not always."

"Where else does he go?"

"He's been on the rink."

"Ah yes. Tress told me. He tried out the new skates she bought for him."

"He goes other places, too," said Am. He did not add that, several times, he'd watched Kenan enter the woods.

"Maybe he'll venture out in broad daylight on Christmas Day. Maybe Agnes and Dermot will invite Oak for dinner, too."

"I doubt that," said Am. "Oak will eat with Tress and Kenan at their house. As he did last year."

"I think you're right," said Maggie. "Kenan isn't ready for any larger family celebration. Yet."

"He will be." Am headed for the tower ladder as if he'd said all there was to say and even that had been too much.

Maggie was thinking about Kenan's upbringing. Oak was a quiet man but known to the town and respected. People took their business to his welding shop. At one time, he'd raised hens. Oak had always been one to rely on. He was loyal. He'd adopted Kenan and raised him in a womanless house, treating the child as his own.

Well, Kenan was no longer a child and Oak was no longer responsible for him. Since Kenan had returned, Oak didn't seem to know what to say to the lad. Was it because of Kenan's injuries? His changed appearance? It was hard to say. According to Tress, Oak arrived to visit when Kenan first came back, stayed ten or fifteen minutes, excused himself and backed away. He continued to visit, of course. It was just that he wasn't strong on conversation.

Maggie heard noises from above. Cards set out, one at a time. *Snap slap*. And then, Am tinkering with the clock. She wondered if he had conversations with himself when he was alone—the way she did when she was by herself.

The person she couldn't help wondering about was Luc. Where would he be on Christmas Day? What sort of Christmas celebration was he accustomed to? No doubt the lodgers on Fourth Street would do something special. She'd never been inside his rooming house, though the building was close enough. She'd heard that the cook could put together a good meal. It was a popular enough place.

The week before, Luc had walked into the parish hall at St. Mark's while she and several other women were decorating for Christmas. She'd been surprised to see him. After he was introduced to the others, Luc spoke quietly about the choral society's upcoming concert. He told the women he'd been given permission to play the piano in the hall when it wasn't being used. He told them he'd wait, or come back later if he was in the way.

But the women asked him to stay. They were thrilled to meet the music director and wanted to hear him play. They invited him to go ahead, and then they moved toward the doorway, where they continued to arrange branches of evergreens. Their movements, their conversation became more deliberate after Luc's arrival. *Notice me*, they were saying, silently. Or so Maggie imagined.

Luc removed his overcoat and tossed it over a nearby chair. Underneath, he wore the jacket with the elbow-shine. He had taken off his galoshes at the entrance. Maggie, aware of the women in the doorway—as she knew they were of her—stayed beside him and gestured to a crèche into which she was placing a doll to represent the Christ child. Unsettled by Luc's arrival, she began to blurt out a story about an old doll from her childhood. He watched her as if listening for some other, parallel conversation. She felt the red spots in her cheeks. She looked past him and saw cracked paint on a cupboard door. She kept on.

"I lived on a farm," she said, "when I was a child. A farm north of here."

"I, too, lived on a farm," Luc told her. Gently, as if to slow her down. She was close enough to see the lines in his face. Not hard lines. Sad. Always sad.

"Ah." *Where?* she wanted to ask. And then she thought, What difference does it make? I wouldn't know the place anyway. She carried on, wondering why she had chosen this story to tell. Nerves, she told herself. My nerves get the better of me, no matter where I am anymore. She continued to speak rapidly, as if she'd been allotted only a short time.

"My sister, Nola, and I owned one doll between us. I'm not sure how we dreamed this up, but we named her Jezebel. She had a red skirt, red bonnet, white petticoat—our mother must have sewn the outfit. And green eyes that closed when she was lying down." *Like mine*, she wanted to say. *I loved the doll because she had green eyes like mine.* "Every December, our church needed a doll for the crèche, so Nola and I volunteered Jezebel. We took off her skirt and bonnet, pulled her hair back as tightly as we could, swaddled her in strips of cheesecloth and renamed her Jesus. She was put on a bed of straw in a wooden manger our father nailed together for the occasion. She had to lie there with her eyes shut tight until we went back to collect her a week after the new year. And once again, our doll became Jezebel."

Luc had laughed. The women looked over as if impatient to hear his music. When Maggie thought about the encounter later, she realized that she hadn't seen Luc laugh out loud before. She couldn't bring one instance to mind. He was serious during rehearsals. An occasional smile, but serious most of the time. Intense. Yes, that was the word. Intensity surrounded him like an aura, no matter who was present.

After meeting him that day in the parish hall, she had written to Nola in Oswego.

I was thinking today of the way we used to tart up our doll eleven months of the year. And then, come December, we turned her out as plainly as we could so she could switch identities and become Baby Jesus. Do you ever think of old Jezebel? Why did we give her such a name? What ever happened to her? Do you have her with you in New York?

She never mentioned Luc in her letters. She wouldn't know where to start. Nola knew that Maggie was to sing solo in the concert, but from her home across Lake Ontario, she would know nothing about Luc. And what was there to share? If Maggie mentioned even one innocent detail, more would come pouring out. But more of what? There was nothing to tell.

MAGGIE WAS IMPATIENT. SHE WANTED TO WORK AT something, but Am was in the tower. She wanted time alone, wanted to practise her solos. She wasn't able to sing when he was around, even if he could not be seen. No matter where he was in the apartment, she was aware. He went up and down the ladder with such regularity, she could tell when he was carrying something and when he was not. She was aware of him standing, sitting, aware of his shoulder slump, his breathing, his imagined expression, his squinting to see, his sighs over whatever pain he was trying to hold in, his right hand pressed to his lower abdomen. She wondered if he had a problem with his bladder. *Dandelion fluid*, she said to herself. *Sarsaparilla mix. One spoonful before bedtime.* But she could not concoct dandelion fluid at this time of year.

She thought she would go to the bedroom to sing, but she heard footsteps above, as if he were deliberately asserting his presence. She could not free herself of the *weight* of him. She heard him descend the ladder, and suddenly he was in front of her. She looked at his face and her body went cold. He was about to speak, but he must not speak. Maggie brushed past, went to the kitchen, busied herself at the table, turned her back. She heard his footsteps on the ladder again as he went up.

She paced in the kitchen, paced up and down the hall, not knowing what to do. She was agitated, tried to calm herself. She told herself she had to practise, focus on the music that was in her head all the time. Notes and phrases and instructions and corrections and encouragements from Luc. She should be rehearsing her part for "Peace, Gentle Peace." The four soloists were to sing, partly with choral backup, but the entire piece was a cappella. Maggie wanted to go through not only her own part but the entire work by herself and perhaps with Zel, and certainly before the next rehearsal. Repetition would help. Practice would help. She had to be certain of every nuance of text. She was attracted by the way the lines flowed, the gentleness, even the tone of melancholy. Why, then, did she feel that at every turn, the words pulled her down, that they clung to her feet like mud?

Thou dost restore the darkened light of home
Give back the father to his children's arms.

Even with the Boer War over, Elgar might not have included "Peace, Gentle Peace" as part of his *Coronation Ode* had he known of the conflagration that lay ahead.

But who was she to know what Elgar might have done if he'd been capable of peering into the future? Maybe it was appropriate after all. That Luc had chosen this to be performed for the ebbing away of 1919, for the greeting of the first moments of 1920. New beginnings. Perhaps the ode was truly appropriate at the culmination of the year the boys had come home, the year the world had vigorously, if confusedly, attempted settlements of peace.

But the hurt, the death toll, the pain, the damage done. Those could not be erased. Maggie had seen the faces of returned men, the faces of wives and children left to mourn. She had watched Kenan's struggles, which were now Tress's struggles, too. These were far from over. What possible belated effort could turn memories of war into hopes for peace? Peace had to be something separate, something untainted by war. Surely.

She glanced up toward the hatch in the tower floor, afraid that Am would come down again. She and Am did not own a piano. If she were to try to sing in the parlour or kitchen or bedroom—with or without accompaniment—ears would hear. Am would hear from above. Workers would stop and listen on the floor below. She wanted no premature audience through wall or floor or tower hatch.

She decided to walk to Zel's and practise there. Zel had

urged her to come to the rooming house whenever she wanted
to use the piano, whether anyone was at home or not. The
boarders wouldn't mind, but Maggie hoped that everyone had
by now departed for their holiday destinations. Mr. and Mrs.
Leary were already in Rochester. The teacher might or might
not be at Zel's.

Perhaps Zel would be home alone and would want to accompany her while she sang. She didn't mind singing in front of her
friend. Zel would be helpful, and sensitive to Maggie's mood.
Zel, singing alto at her side, had a steadying effect.

If Zel happened to be out, Maggie could accompany herself.
She gathered up the music for the pieces she'd be singing, called
out abruptly to say where she was going and left the apartment.
If Am had heard, he did not reply.

A brittle, metallic sun shone through the afternoon cold.
She could hear skaters before she could see them, the voices of
adults and children laughing and calling to one another while
their blades criss-crossed the ice. The echoed depth of the bay
declared its presence beneath the frozen surface. She crossed
the street to be closer to Tress and Kenan's house, and looked
toward shore. The sight of the rink and the skaters gliding
around the oval tugged at her, made her want to join in. Music
started up near the skaters' shack while she stood there—*The
Skaters' Waltz*—and she stopped to listen. The music calmed.
She felt lighter, as if she were out there gliding around. She
decided that she would go out on the bay this very week. All
she had to do was pull her skates out of the closet and check the
blades to see if they needed sharpening. Maybe she'd skate with
Tress on a day when neither of them was working. Or with Zel.

The length of the skating season was unpredictable because it was dependent on weather, so most people in town took advantage of the ice while it was in good condition. Even the older residents came out to the rink. One of the frequent visitors to the library, Mrs. Woodley, was on the ice every year in a kind of improvised wheelchair. She wasn't strong enough to skate anymore, but she was sure to be seen, her grandson steering her chair from behind, the two of them having a grand time. Mrs. Woodley's chair had narrow metal blades that glided over the surface like sled runners. The boy took wide-legged strokes as he pushed the chair over the ice. Like a grand duchess, his grandmother wrapped herself against the cold, her eyes and a bit of nose showing. A multi-coloured scarf was always twisted around her head and face, and knotted at the side so that the ends drooped like petals over one shoulder. Maggie hoped Mrs. Woodley would be out again this winter in her specially designed chair.

Maybe, Maggie thought, maybe I'll ask Am to skate with me some evening after supper. But after refusing to listen to him today, she didn't know how she would ask. There were tensions between them that she couldn't explain. If she did ask him to skate with her, he might say no. She didn't want him to refuse her. She didn't want to be refused.

She walked to the edge of town and passed the falling-down barn on Zel's property. A new wooden sign had been hung outside the door of the house: JACKSON ROOMING HOUSE, APPLY WITHIN.

Zel was ready to take in more boarders. She had cleared and prepared the last of the available rooms. Her house had two sets

of stairs. The stairs off the kitchen were located behind the pantry and led up to the private area of the house, which included
Zel's personal quarters. Her roomers used the stairs that were
closer to the front door, though the front door was rarely used.
Zel had told Maggie that she'd be advertising after the new year,
for either a couple or two single persons.

There was no light in the kitchen when Maggie approached
the house. Despite the dimness inside, she rapped at the door.
She rapped again and let herself in. She took off her coat and
hat and turned on the kitchen light. The stove was lit; she'd
seen chimney smoke as she walked up the road. Zel was burning coal now, as was most of the town. Maggie warmed her
hands over the stove and took her music through to the dining
room. Where the piano had stood only a week before, a small
table was now pushed against the wall. How had the piano
been moved? That would have been a heavy job. And where
had it moved to?

She was about to put on her coat to return home in disappointment, but she remembered that she had also seen smoke
coming from the chimney of the small building next to the
house. Zel must be out there. Maggie gathered up the pages
again and ran, coatless, from house to workroom. She gave a
quick tap at the door and pushed her way inside. Luc was sitting
at the table, reading. He was alone and startled to see her. Zel's
piano stood against the wall on the left. The room was warm,
warmer than Zel's kitchen.

"I'm sorry," said Maggie. "I'm sorry, I'm sorry. I didn't know
you were here. I was looking for Zel."

Her glance took in the changes as she spoke. A thin wooden

partition, newly raised at the end of the room but not quite reaching the ceiling, concealed a bed and dresser. Partly concealed—there was no door between the main room and this new small bedroom. A makeshift curtain had been pulled back and was tied with cord at one side of the improvised doorway. Maggie recognized the fabric: part of Zel's supply, which they'd recently inspected while choosing what to use for their carnival costumes.

Embarrassed at being in the man's private rooms, Maggie turned, almost tripping on an outer ledge, and went back outside and into Zel's house.

But Luc followed.

"Wait." He was calling out behind her. "You had no way of knowing. I've been here only two days. Zel permitted me to move in earlier than planned. The place . . ." He caught up, hurrying, and gestured in the direction of the workroom. "The place is so much better than what I had in town. Here, I have privacy. I can play the piano as much as I wish and only the trees and barnboards can hear. Zel was kind enough to allow me to move in now instead of waiting until spring."

The two of them looked at his hands, which were held out as if hovering over an unseen keyboard.

"I must go," said Maggie.

"Why must you? Stay, Magreet. Zel will be back shortly. The teacher, too, will be back. Why does everyone call her 'the teacher' instead of her name? Well, that's what I call her now, too. You could make a pot of tea. You know where Zel keeps her things? Perhaps when she comes back, you can practise. That is why you came, yes? To use the piano?"

He pointed toward the pages Maggie had dropped onto the kitchen table, as if this gesture would stop his own questions.

Maggie considered. Zel would not be upset. She would return to her house and find the two of them at her kitchen table, and she would join in as if this were an everyday occurrence.

"All right," said Maggie. "All right." She sank to a chair and added, "Lukas."

"Luc."

"Luc, then." But his name came out differently when her voice spoke it into the air.

"Something like that."

He sat across from her and rested his arms on the table. Maggie knew she was holding her breath. They both rose at the same time: Luc to check that the kettle was full, Maggie to bring cups to the table.

As predicted, Zel was not surprised to see the two of them together. She strode through the door and pulled off her coat just as Maggie was about to pour tea.

"Aha! I saw the light in my kitchen and had a feeling it was you, Maggie. I knew the teacher was in town because she was in the drugstore not fifteen minutes ago. Sorry I wasn't here when you arrived."

"I'm sorry I didn't give any notice," said Maggie. "If I'd known that the piano had been moved out, I wouldn't have presumed . . ."

"The move happened without much of a plan," said Zel. "Lukas and I worked out the arrangements and one of the men from town arrived to deliver coal, so we enlisted him to help while an extra pair of hands and a strong back were available. Actually, he did more pushing and pulling than lifting. Lukas fashioned a trolley on wheels to move the thing out. I did the guiding. The path is short, thank heavens."

"We should have left the piano in the dining room." Luc was apologetic. "Magreet came here to practise."

"And so she shall," said Zel. "Let's have the tea you've made and then the three of us will go out to the workroom."

Maggie poured another cup, and watched as bubbles formed on the surface. Zel scooped them up with a spoon while Luc looked on, amused.

"Bubbles mean money," said Zel. "Income. More boarders after Christmas. Now, Maggie, how shall we proceed? I can play accompaniment and Lukas can help with problems. What do you want to work on?"

"Everything," said Maggie. "But it's the Elgar I'm worried about. I'm late coming in at entrances. I'm worried about not making it through the phrases."

"Leave that behind," said Luc. "All of it. You worry about the wrong things. Use your body to express each phrase. Continue your thought all the way to the last word. That's where I would like you to start. Also, you must change moods in the second half of the concert—from Gilbert and Sullivan, yes, to Elgar— but I will be playing Liszt between the two. For you, a metamorphosis from sun and moon to . . ." He was not reaching her and he could see that.

"Let's go to the workroom and begin," he said. "Already, you have honoured the music with the beauty of your voice, Magreet. You will accomplish much more than that, too."

Maggie did not, could not, tell him or Zel that the words were dragging her down. That when she sang "Peace, Gentle Peace," she was capable of becoming one with the text, yes, but she was also becoming part of "the bruised and broken earth" the text described.

Chapter Fourteen

SATURDAY MORNING, KENAN WOKE WITH TRESS curled against him. He pulled her closer, moved his hand up under her gown and along her thighs. She adjusted to his good side and turned toward him. He did not know how long she'd been awake. With not a word between them, they made love. The room was dim, shadowed; fingers of light reached in around the curtains. Tress was intense and silent. Before he drifted off to sleep again, Kenan considered how the unspoken words between them were accumulating, and how each of them was aware of this.

When he woke for the second time, it was because Tress was sliding over to the edge of the bed. Instinctively, he moved to the warm spot she left behind, but already it had begun to cool. He reached for her as she slipped into her robe.

"No interference," she said. "I'm hungry and I'm going downstairs to make breakfast—as long as you promise to take your turn tomorrow."

"I do," he said. "I promise." Lately, he had begun to share in meal preparation. More cooking than he'd ever done at Uncle Oak's, though his uncle had ensured that he could put a meal together. Kenan was comfortable in the kitchen and he cooked supper once in a while when Tress was working late. With one hand, he could negotiate the stove, the icebox, the utensils, the frying pan, the wiping up. Even peeling potatoes could be done if he sat down, kept the potato steady by using his dead hand as a weight against it.

He could hear Tress in the kitchen below, filling the kettle, putting dishes on the table. She had no shifts at the hotel for the next three days and had declared that she planned to relax, visit friends, catch up on Christmas baking, skate—if weather allowed. There had been two or three stormy days the past week, but when the rink was clear again, she had gone out skating with Kay. When she returned from the rink, her face was glowing, her body brimming with a vitality he hadn't seen in her for months. His fault, he told himself. His fault she wasn't like that all the time. But he knew she didn't blame him; Tress wasn't one to lay blame. Nor did she push him to talk about going out on his own skates. This was no secret, since it was obvious that he'd worn them.

Now he lay in bed, tracking her steps as she moved about below. Weeks had passed since he'd listened to her stories. She had become more and more silent. She was going out frequently with friends.

The frying pan connected with the stovetop. He heard the sizzle of grease. She would be cooking eggs, two for him and one for herself. He wondered if she ever gave any thought to the fact that he had not been permitted to eat eggs when he was a child. Well, that wasn't entirely true. Once a year, Easter morning, an egg had been put before him at breakfast. The rest of the year, he craved what he couldn't have. He watched other children open their lunch buckets at school and lift out hard-boiled eggs, or eggs sliced between slabs of bread. A couple of times he traded a sandwich with classmates, or cheese and honey, all for a bite of egg, just to get the taste. He used to wonder how he could ever imagine the taste when he was allowed only one egg a year. Now he could eat as many as he wanted and he still couldn't describe the taste. An egg tasted like an egg.

His uncle Oak had raised hens for a decade and a half in a tiny area that was mostly a scrubby patch west of their house on Mill Street. There had been hens in the coop for as many years as Kenan could remember. His uncle wore his overalls while tending, feeding, cleaning. Every year in April, May, June, the good laying months, the eggs were put by for storage. One of Kenan's after-school jobs was to immerse the eggs in crocks filled with water glass, a syrupy, jelly-like substance he didn't like to put his hands near. He was taught to pack the eggs carefully, small ends pointed down so the yolks wouldn't settle. It was also his job to check the crocks and add cooled boiled water so the eggs would stay immersed.

Uncle Oak's eggs tasted fresh, even in the middle of winter when egg prices were at their peak. Or so it was said by his loyal customers. How would Kenan have known the taste of a fresh egg from a stale one? No egg had ever been put before him at mealtime. Every egg was a source of income. Uncle Oak relied on the egg money to support the two of them, along with what he earned from the welding shop. What Kenan did know for certain was that in wintertime, his uncle's storage eggs satisfied the demands of their end of town.

And so it evolved that the day for his once-a-year egg during childhood was Easter Sunday. On that morning, two eggs appeared on the kitchen table in a white oval dish that had a thin gold line around its edge. Kenan had easily imagined that a storybook king was about to arrive, or a prince. The two eggs out of sight under the gold-edged lid were hot and promising in their shells. One for Kenan, one for Uncle Oak. Kenan did not know where the special dish had come from. It was stowed on a shelf in the cupboard. Perhaps it had once belonged to Uncle Oak's parents. Apart from Easter morning, the fancy dish with the gold-rimmed lid stayed in the cupboard. It was probably there still.

Why had he been allowed an egg only at Easter when there was an abundance under their noses?

Every year at Easter, when his uncle carried the dish to the table, he said the same thing to Kenan: "This will keep your gizzards functioning." And he smiled to himself as if it was a great joke.

His uncle Oak was a tea drinker. He drank tea in the morning and tea after supper at night. The teapot was his luxury and it matched the dish that held the eggs, a thin gold line rimming the lid. When his uncle was done drinking his tea, he stood on the stoop at the back door of the house and threw the remnants, including the tea leaves, off to the side and onto a flat patch of dirt. Not only were the dregs of tea thrown there, but dishwater, too, was pitched to the side after the dishes were done at the end of the day. In winter, when the earth was frozen, the dishwater and tea collected on the surface of that patch of yard, and froze. The icy patch, no more than ten feet across, was the first small rink upon which Kenan had tried out his skates. If a clump of tea leaves became trapped in the ice, he tripped. He fell more than a few times, but that little frozen patch provided him with his first experience on skates. Long before he went out to the rink on the bay.

This year, Uncle Oak would be joining him and Tress for Christmas dinner. Kenan knew that Tress's parents would like to have them all over to the hotel dining room for dinner, but he wasn't planning to be company for anyone. Not now, not yet.

His own memories of Christmas were of Uncle Oak ensuring that they always had a modest celebration. Every year, Kenan had found a quarter wrapped in a handkerchief under the tree. That, and an orange in his stocking. A wonderful, sweet-tasting, full-of-juice orange that he took his time about eating. Some of his friends from school received an apple Christmas Day, instead of an orange. A Snow apple, or maybe a Spy. But Kenan felt himself lucky to be given an orange. When he was overseas, oranges appeared a few times but had to be divided and shared by three men. A third of an orange was an enormous treat and never failed to bring back memories of Christmas Day.

On Christmas afternoon every year, while Uncle Oak was cooking a small goose for the two of them, Kenan stopped by the house next to the hotel to visit with Tress and Grania and their two brothers, and to see their Christmas gifts. There, Tress's mother gave him special candies. Agnes knew that satins with pale stripes were his favourites. He'd have been happy to have one every day of the year. But satins were sold in the stores for one month only, and that was December. Every Christmas afternoon, Agnes gave him his own small bag—a drawstring bag she made—filled to the top. By exercising willpower, he could make his sticky candies last into the new year.

Agnes also made a special orange pudding for her children on Christmas afternoons, and she included Kenan in that treat as well. The pudding was a sweet custard containing pieces of cut-up orange. Kenan looked forward to the dessert as much as he looked forward to the satin candies.

His uncle went to the bother of putting up a Christmas tree. A small tree in one corner of the dining room. He kept a supply of hickory nuts by the kitchen stove all winter so that he and Kenan could crack them open with the iron poker. One year, his uncle carved a tiny basket from a walnut shell and hung it on the tree. Kenan lifted it off the branch and marvelled at its delicate handle. He was given a jackknife that year, and Uncle Oak taught him how to whittle. After that, Kenan made his own carvings to hang on the tree.

In 1913, Uncle Oak gave up the hens and the egg business. By then, he had more than enough welding to do and there was no shortage of repair work. People were making equipment last instead of buying new. That was the same year he acquired his pup, the bulldog that sprawled in the back doorway, especially if there was a spot of sun to lie in. Oak named the dog Jowls, and Jowls had to be stepped over or pushed out of the way whenever Kenan or his uncle wanted to enter the house.

In that same year, Kenan turned nineteen. He finished school and began to train as a teller at the bank on Main Street.

He and Tress married when he was twenty, and Dermot and Agnes became his in-laws. It was no surprise to anyone when he and Tress announced that they would marry.

Jowls was a year-old pup when Kenan left for the war. When he returned, Jowls was reported to be at his post, though Kenan had been inside no one's house but his own, and in the tower above Maggie and Am's apartment, since coming back. During Uncle Oak's most recent visit, at the end of November, Jowls had been at his heels. The dog hadn't forgotten Kenan, but after the initial excitement of seeing him, he slumped in the doorway of Tress and Kenan's kitchen, transferring his habits from Oak's house to theirs during that short and somewhat less awkward visit. The dog's presence must have helped, because Oak spoke more freely that day and even described a moving picture he'd seen at Naylor's. An exciting picture about the Martin and Osa Johnson expedition to the South Sea Islands. He couldn't stop talking about the threat of cannibals. It was clear that he'd never given cannibals a thought until he was presented with evidence of them at the pictures.

KENAN KNEW HE SHOULD GET OUT OF BED. HE COULD smell sausages frying. There was bread left over from yesterday's baking. Tress would have heated that in the warming oven. He thought of bread and golden syrup, a ration that had been a popular treat at the Front. Every man he knew there had a craving for something sweet.

He decided to go downstairs before Tress called up to him.

But he didn't move. The memories of the yearly egg, the

dish with the gold-rimmed lid, the satin candies, the orange pudding were as vivid as if he had stepped away from them the day before. What he couldn't reconcile was that those parts of his life were disjointed; they didn't fit together inside the person he was now. He also knew there were memories he didn't have. Missing memories. He had never asked about his background, his parents. He had been adopted and brought up by Uncle Oak. Why hadn't he pushed for an explanation? Why hadn't neighbours, teachers, friends, anyone, spoken about his real parents? Why didn't Tress's family ever say anything? Most of all, why had he not thought it strange that everyone had remained silent?

Because Uncle Oak had set the tone while Kenan was growing up, that was why. The tone meant: life is treacherous, no questions asked. And someone—perhaps Oak, perhaps not—had sent out a great hush, a devouring, silencing hush, a wave that had rolled over anyone who might have knowledge of Kenan's birth.

There had to be a simple explanation. Kenan was an orphan and had always been an orphan. Uncle Oak had no doubt adopted him from the orphanage in Belleville when he was a baby, and Kenan couldn't imagine an orphanage giving up its secrets. The life he'd had growing up in his uncle's house was the only one he knew, and he had memories of no other. But what did that explain—knowing you were an orphan? Nothing satisfactory that he could think of. His family attic was empty of skeletons.

Someone might have knowledge of his mother and father. Now, this minute, he craved the tiniest detail, a rattle of bones from the past. What had his mother looked like? His father? Whom did he resemble? Where was the rest of the family—relatives of either parent? Why he wanted to know details now, when he was twenty-five, he couldn't explain. Nor was he certain whom to ask.

Why hadn't anyone come forward? Probably because there was no one. Perhaps he'd sailed from Britain with the Home Children. But whatever his story amounted to, it had also belonged to others. He hadn't arrived in the world by appearing on a log in the middle of a swamp. If he knew where to look, perhaps he would find a person who could tell him. He could, he supposed, ask his uncle point-blank. He made up his mind to do just that if Oak stopped in to visit during the week.

Some people spoke freely and some did not. Some told and others withheld. Kenan's memory shifted suddenly, and he recalled that while he'd been convalescing in hospital in England, the soldier in the bed next to him couldn't stop spilling out everything he knew. Why should he think of him now? At the time, the nursing sisters had repeatedly asked the man to be silent, but he waited until they were busy and then started up again in a low monotone, as if his voice were controlled by a mechanical speaker. The man was small, short; he'd been nicknamed Peewee by his mates, he said, the day he joined up. Most men in the hospital with blighties wanted to stay in bed and do nothing but sleep, but not Peewee. He wanted to talk.

"I inherited from my mother," Peewee said to Kenan—he was lying on his back and turned his head toward Kenan's bed so as to aim his conversation directly— "I inherited the tendency to believe that I could smother at the slightest of causes. My mother disliked closed doors, drawn curtains, rooms deprived of fresh air."

What is he going on about? Kenan thought, not wanting to listen, not wanting to hear about smothering at the slightest of causes. But Peewee would not be stopped, and he knew very well that Kenan was not capable of interrupting. Not then.

Kenan turned on his side to stare the man down with his unbandaged eye. But Peewee remained on his back with his head turned toward Kenan, and was not intimidated by the glare. While he was speaking, however, his hands and arms were in constant motion, and this caused Kenan to stare even harder. Peewee's short arms whirled almost comically through the air above his torso, as if some separate momentum might cause him to rise up from the sheets and perform a sudden cartwheel between their beds.

Peewee's story came out in bursts over several days. He had been crushed under the weight of sandbags and other debris. A shell had exploded in the trench and he'd been buried under three feet of earth, along with four other fellows. The other four had suffocated. Peewee was dug out, dragged out—with cracked ribs and fractured leg—the only one of his mates to survive. Fortunately, a stretcher bearer was nearby with spirits of ammonia to buck him up and get him breathing again.

Once he began to talk about his survival, Peewee wouldn't or couldn't shut up. His constant talking irritated and angered Kenan, though he recognized Peewee's right—the assertion of that right—to spill out his story. Wasn't that what the large gestures of war broke down to? Into smaller bits that were each man's story? Peewee had lived, his friends had died. Peewee had hung on to life, even while every excruciating breath was under threat of being sucked away. He had not wanted to die and he had not died.

On the ward, Peewee wasn't anywhere near death. He survived his wounds and was eventually sent home to his parents, smiling broadly, sitting upright, his chest tightly strapped. His leg was immobilized and propped on a leg-board, a narrow extension that slid under the cushion of his invalid seat. He waved goodbye to Kenan with one of his short arms while he was being wheeled away.

Kenan called up every part of this memory in clear pictures, almost as if *he* had been the one who'd survived being buried alive. Kenan had not wanted to hear the drawn-out episodes of Peewee's story, including intimate details about his mates, but he was forced to listen. He was a silent, unwilling partner in a one-way conversation. He'd have stopped the man if he could have, but at the time he could neither speak nor make a move to set his own limbs in motion to get himself out of bed and shut Peewee up.

Chapter Fifteen

THE VISITS TO LUC CONTINUED. WHEN SHE
wasn't working at the library, Maggie walked up the
hard-packed snowy road to Zel's home several times a week, to
practise and to sing privately for Luc. The teacher who boarded
with Zel had left to spend Christmas with her parents. Mr. and
Mrs. Leary wouldn't be back for many weeks. The concert date
was fast approaching. Luc had assured the singers in the group
that they were improving, and this had been a boost to everyone. Confidence was in the air, a sense that they could, indeed,
call themselves performers, that they might actually be ready by
the end of the year.

When Maggie was with Luc, there was no one around to
censor or judge. There isn't anything to judge, Maggie told
herself. She was out of sight of the eyes of the town. Most of
the time, Zel was in her house. Maggie stopped in to see her
friend but then went on to the workroom, where only Luc was
present. Zel did not try to join them, or suggest that she should

or would. She cautioned Maggie only once. "You are stretching away, Maggie, moving toward an edge. Think of what you have, measure what you might lose." Maggie listened, and heard. But she knew that her friend did not think less of her.

Sometimes, after Maggie sang, Luc stayed at the piano and played for her. Beethoven, occasionally Debussy or Liszt. Once, a sonata by Haydn that Maggie asked him to play again because she loved its deliberate pacing and demanding fingerwork, its delicate mood and dynamic pulsing. Whatever Luc played, whenever he paused, the silences between the two ebbed and flowed naturally. Sometimes they spoke little throughout an entire visit. Their hands did not touch, but an undercurrent flowed between them. Each was aware, always aware.

A very different Luc from the one who stood before the choral society in the evenings. At the theatre, he praised, cajoled, corrected and coaxed the singers to believe that they could create harmony with their voices. That they could create beauty. The singers stood, sang, responded. Gathered up their music and left with satisfaction, with a feeling of accomplishment. Maggie marvelled at the way Luc could lead with such authority. But when he was alone with her, he allowed himself a quietness that calmed them both.

One afternoon, he began a conversation he had not entered before. Scores and pages were spread out over the table. Luc left the piano and sat across from Maggie.

"My father, Magreet," he said. He paused, seeing Maggie go still, and he started again.

"There were three of us—I had two brothers," he said. "I was the youngest. We were never close to our father. He was difficult, hard on us, strict. He had been that way with our mother, too. Demanding, always demanding. When I was nine years old, I saw him strike my mother and she fell to the floor. I was certain it was because of him that she died so early. Her name was Hanna. She was only in her late thirties."

Luc looked down at his hands spread before him. He shifted in his chair.

"My mother's death was not easy to forgive. When I was older, I realized that my father had probably behaved toward her in the same way he had observed his own father behave. What else did he know? And yet, my brothers and I were not like him at all. There was a distance between him and us. We wanted that distance. We knew our place after our mother died. We knew that she had partly been our shield. We learned to survive, but we were not like our father."

He looked at her, but Maggie did not comment, did not interrupt.

"Our house was at the edge of town and our field spread out beyond the lane behind the house. That's the way small villages and towns were organized: in a circle, more or less. Houses together at the centre, the land to be tilled in the larger circumference of the surrounding fields. My brothers and I worked in the field our father owned, worked hard at school, helped in whatever ways we could. We learned to stay out of trouble.

"I did well at school, and from my earliest years, I loved to listen to music. In our town—even a town as small as mine—lived a man who made flutes. The flute maker had met Liszt and had heard him play his own compositions on the piano. Imagine what that meant to me when I was a small boy,

Magreet. Knowing a man who also loved music and who had met Liszt!"

Maggie was watching his face. She knew instinctively that he had not talked of this for a very long time. And yet, he spoke carefully, formally, as if he had told himself the story countless times.

"As it turned out, there were several people in our town who cared about music. One special teacher encouraged me and arranged for me to take piano lessons. At the end of my schooling I was awarded a scholarship. My teacher had recommended me and applied on my behalf. I came home and announced this proudly. Too proudly, perhaps. My father was not interested in having one of his sons accept a scholarship in music. Of what use was music to him?

"I knew what I wanted to do, so I accepted the scholarship without his permission, and I left home. At the time, I was glad to leave, though I felt very much alone. The day I departed, my father told me, 'Nothing will ever come of you. You will be back with your hand out.'

"Of course, I did not go back with my hand out. Because what I was becoming was a musician. I travelled to the city and found a rooming house where I could stay. My room was on the top floor and had a narrow window. In several directions, I could see tiles, jutting chimneys, coral rooftops. Houses were seamed together, laddered upward because there did not seem to be enough space on the ground to hold everyone. So many people, crammed into one place. The entire scene made me think of England, though I had never been to that country. When I did finally travel to London, I realized I had invented the idea from some scrap of story or myth that could not be prised from my imagination. All this time, years were passing, and still I did not return home, not even to visit."

Which country? Maggie wanted to know. *Which town?* But she did not ask. What did it matter? Something would always be withheld. Parts of Luc's story would never be let go.

"Leipzig," he said, because he was aware of her silent question. "Leipzig was the city where I first began my studies. But after several years, I received a letter from my oldest brother, asking me to come home. The letter was more of a telling than an asking. He wrote that our father was ill and had been taken to the hospital. He wrote that our father was dying. At first, I wasn't certain whether to believe him. Maybe my father was trying to force me to come home and had asked my brother to write. I knew our father hated the thought of me becoming a musician. I was no longer under his control. But when I considered, I realized that my brother would be loyal to me after what we had been through as children.

"At the time, it was unusual for someone to be admitted to hospital, especially someone like my father. This was long before the war. If a man was dying, he died at home in the presence of his family. But my father was too ill to be cared for at home by my brothers."

"It's the same here," said Maggie. "In the country and in town. People are cared for in their homes, at the end. The wake is held in the parlour, the vigil in the coolest room, whichever that might be."

"My brother had written that I should make plans to depart immediately. This was not easy; I was forced to borrow money, and I was a two-day journey away. But I made the trip, partly by train and partly on foot. When I arrived in the town of my birth, I went directly to the hospital, as my brother had asked me to do.

"I entered a long ward that had rows of narrow cots on both sides of the room. Both my brothers were present, and they turned when they saw a nurse pointing me in their direction. I saw them at the same instant; it was like seeing myself in duplicate and triplicate.

"My father had been a robust man when I left. In the hospital cot, he was thin and weak and his skin had an unhealthy pallor. When I approached, I saw how truly ill he was. My brothers embraced me, and said they would wait outside so that I could be alone with him. When Father realized it was I who was sitting by his bed, he stared at me as if to convince himself that he was not imagining. There was no greeting, no hello, no joy or admonishment. Instead, he said: 'Lukas, go and bring me a glass of water.'

"I was confused. I suppose I expected to be greeted or welcomed, even railed at. I looked around for someone who could tell me where to get a glass and some water, and I was sent to an area between two wards. When I returned to my father's bed, I put a hand beneath his head and helped to prop him up as he sipped from the glass. He looked at me with an expression of sadness and said, 'Now I am ready to die. Each of my sons has brought me water.'

"He died within the hour. He never once asked what I was doing, or about the music I loved or the years I had been away. He had never written a letter to me. I'd always believed that he was disappointed in me, angry. He said nothing to prove me wrong."

"Even so," said Maggie, "that was a reckoning of sorts. In the hospital. For him, and perhaps for you? It might have been the only way he was capable of making peace."

They sat for a while without speaking.

"Did you marry?" Maggie looked down as she asked.

"Much later," he said. "I met my wife in London, though she was Belgian. Her life ended shortly after the war began. She was killed, massacred along with her parents. Her father was an artist, a painter. She had returned to Dinant, where she was born, to help her family. She was hoping to bring her parents to England soon after the war broke out. There was a rush to travel, to make decisions, to catch a train that could get her to the coast quickly. There was no time for goodbyes because I was in Manchester, directing a choral performance. She left without words. Only a written note. But I remember the words that were spoken before that last trip. All of the words from our years together are gathered in memory. I have all of those."

He stared at the wall behind Maggie.

"We had no children," he said. And added, "I should have travelled with her. To Belgium."

"What would have happened to you?"

"I'm not certain. The same, perhaps. Executed. Shot. Or I might have been able to save her."

"What was her name?"

"Marie." His face was contorted. He got up to shake down the coals in the stove. The ashes fell heavily, abruptly, and jarred the silence. Luc returned to the table and pulled his chair around so that he could sit beside instead of across from her. As if reconsidering, he stood and reached for her hand and tugged her up so that she faced him.

The movement toward each other came from both in the same instant. At least, that is the way Maggie saw herself and Luc when she went over and over the scene, later, in her mind. She took a step forward while being pulled into his arms, and he pressed her against his body and they breathed deeply and quietly. The weariness in his face, the weariness attracted her, the sadness. She had allowed herself to be pulled up by him, to be held; she had allowed herself to hold.

After a time that might have been long or short—she would never be certain—she stepped away and slipped into her coat. She turned to look at Luc before she left, and she walked slowly back to town and the tower apartment. She did not stop in at Zel's kitchen to say goodbye. She saw nothing around her during the walk home. If skaters were gliding around the rink, she did not hear their laughter or their shouts. Neither she nor Luc had spoken after that moment. Her awareness, her consciousness, was alive with song.

Chapter Sixteen

Emyvale, PEI: December 10, 1919

Hello Old Stuff

I can't tell you how happy I was to have your letter put into my hands this morning. There have been changes in your life and mine since we served together over there, and we both seem to be recovering, though my progress has been slow. At least that's the way it has seemed through the months I've been here. I was forced to "settle in" and I did exactly that. You, too, might regard your progress as slow, but it sounds as if you're getting around on your own now—that's what I read between the lines. If you're as good as you say you are at getting around in the dark with your good eye closed, perhaps you'll be persuaded to look at what's beyond when it's open. One way or another, I think we could cheer each other up if we had half a chance. With a bit of luck, that might happen in the spring months, and sooner rather than later.

Since I first wrote to you I have been moved downstairs to a ward we loosely refer to as a "halfway" world, which means that anyone moved here is almost—but not quite— ready to leave for good, and will not be carried out in a box. In other words, I am no longer considered a danger to others or to myself. This gives me more relief than I imagined it would. I've become used to the routine, and the place gives support in many ways. I know my parents are eager to see me out of here, and no doubt my father has plans for me. He has been a schoolteacher in Charlottetown for many years and would like to see me in the same profession. However, I haven't decided about that and I am not ready to return to studies until I've been out of here for a while. I don't intend to be one of the invalided soldiers who becomes an "unemployable," but before I do anything, I want to travel to Ontario to visit you.

You tell me that you read every day, and I, too, have become a perpetual reader. There is a library of sorts at the end of my ward. My father sends books, but those will have to remain here when I leave. I pull just about anything off the shelves, from The Old Curiosity Shop *to* The Weavers *to* Owen Johnson's *novel* Making Money. *We have our own famous author from this island, our Lucy Maud Montgomery. You might have heard of her. She has written stories and books about a girl named Anne. My father knew Maud years ago, before she married and moved to Ontario. She was born north of here and there are still plenty of cousins around. Her mother died of the white plague, same as the one I'm almost cured of.*

I am still required to remain relatively quiet, but I am permitted a bit of walking and mild exercise. Mild in the extreme after what this body was once able to do during our long marches. In the halfway world where I am now, we fellows have the choice of sitting in a comfortable lean-back armchair or lying in bed for our cures. Either way, we still have to bundle up and move outside to the fresh-air pavilion every day. I stay out as much as possible. Weather doesn't always cooperate, but when it does I enjoy the sting of cold on my face. The best days are when sun is mixed in. Now that winter has fully arrived, the biggest change is in the sky. Our island sky is like no other, and if I had even one speck of drawing talent, I'd try to capture what I'm forced to look at so many hours of the day. There are some here who are good at art and who have done a passable job of painting outdoor scenes. But my enjoyment comes from watching. The clearest blues can shift in moments to visions of fire, layers of red and pink as the day wears on. Every morning, a different scene is revealed. Sometimes I think a giant spoon has stirred up the colours. Sometimes the lineup of clouds makes it seem as if someone has laid out an obsessively neat pattern. It's as if nature knows that we are shut-ins, and puts on her display for our eyes alone. And that's enough about me being a nature watcher. If I could, I'd try my hand at painting. Alas, that's not something I am able to do.

One of the locals who works in the laundry here insists on placing an empty chair outside the building if someone succumbs to this disease. A kind of tribute to a life lived. A stark reminder, and no one objects—neither patients nor those who are in charge. The empty chair appears on the lawn—or in the snow—at the front of the property the morning after the death, and is carried back in before dark. Fortunately, this doesn't happen often, but when it does, word spreads through the building quickly. Imagine if we had placed a chair in no man's land for every loss. Such a ritual would have stopped the war. No one would have been able to move through the mountains of lumber.

I try not to dwell on thinking about the bigger questions of why we were over there in the first place and what good it all did in the final run. How could we not be angry at the staggering waste of life—well, the millions of empty chairs? Somehow, we have to move on. We have to gather up what is left to gather and confront the world head on. I'm determined to keep my spirits up.

I was glad to know that you recognized the place where the photo was taken of the three of us, you and me and Bill. It's strange, isn't it, how we remember different angles of the same picture. Memory is a crazy thing—and I don't mean that you and I are crazy. Just that one person can swear that such-and-such happened and so-and-so was present, or was standing just outside the frame of the picture. Another at the same scene will swear the opposite. What happened to our mate Bill? We could piece fragments together to try to figure out the answer. Or maybe it's best not to dwell. Disappearances happened so quickly and brutally, I shouldn't even be writing this down. Some episodes are best forgotten.

That's about it for this missive. Not too much happens around here. We rely on news the staff brings in from outside, and from letters, to know what's going on.

Well, Old Stuff, I send my best to you and your wife for a happy Christmas, and I mean that. Don't forget to tell Tress that I look forward to meeting her. I'll keep you posted as to my progress and when I'll be discharged. I do wonder sometimes if I'll be able to understand the outside world again when I'm let loose in it. A big part of me wishes my father were not waiting in the wings, hoping to convince me to enter his profession. It's possible that anyone who has expectations is sure to be let down.

And speaking of "down," keep your head down, mate, and stay out of trouble.

Yours, Hugh

P.S. One of my roommates was running a fever a few weeks back and kept insisting that the nursing sisters bring him salt herring to place on his feet. They refused to comply. I don't know if they couldn't get any herring or if they thought the practice barbaric. He was upset when the salt herring didn't materialize, but his fever subsided without it, nonetheless.

Chapter Seventeen

FULLY DRESSED, KENAN STOOD AT THE BEDROOM window upstairs until the lights at both ends of the rink flickered and went out. Ten o'clock. He checked the sky, checked the surface of the bay. From here, it was difficult to appraise the condition of the ice. Not much of a glow from the moon, a thin sliver now. He watched while the caretaker of the shack crunched up the path toward Main Street.

Behind him, in bed, Tress was asleep. She had gone to bed early because she would have to leave early in the morning for the breakfast shift. Agnes needed her to fill in again for someone's day off. Kenan didn't keep track of who worked when; he paid attention only to Tress's hours and schedule.

Safe in the darkness, he padded down the stairs in his socks. He tried his best to be silent at the front of the house while he lifted his jacket from the hook. He slid his dead arm down into the sleeve, fastened the toggles, pulled on his mittens and a warm hat with earflaps. He grabbed up his skates on his way out the side door.

The air was blue-black, crisply silent. He walked through the yard and down to the shore and along the path. When he reached the shack, he checked to be certain that no one was around. Two snow shovels had been propped against the outer wall. He let himself inside and sat on the bench. His feet slipped into the new skates more easily this time, but his fingers and hand were still awkward at tightening the laces. The shack was warm; the fire had not yet died in the stove. The woodbox at the end of the room was stacked high in preparation for the next day. A low glow cast shadows through the room. He needed no other light.

He hadn't forgotten the hard fall during his first skate, and he was determined not to stumble this time. He reached the ice, tested, felt his blades scratch against the hard surface. He tried to relax, to let go, and surprised himself with a sprint that took him to the far end of the rink. He had not fallen. He had not once looked toward the wall of snow. He couldn't stand the sight of it.

He stood still after the sprint and considered what to do next. His body would cool quickly if he stayed in one spot. A low wind was blowing in off the bay and he wanted to keep moving. He pushed off again, kept his knees bent, felt his blades carve ice, heard the sound—harsh, familiar, satisfying against the night silence. He tried to warm up, move faster. Tried again to let go, drop his weight, allow his legs to prove their strength. He skated the length of the rink, straight up the centre, reached the far end and almost panicked knowing he'd have to turn.

Then, one foot crossed over the other, right foot over left, and he executed a quick three-step on ice, the dance of the feet, naturally, smoothly, the way he'd always done. One of his blades struck an uneven patch, a ridge in the ice, and he went down, but not so hard this time. He sat on his ass and laughed abruptly into the dark.

He got up again, not easily, but wanting nothing more than to lean into the skate, to keep his legs moving, to feel the release from the long months he'd spent indoors. The wind picked up and he felt, in some half-frozen, half-crazed way, that he was back. Back to something he knew, something that gave him history, his own small place in the larger botched-up, buggered-up world. He was disfigured, yes, but he wanted to be untainted by war. And now that he'd thought of war, there was no pushing it away. He was tainted. He'd been part of it, a party to it. He'd rushed off in 1914, responding to the call. He'd been a child doing a tap dance in his boots on the steps of Tress's parents' hotel.

Charlie Chaplin went to France
To teach the ladies how to dance

Who could have known? Who could possibly have known what awaited?

He tried to adjust to the imbalance of his body, tried to compensate. Let his good arm swing as it would, left to right and back again. He picked up speed, tried once more to free his thoughts. He wondered if his desire to fly across the ice this moment was anything like what it had been for pilots when their machines left the ground as they'd flown their Blériots or Bristol Scouts or

Sopwiths—some that gave the appearance of being alarmingly flimsy—over the trenches. He'd met a pilot from Nova Scotia when he was on leave in London during the second year of the war. They'd shared a table for breakfast in a crowded restaurant one morning, and he'd listened, fascinated, while the man described what it was like to be up there in his machine, separate from earth, a new winged creature inserted into the territory of the sky. Kenan was envious until he heard the rest of the stories: forced landings, cylinders missing, engines cutting out, pilots forced to glide to earth in order to land. Later, he chanced to hear that the same pilot had dropped to his death over an occupied French village. He had fallen from his upside-down plane during a machine-gun fight in the sky. The pilot was given a military funeral by German officers, and written confirmation of his death was dropped in a package from a German plane over British lines. A strange sort of honour among enemies in the midst of war. Kenan had been thankful to have his own two feet on the ground, even if it meant living between subterranean walls of dirt much of the time.

There'd been other pilots, too. In Belleville, the year before the war began, Kenan had gone to see the flying tricks of Lincoln Beachey, Death-Defying Aviator. Two years later, Beachey fell from his own plane while performing manoeuvres over San Francisco Bay. Kenan never forgot the thrill of watching Beachey loop the loop over the skies of Belleville, and he'd been saddened to read of the man's death.

As for his leave in London, Kenan had begun to wish he'd never gone. The city was no part of any reality he knew. The clothes, the presence of real flowers, the shows, people laughing in the streets—all combined to make him understand that no one could possibly know what was going on across the Channel unless they were there themselves. He ended up walking the streets like an alien.

Kenan skated around the perimeter of the rink more than a dozen times, paying attention to the cues of the night, mindful of his balance, thankful for the generous length of cleared ice. He'd lost track of, did not care about, time. After a while, he slowed with deliberate ease. He kept his blades on ice without lifting either skate, and then widened and narrowed the gap between his feet, widening and narrowing again and again while making a continuous and regular pattern, his own mark, the length of the rink and back. He turned to look with satisfaction at the undulating lines, the double tracks, his path etched onto the surface. He faced the wind full on, but at the same time faced the low wall of snow. He felt his heart race suddenly, and he cursed and glided over to the opening where he'd entered the rink. He moved along the path, almost tripping, his blades cutting ruts in the hardened snow. He reached for and grabbed one of the shovels that leaned against the shack. This time, he made his way to the far side of the rink and swung the shovel. One-armed, he battered at the wall, his weapon flailing. Snow exploded back onto him, some of it splattering over the ice. He left a mess of white clumps scattered across part of the rink.

He dropped the shovel and returned to the shack. Removed his skates and buckled his boots. Walked quickly toward the house in the dark and locked the door behind him. He threw his hardened mittens onto a rack beside the stove. Brooding, he went upstairs to bed.

Tress murmured in her sleep. He reached for her and she shivered and woke up.

"You're freezing," she said. "Where have you been?"

Kenan had nothing to say. He was shaking uncontrollably. Words and images spun in his head. Hugh shouldn't have reminded him of Bill in the letter. Kenan wanted to forget. He wanted to forget Bill. He wanted to forget Peewee, who'd been in the hospital bed beside him and who had inherited the tendency to believe he could smother at the slightest of causes. He wanted to forget every one of the boys he'd fought alongside and every one of the boys who hadn't come back.

He and Tress held each other until he was no longer shaking. The heat of her body, the warmth of the blankets began to spread through him. He slept.

DESERONTO POST, December 1919

Local Items

A few folks in this town are determined to find trouble, no matter what the season. In summer, they are bold enough to steal sheets off clotheslines, right out of their neighbours' backyards.

Now it comes to our attention that a peculiar mystery is brewing while our small town braves early winter's devices. Someone has taken to battering down the snow wall beside the rink on the bay. It'd be enough to make you laugh your kneecaps off, except that the snow wall was built up by men good enough to volunteer their time. These hard workers trudged out onto the frozen bay and scraped the ice and cleared paths and shaped a place where we could skate. A goodly amount of toil, but they didn't stop there. They also built the skaters' shack, using last year's lumber. All for no reward except to know that our residents are assured of having healthy recreation throughout the winter. Now, for all their troubles, the men found a mess of snow scattered over the ice early one morning this week. Fortunately, there was no damage to the rink's surface.

A warning to the troublemakers who are reading this: Set yourselves about skinning your teeth or finding some other pastime, and leave the rink and snow removal to those of us who are not full of useless mischief. Is this the joke of an errant night snowman?

To keep to the same line of thought, remember the snow by-law and let the boardwalks be kept clear for the next several months. This municipal regulation is not to be disregarded as heretofore has been too frequently the case.

Stomach trouble comes when the blood is weak and watery. Thin-blooded people generally have stomach trouble. Thin blood is one of the most common causes of stomach ache. Dr. Williams's Pink Pills act directly on the blood, making it rich and red.

Chapter Eighteen

AM STOOD IN THE DARK BEHIND THE CLOCKS, the apartment below silent with unease. Mags had gone to bed immediately after practice. She was always tired now, or so she said. There was a time when they'd gone to bed together, same time every night. He didn't try to remember how long ago. Instead, he thought of how Mags used to look when she unpinned her hair and slipped her nightgown over her head while he was in the room. She didn't do that anymore. If he was in the bedroom, she dressed and undressed in the bathroom. Or she went to bed early and was under the covers by the time he came to bed. He thought of her slim body, her hip bone pressed against him as she lay on her side—when they used to sleep close. He thought of the flush of her cheeks when they'd been man and wife. Well, weren't they man and wife now? They were. They slept in the same bed. But there was little connection between them. There was no comfortable silence between them. Not as before. Whose fault was that? They had once owned a silence so easy and peaceful, it went unremarked—until it was gone. Any silence now was fraught with tension, something he couldn't name. One will rising against another, perhaps. Did he ever reach for her, or she for him? Was he afraid? Afraid that he had lost her? If so, what had he done about it? Well, maybe Mags was afraid, too. Or was she just plain angry?

When they lived on the farm, it had been Am's habit to sit by the stove in the evenings, mending tools or fixing something or other, while she sewed or read or ironed after supper. In those days, they had talked into the late hours. Mags placed her sad-irons on top of the stove and kept an upside-down cake tin over them to hold in the heat. She smoothed a thick blanket over the end of the table, an old flannel sheet overtop, and used that as her ironing surface. While she ironed—this always looked awkward to him because she ironed with her left hand—she amused him with memories about herself and Nola growing up on the farm adjacent to the one that had belonged to his parents.

One evening, a cool summer night, she made a special bread pudding for him, adding in raisins and small, tart cherries. When the pudding came out of the oven they sat there with two spoons and finished the whole dessert between them. They'd laughed over that. Another evening, he came in from the barn, unable to hear properly. Something had bunged up his left ear. Mags knew exactly what to do. She mixed sweet oil and turpentine and, with a feather, dripped the mixture into his ear, one drop at a time. His hearing was as clear as could be after two days. If he had a boil, she mixed brown sugar and yellow soap. Mags could cure just about anything.

Am and Mags had known each other forever. A few of her

stories he'd heard; many he hadn't. Especially stories about church. He'd been brought up Catholic. Mags Healy belonged to one of the Protestant families in the area and had farther to travel to get to church, unless a visiting minister came by and preached in the schoolhouse in winter, or in one of the homes. But being of different religions had not stopped them from marrying. Am's own family had uncles who'd married Protestant and switched. Mostly, it was the other way around. One thing he knew for certain: no one really knew what went on in someone else's private space—he'd learned that much, even though he and Mags had been neighbours as children. There were things he didn't know about her then, and things he never would. He understood that now.

Occasionally, he made an effort. He'd announced only this week that he was thinking of buying her one of the new electric irons Nola had recently described in a letter from Oswego. But Mags said she was afraid that if she used an electric iron, it would give her a shock and she would disappear. Someone had told her electricity could do that. They'd laughed, a rare laugh between them these days. A softening, perhaps.

They'd first lived with electric lights after moving to the tower apartment. What a marvel that had been. Walk into the kitchen, push a switch. Walk into the bathroom, push a switch. Mags had complained about the rules that went with having plugs and outlets and wiring throughout the building. "Why does lamplight have to be over my left shoulder when I read?" she wanted to know. "What difference does it make whether electric light beams down on the page from left or right?" He didn't have an answer for that.

Other things were different, too. When they'd lived on the farm, after frost, sometime in November or early December, he worked around their small orchard, removing loose bark from the apple trees, exposing the larvae of coddling moths. Just before winter each year, he slaughtered a cow and a pig. He and Mags didn't have much to buy in the way of supplies. Kerosene, flour, sugar, tea, raisins, soap—though Mags knew how to make her own soap and often did. She still made her own laundry soap. Even though everything was available in the stores in town.

AM STAYED IN THE TOWER AN EXTRA HALF-HOUR AFTER he was sure Mags was asleep. He liked to use a lantern in the tower instead of electric light. Sometimes he lit the lantern; sometimes he didn't. He just liked being up here. And not because he was in pain and needed to be alone. Right now he had no pain, but something else was amiss. He'd been edgy all day. The edginess had begun after he'd read an article in the *Post* about someone in town battering at the heaped-up snow at the side of the rink, scattering it over the ice. This had happened earlier in the week, but no one knew who had done such a thing. He recalled peering through the clock one morning, watching two men out there scraping away at the ice.

From the tower now, the ice was the colour of thin porridge. Cold porridge. At night, especially when the moon was up, he was sometimes deceived into thinking he could see puddles illuminated over the surface of the bay. He knew the ice was solid. He knew his vision was being tricked.

Did it matter if snow accumulated out there? Probably not. Initially, the snow wall was intended as a bit of a warning, a deterrent against going out too far and onto thinner ice. Now, more and more people wandered out, knowing the ice was thick and safe across the bay. What mattered was who was battering at the snow and why. What was the point of scattering snow in a place where everyone in town enjoyed skating? Someone was up to mischief, and that meant extra work for others. Someone who had no reason to do such a thing except to make trouble.

In a few weeks, after the new year, the annual horse-and-sleigh races would be held on the bay, out past the rink, where the whole town could see. One year, when he was a young man and still farming, he had entered the races. Dermot convinced him to come to town for the events and Am had won ribbons with two separate horses. Cold days. Exhilarating days. The horses stomping on the ice, ready to let fly, Am talking them down in low tones under his breath while they nickered restlessly at the start line. In those days, the Rathbun Company employed five thousand workers. The streets were crowded, skaters swarmed over the rink, the town prospered. Today, the population was not even three thousand, and local industry was collapsing in on itself. Mills and plants were closed. There could be no mills without lumber. Even the Big Mill had closed in 1916, during the war, because of the dwindling supply of logs.

Before that, the Great Fire of 1896 had destroyed other industries: the bran house, the cedar mill, several piers along the waterfront. That was when Am was still living on the farm. At the time of the fire, his brother lived in town, but he hadn't yet purchased the hotel. Fortunately for everyone, Dermot's home had not been damaged. The family remained safe, though Grania was born the night of the fire. Am and Mags had always loved the child as if she were their own. Grania was twenty-three now. The whole family looked forward to her return in the spring. And to the birth of her first child.

Am decided he would walk over to the rink and take a closer look at the ice. It was dark outside, clouds were built up in the sky, not a whisper of moon to be seen. He would take his brass lantern with him but wouldn't light it unless he had to. He thought about the farm again and how he'd always tried to get his chores finished during daylight hours so he wouldn't have to take a lantern out to the barn. There was a constant worry about fire any time there was a lantern in a barn.

He peered out through the clock again and saw a man below, dragging a small sled along the street, the sled covered with boxes tied down with rope. The sight made Am remember how he'd once caught a snake on his father's farm. He was four or five years old and had a small wagon his father had banged together for him. Every day in summer he dragged the wagon behind him through the farmyard and through a small orchard of apple trees. One day, he collected two grasshoppers in a jar, an old bird's nest and the snake, all of which he stowed in the wagon. He headed home to show his father, but when he reached the house the snake was gone; it had slithered out of the wagon and escaped. He never forgot the enormous disappointment over the lost snake he'd wanted to show his father.

Memory. It whipped him around in all directions. And who was he to say whether his memories were accurate or not? He never knew what would be laid bare. There were days when past events drifted through him until he felt he'd become a medium. Like stories he read in the paper about people who claimed they were able to communicate with the spirits of boys who'd been killed in the war.

Or maybe his memory was slapping him with cold truth. Which he did not always want shoved in his face. He climbed down the tower ladder as quietly as he could, tucked a box of matches into his pocket, put on his coat and gloves, and wrapped his scarf around his neck—the striped one Mags had knitted and presented to him in a quiet moment of tenderness. He pulled on a cap and left the apartment.

When he reached ground level and shut the outer door, a sudden movement behind the post office startled him and he stepped back quickly. He stopped and peered into the dark and realized that nothing had moved but himself. A stack of wood piled up behind the building loomed in the shadows. His vision was failing; he hated to admit this to himself. He should probably be wearing glasses, but up to now he'd done his best to ignore the signs.

The first time he'd become aware of his diminishing eyesight was late spring, when he was with his brother in front of the drive shed behind the hotel. He'd been called over to admire the Dodge Brothers Touring Car his brother had purchased from a Kingston man. Dermot was proudly showing him the features of the auto when Am glanced off to the side. From the corner of his eye he saw a small wedge of wood balancing unreasonably on its end. Curious, he let his attention drift away from the auto. He looked more closely, and watched the wood hop and become a robin. The episode startled him, made him uneasy about the way he was seeing the world. Ever since that day, or so it seemed, one thing could become another without any effort on his part. A dark speck roaming around his eye could become an ant crawling across a stone. An ant could just as easily become a speck in his eye. A thickness halfway up the branch of a tree in the woods at the edge of town could be an owl listening for the scratch of mice under snow. He began to wonder if anything held its true shape, if the world of sight had always been a deceit. If he were to see a snake in a field in summer, he'd probably mistake it for a length of rope. Light and shadow confounded him equally. He supposed he should mention all of this to Dr. Clark, but he had enough to worry about on the days he had pain in his gut. He'd begun to take the pink pills he'd read about in the *Post*, hoping to solve the problem. He'd gone to see Hal Edwards at the drugstore when he bought the pills, and told Hal to keep quiet and not to mention anything to Mags.

If he told Mags about his eyes, she'd want to apply bread-and-milk soaks, or she'd tell him to buy glasses, an obvious solution. He had no intention of mentioning any of his problems to anyone. Especially when the only danger—as far as his eyes were concerned—was misjudging depth when he stepped off the end of the boardwalk. He'd almost taken a tumble a few days ago, but had corrected his balance just in time. An inconvenience that small could be lived with. His eyes were strong enough to recognize his fellow citizens out walking on the street when they were close enough to say how do you do. And the ladder that led up to the tower had never tripped him. He knew every rung; he could go up and down with his eyes closed if he needed

to. No ailment of his had ever affected the work he'd been hired
to do. He had considered getting a dog for himself so the animal
could walk by his side on the street, or so he'd been thinking. In
August, he'd wanted to take in a large setter that had to be given
away when its owners moved. The dog had a dignified expression, silky ears almost a foot long and smooth hair that hung
past its belly like a saddle blanket. The dog ended up going to
some other owner because Am hadn't acted quickly enough.

Am strode east along Main Street and entered the path to
the rink. He glanced to the left but there were no signs of activity coming from Kenan and Tress's narrow house. It was late
and they'd be in bed. The snow on the path between the wire
fencing glistened and guided him down the slope to the skaters'
shack and then forward to the rink and onto the ice. He didn't
have his skates with him and wished he'd thought to bring them.
How good it would feel to be out here alone, skating on the bay.
Free of fatigue, free of worry over whatever was going on with
Mags. She didn't tell him a thing anymore.

He looked along the length of the oval. It was late, and
everyone at his end of town was in bed. At the other end of
Main Street, in Dermot's hotel, men would be playing cards,
holding forth on politics, opining about the dozens of coun-
tries in Europe that even now were battling out the lines that
had been drawn around their precious territories. Who won the
spoils? Whoever shouted the loudest. That's what it came down
to. He had no use for the killing and spent no time wondering whether he'd have signed up if he'd been a younger man
in 1914. What he could plainly see was the effect war had had
on young Kenan and on other families in the town. Bereaved

people walked into the post office building every day. War was an utter waste of youth, as far as Am could tell.

He decided that he would go and visit Dermot later in the week. Have a drink with him at the hotel. Dermot always had a supply of liquor and Am never asked about its source. Dermot would want to talk about his touring car. How he'd been lucky to buy the winter version, which he drove when the roads were hard enough. Am thought the winter version was a waste. Sometimes it was all anyone could do to get a horse and sleigh out of town. Admittedly, Dermot had driven his car on local roads after snow had fallen. The car was sleek and black, all steel, with a solid winter top, a solid wood steering wheel. One day the past summer, Dermot had driven north to the Ninth Concession, where he and Am had grown up, to show their father. He'd asked Am to accompany him. The two brothers had taken their father out for a little tour, the car bouncing along the roads. Their father, now in his eighties, had put on his only tie for the occasion.

Am thought he heard music, but his mind deceived him. How many times had he and Mags skated to the music of a clockwork-driven Victrola, on small rinks, on large rinks, the muffled, tinny sound drifting into cold air while accompanying bundled-up, gliding bodies? How many times had he and Mags skated into the night along country cricks and ponds with no music at all, the only light being whatever the moon and stars had to offer, or the lantern's glow?

He glanced at the stretch of ice before him and thought he saw two children skating hand in hand. When he looked again the rink was empty. What had he just seen? Mags was the one who reported seeing wisps, or spirits. His vision might be shrinking, but now his imagination was expanding in the opposite direction. He wondered if he was experiencing some sort of madness.

He thought of music again. This time, he *did* want to remember. Mags had always loved music. She had sung since early childhood. At home, at weddings, at school concerts, at parties, with her legs dangling over the edge of the haymow when they climbed up there together and threw open the big wooden doors. When they were first married, she sang while she went about her daily work on the farm. She was hardly aware that she was humming or singing, inside the house or out—while preparing meals, while heating the sad-irons, while helping to pick apples or sewing or knitting, canning, preserving. And then the singing stopped.

But not now. He realized with surprise and sudden clarity that she had begun to sing again. Or was this another way his mind was playing tricks?

He tried to recall. Early this morning he had been in the bedroom while she was in the kitchen. He had looked over to her side of the bed, the imprint of her still on the pillow, which was scrunched the way she liked it. She'd always pushed and pulled at her pillow until it supported her neck and shoulders exactly the way she wanted it to. Mags was up before he was every day, even though he started work at seven. And this morning, he had heard her humming. Not one of the concert solos, not one of the hymns she sang in church on Sunday mornings. She'd been humming in the kitchen the way she used to when they were younger. She had been doing this so naturally, he wondered if she was even aware. It was as if some moment of happiness had brought her back from a place that for a long time had kept her silent.

What was happening to Mags?

What was happening to him? Was he getting old? And cranky, too? There were things he wanted to say. He had tried. He had climbed down out of the tower and stood face to face with Mags, but she had retreated. She had stopped him.

He looked down at the ice under his feet. From a standstill, he pushed off in his boots and, with a gliding motion, slid sideways across the width of the rink. Not at all satisfying without skates. He looked at the wall of snow on the bay side of the rink and wondered why on earth it had been thrown up there in the first place. What was the point? Snow had to be cleared, yes, but did it have to be put in one place? Snow acted as insulation. After a time, it could weaken the ice. If people wanted to wander out farther, even on thin ice, they would. The wall shouldn't be there; it was cold, barren, an impediment. Hostile, even. In part, it blocked the view of the bay from the rink. No wonder someone had tried to knock it down. He felt the pain starting up in his gut. He had a mind to reach for a shovel himself.

Local Items

They're at it again—the hooligans who are putting a damper on the enjoyment of the rest of the citizenry. Are we so derelict in this town that we have to consider posting a night sentry at the rink during the wee hours? Once again, without reason—for why would anyone with reason act in such a way?—snow has been scattered over the cleared portion of the ice. Let the scoundrels cease and desist!

Your local Butcher Shop intends to make the finest display of Beef, Pork, Lamb, Mutton, Veal, Game, Poultry, Vegetables, and every variety of Fresh and Salted Meats this Christmas that has ever been seen in Deseronto, or in fact in Ontario.

We are already booking orders for Turkeys. Now is your time to do likewise, and thus be sure of your Christmas dinner before the Turkeys see this ad and strike. Come along and have a look, and if it does not make you hungry to see so many nice things ready for the oven, it won't be our fault.

Come to Ford Jewellers to buy your lady the new and popular bracelet watch. Assorted fancy dials, gilt finish, reliable timekeeper. A Christmas gift that is sure to win her favour. Only a few days left to complete your shopping.

Get your Butter Paper, printed or plain, at the Post *Printers.*

Chapter Nineteen

TELL," HE SAID. HE WAS STRETCHED OUT ON HIS back. Tress was lying next to his dead arm, the dark shadow of its crease. His good arm was free. He left the small lamp on beside their bed.

He stared at the ceiling, aware of her face close to his cheek. "What shall I tell?"

"Anything. What you did at work."

"I can tell you who was in the dining room, whether they ordered hot pot or chicken pie, whether they had room for dessert, what they left behind. And Mother sends her love. She'd like us to be there Christmas Day, but she understands. She truly does. She already knows that Uncle Oak has been invited here for Christmas dinner."

Kenan knew that Tress passed along abbreviated versions of what was going on, the way she'd learned to do while growing up with a younger sister who was deaf. She used to tell Grania, "This is what Father said." "This is what Mother wants." But what was told was Tress's shorthand version of events. She had been the interpreter, the go-between, from the time the sisters were small. They still had a private language, one they'd made up between them before Grania left to go away to residential school. Kenan had been excluded from that, though he'd been a friend to both.

Kenan knew, too, that Tress continued to supply her own version of events. She altered stories in any way that suited her. Well, he thought, *what I pass on is never the whole story, either. It's the way things have been since I've come back. I haven't told her about Hugh's letters, have I? Jack Conlin delivered both to the front door, but someday Tress will reach her hand into the mailbox at the post office and pull one out for herself.*

Tonight, Kenan didn't wait for Tress to launch into an account of the hotel dining room. He had something of his own to tell. Tress stilled to listen. What had happened while she was out?

Uncle Oak had visited, that's what had happened. A short visit, as always, but he'd also brought an offering: a photo. A postage stamp of a photo, maybe two inches by an inch and a half. Small, but one that neither Kenan nor Tress had seen before.

Kenan produced it now, sliding it out from beneath a book on the bedside table. He wanted to show her, tell her, in a certain way. He held it in the air, in the space above them. Tress raised herself on one elbow and took the photo from his hand.

Two women. The older grey-haired woman was seated on a high-backed kitchen chair that had been set outside in the snow. The younger woman, perhaps a daughter, was standing behind.

The older woman was spilling over the seat of the chair, which seemed entirely too small for her body. The word *ample* came to Tress's mind. A bibbed apron with a guinea-hen pattern was looped crookedly over the woman's dress, as if she'd put it on hastily or half pulled it off. In the background were a snow-covered roof, bare trees, a stoneboat propped against the side of a milk house. It could have been Tress's grandfather's farm, or anyone else's farm north of town and for miles and miles as far as Maynooth, for all she knew.

Despite the snow, neither woman in the photo was dressed for the outdoors. Both were coatless. The older woman's legs—thick and swollen—were stuffed into splayed galoshes. She was balancing a cake on her lap, her thick fingers tucked under the edges of a rectangular platter. But who would have, or could have, owned a platter so large? The cake must have been resting on a covered cookie sheet or a piece of strong cardboard.

Someone had gone to the trouble of decorating the cake. Tress could make out a single word across the top—MOTHER—with scrolls of icing on either side.

She held the photo closer to the light. The second woman, the one who stood behind the chair, was tall and thin and she was grinning. Her hair was long and thick and dark, the colour difficult to discern. Possibly red. Red hair would be dark in the photo.

"Maybe the young woman baked the cake for her mother," said Tress. "Maybe the two women are members of the same family. Is this Uncle Oak's family? Is this your family?"

"Partly," said Kenan, as if he were unclear about details. "Oak gave me the photo. He said it's the only one he had. It was taken at the older woman's farm. The younger woman had just baked a cake for her mother's birthday. Oak said he'd been given the photo, which could have been one of several taken that day. He was not present at the birthday celebration."

"But how are these women related to you?"

Tress studied the faces in the photo: hairlines, cheekbones, eyebrows. She searched for signs of pleasure in the women's lives, jokes in the kitchen, that sort of thing. But the older face was tight-lipped; jokes had not been captured by the camera. Still, both women must have enjoyed the moment, displaying the cake outside in the snow. The photographer would have needed the outdoor light and would have persuaded the two to go out.

"So," she mused, "there was a quick dash out to the snow, a pose, a quick run back. No, the older woman—whoever she was— wouldn't have been able to run on those swollen legs and feet."

Kenan listened while Tress invented background. She turned over the photo. No names, no date. She looked at the younger woman, looked at Kenan, looked at the photo again. She wanted likeness and found it, in the smiling eyes, the grin, the curls around the forehead, the undisguised waves in the long hair, though most of the woman's hair was fastened behind her neck. Still, the waves, the curls were there to be seen. Kenan's hair had always been thick and curly. It still flopped over his forehead—on the side of the obliterated eye, which Tress was glad of.

"Did Uncle Oak give a name?" said Tress. "More importantly, what did he say? I know he doesn't talk much, but he must have given some clue."

Kenan could hold in the information no longer. "Roberta.

The young woman's name is Roberta. My mother. With my grandmother. Taken several years before I was born, Oak said. Only that, and that the photo rightfully belongs to me and he's been meaning to give it to me for some time."

"Your mother, before she married? And your grandmother? Why now, all of a sudden? He must know more than that. Has he always known? Why didn't he show you this when you were a child? Or when we were first married? You're older now than your mother was in the photo—she doesn't look more than seventeen or eighteen. If this *is* your mother, did she marry Oak's brother? After all, it's Oak's surname we both carry now. Or is Oak your adoptive name only? No blood relation."

"Oak obviously has more to tell, but knowing him, he won't be in a hurry. Last week, I asked him if he knew anything about my birth. He mumbled around but then showed up today with the photo. If it took him this long to bring one photo, it might take another twenty-five years before he adds in another detail."

"That isn't good enough," said Tress. "We'll ply him with questions. He'll be here Christmas Day and we can demand answers. Well, not demand, but ask."

Kenan, who was hearing *"life is treacherous"* in his uncle's tone of voice, was not convinced by the suggestion and could see that Tress understood this from his expression. He knew Uncle Oak and his ways better than she did. But he was also recalling the unfamiliar sense of belonging he'd felt when Oak had handed him the photo earlier in the day.

Tress examined the faces again. "Let me make up the story, then," she said. "But we have to find out more. Maybe not right away, but soon."

She rolled onto her back. "An unseen young man took the picture. After the photo was taken, the photographer—your future father, maybe? someone who was in love with your mother?—carried the camera, and probably the chair, back inside. The chair was carved and ladder-backed, like Aunt Maggie's beautiful kitchen chairs, the ones Uncle Am made after they were married."

"We don't know that. We can't see the back of the chair." Kenan smiled to himself, listening to her voice, waiting for more.

She carried on. "Your mother carried the cake back to the kitchen, being careful not to slip in the snow. She had a grin so wide you'd remember it one entire day and into the next. She had a mischievous sense of fun. When she was a child, she ran the circle of snow in Fox and Geese, yipping like a mother fox when it was her turn to chase. And long legs. She could catch up and overtake everyone, even the older girls. Her face was beautiful," she added, and thought to herself, Like yours, which is still beautiful, no matter what you believe.

"As soon as the women—and the unseen photographer— were back inside the house, they set down the cake and dug in because they were hungry for dessert. No, wait. There was a fourth person inside, an older man, your grandfather. He was a man who pronounced the word 'bury' as *burry* instead of *berry* when he paid his respects at the graveyard. He had been watching the photo session from a kitchen window that was either patterned with frost or dripping with condensation, and now he was impatient for his tea. What a fuss! To take a cake out into the snow. Your grandfather had a habit of pouring his tea into his saucer to cool. Your grandmother had learned long ago to ignore the slurping. Neither of the men complimented the women on the cake. Spice cake? Marble cake? If they did, no matter who had done the baking, the men would find themselves eating the same kind of cake for the next six months."

She checked the photo again.

"I've changed my mind. The size of the cake indicates a larger celebration. There are more than four people present. Fiddle strings are at the ready and the room has been cleared for dancing. The younger generations will have pushed the kitchen furniture back against the walls. The food is ready, laid out under clean linen cloths on a long sideboard: scalloped potatoes with a sprinkling of flour between each layer and melted cheese overtop; an extra-large ham, glazed to perfection; a bowl of mashed turnips; a dish of mustard-bean pickles and another of gherkins; a plate heaped with slices of buttered bread; a container of applesauce. All of this will be served before the dancing begins. There are too many people to sit at one table, so they'll carry their plates here and there, or find a chair, or lean against a wall. The non-dancers will move to the living room or the parlour after they eat. They'll sit there and gossip and play cards until the young people finish dancing in the kitchen."

"Which kitchen?" said Kenan. "Which farm? Do you recognize anything?" He took the photo from Tress and said, "Roberta. My mother. Her name was Roberta." He stared into the face of the young woman who had a grin like his own.

"Bobbie," said Tress. "She would have been called Bobbie if her name was Roberta. We do know the date of your birthday—or we think we do. We've never asked if we could try to look up birth records from twenty-five years ago. Isn't that something that could be done? Your birth has to be registered somewhere. And we have your mother's first name. That's something."

"On my Attestation Paper, when I signed up, I was told to write 'Deseronto (Adopted)' on the line for my place of birth. You were listed as my next of kin."

He placed the photo on the bedside table and reached for the lamp switch. The light flickered and went out, and he understood within the space of that flicker, within the quick ripple between light and darkness, that he and Tress had, in those few moments, crossed into new territory. A thin path with barely trackable footprints, a new-old territory that offered an elusive shimmer of light that burrowed back and cast a glow over what they had once had. A past together. One that allowed imagination, sharing, spontaneous eruptions of humour and wit that could be exchanged between them.

Roberta, he said to himself in the dark. *Bobbie.*

Was this what was to be important in his life? Did everything distill to a moment of peering into a photograph the size of a postage stamp and seeking his place inside a family? Well, he had a family. He had Tress. He knew she loved him. He had Aunt Maggie and Uncle Am, and Tress's parents, and her brothers, and Grania and her husband, Jim. He had Uncle Oak, and maybe Oak didn't want to be pushed into telling what he did not want to tell. He had his friend Hugh, whom he hoped to see the following year. He could tear this photo to bits and he would still have a family.

But he had thought of Hugh and now the cloud of war was in the room. It had drifted in without announcement, and shadows were circling. War was about defending and protecting. About allegiance, alliance, seizing and grasping territory. War was about death. A mass of lives, a tangle of human lives, young lives, had been clumped together to form exactly that, a mass. Millions of empty chairs. But couldn't the mass be disentangled, looked at as one life, and another, and another? Each with a story, a photograph, a history, a family to love and who loved?

No one person ever stood alone.

And then, as he felt himself hovering on one side or the other, belonging or not belonging, Tress moved to stretch her legs. She slid over against him, the heat of her bringing him back. She wiggled her feet, settled in for sleep. And at that moment, a thought flitted through his mind and he wondered, crazily, if the young woman in the photo, Roberta, his mother, had ever eaten an egg.

Chapter Twenty

SUNDAY MORNING, MAGGIE WAS ON HER WAY TO St. Mark's to sing in the church choir. The sky was perfect and unbroken, as blue as sky could be. Words swirled in her head as she walked, but these were not the words of hymns. She was thinking of lines from *The Mikado*, the intuitive framing of sun and moon. Three minutes of song headed toward the final consonant, the *k* in "awake." She began to hum, thinking of how she must allow the music to slow and gather, ending with the weight on the final line.

During Thursday evening's rehearsal at Naylor's, she had experienced a sudden, wondrous sense of being borne along, up and up, adrift on the moving notes. Zel was at the piano, or Luc, one or the other, changing back and forth as the songs were repeated. The rehearsal went on and on. Maggie, herself, might have been floating. And then, she focused. The rippling movement of the keys carried her forward; she approached the end, became aware of her voice slowing, slowing, finally, to "The moon and I!"

A small triumph. A tiny one, but she had felt it, nonetheless.

But before any triumph, every line had to flow. She must not let her pitch drop on a repeated note. She must enunciate. "If you don't enunciate, the audience won't understand the words, Magreet. Gilbert and Sullivan have done their work; now you must do yours."

Why didn't she sink into the songs that way every time? Without worries. Trusting what she knew and had practised, trusting what she loved about the music, the lyricism. Singing joyfully in the company of others who also loved to sing. Why?

Well, there were lines of "Peace, Gentle Peace" to muddle through, though she felt somewhat better about them now. Other singers would be standing around and behind her, the entire choral group, despite the fact that she was one of the soloists. After that, there would be volume, plenty of volume for "Hope and Glory." Under those circumstances, surely it would be impossible to hear individual voices. The audience would join in and sing loudly and enthusiastically. She tried to imagine how much sound that would create.

She wanted to perform well. She did not want to feel as if someone had seized her by the throat behind the curtains. Only one rehearsal remained, and that would be a final run-through of the entire programme, start to finish, the night before the concert.

Andrew's "Annabelle Lee" was to have choral backup. Maggie's gypsy solo—it had been decided at the end of rehearsal—would be accompanied on piano by Zel. Luc would play accompaniment for her solo from *The Mikado*. The programme was sent out for printing the next day and there would be no further changes.

She reached the top of the hill, paused to look at the sky again and hurried up the outside steps of the church. In the afternoon, there were things to do. Christmas Day was on a Thursday this year. She had one more day's work at the library, and after that it would be closed until the second week of January. She had gifts to wrap, food to prepare. She had Christmas carols to go over, songs to sing, notes to remember. *Remember the text and you'll remember the notes.* Who said that? She had sewed a thick, warm shirt for Am that she knew he would like. She had made a cloth handbag for Zel in beige with crimson lining, a matching crimson cord woven through the neck as a drawstring. She had finished knitting a scarf for Luc. A gift no one could or would notice or talk about. She had worked on it when she was alone in the apartment, and had buried it at the bottom of her knitting basket until it was finished. The wool she chose was dark and vibrant, evergreens in winter. She would not make a fuss; she would leave it in his room next time she visited. If there was a next time before Christmas.

She would make a next time. She was invigorated by the thought. She would visit this evening, after supper. She would tell Am she wanted to deliver a gift before Zel went off to Belleville to her brother's home for Christmas. She would wrap the new handbag and take it with her. She would visit Zel first. After that, she would take Luc's scarf to him. She wanted to be with Luc. There. She said it again. And again. She could not stop herself. She hummed, the sun and moon.

She arrived a few minutes before the service began, threw her choir robe over her shoulders and grabbed up a hymn book. Zel waved; Andrew raised his eyebrows, one high, one low. Several late-arriving children were led to the Sunday school room. The choir proceeded solemnly up the aisle. The service began.

During the last hymn, Maggie stood tall, trying not to sway as the others seemed to be doing. Why were they swaying? This morning, everything was in harmony, in its proper place, in its proper rhythm. The minister said the final prayer and raised his shoulders as if he were about to be lifted by diaphanous wings.

Maggie did not stay on after the service. She whispered to Zel that she wanted to drop by after supper. Zel nodded, squeezed her hand, told her she wouldn't be leaving for Belleville until Tuesday morning, two more days. The others put on their coats and boots and left the church. It was Christmas week. The choir members had sung well; now they had children to amuse, last-minute errands. School was out until after the new year. The shops were closed Sundays, but the windows were brightly decorated, as was fitting at the end of the year the boys had returned from the war. Citizens had taken to strolling up one side of Main Street and down the other, exclaiming over the efforts the shop owners had put into beautifying their properties. On side streets, wreaths hung from front doors. The town was dressed in its finest for Christmas. The houses settled back and allowed a dusting of snow to drift through the narrow lanes between. Branches of the tallest trees nodded over the streets of the town.

IT WAS AFTER TEN O'CLOCK, AND MAGS WASN'T BACK. SHE had left the apartment after supper, between six-thirty and seven. Am knew she was concerned about her performance. More than one performance—she had several pieces to sing. He knew she was concerned because of the way she'd been pacing around the apartment. For days. This evening, she had walked up the road to deliver Zel's Christmas gift and to practise.

He didn't know what to do with himself. Go out, maybe. Visit Dermot, listen to his brother talk about politics or his auto. The hotel would be warm and welcoming; fireplaces would be blazing. There would be a large tree in the lobby and another in the dining room, the glitter of tinsel offset by velvet ribbons and bows. Even along the bar there would be pinecones, loops of evergreens, sprigs of red berries.

Kenan hadn't been by to visit Am for several nights. Am was restless, knowing that Mags was out. He wondered if Kenan would arrive. He didn't feel like reading newspapers, didn't want to play solitaire. He had nothing to do on a Sunday night except keep the heat going in the building.

He climbed up into the tower and decided to wait for Kenan, who might or might not visit. If Kenan did leave his house tonight, he might head in the opposite direction. From the peering-out space in the clock, Am could tell if Kenan was coming toward the tower. If there were too many people on the street, Kenan walked east out of town, the same route he'd taken the first night he went out. He'd have tracked a good path through the woods by now, wherever it was he disappeared to.

Am reached for the flask of whisky he kept stashed behind a beam. Dermot had handed it to him the last time Am visited the hotel. Wrapped, concealed, a heavy, oversized flask. Dermot had smiled behind his moustache and wished him a Merry Christmas. Told him to keep the gift under cover.

Am took a large swig and decided he would not wait for Kenan. Instead, he would go out onto the bay, maybe take his skates this time. He'd pulled his skates out of the closet the day before and they were ready, waiting for him to slip his feet inside. He had placed them on the mat by the door where Mags had put hers. This was probably as good a time as any to go out and glide around the ice. There'd be no one around. He dressed warmly, pulled on a toque and wondered if he should leave a note for Mags in case she returned before he did. No, he wouldn't bother. She'd figure he'd gone to visit Dermot at the hotel.

ONCE HE WAS ON THE STREET, AM REALIZED THAT HE WAS overdressed. The temperature wasn't nearly as low as it had been the past days and weeks. The night was mild, the air almost balmy. Soothing, in winter. But the ice would be good. Except during heavy snowfalls, skaters had been out every day since the rink opened. Every evening, too. He'd like to skate with Mags but he didn't want to ask in case she refused. Maybe after Christmas. But she would have the concert to worry about. After the new year, then. He'd ask her after that. On New Year's Day. The rink would be full. There would be cheer to spread around. It would be good for the two of them to be in a crowd.

He crossed the street and took his time walking to the rink, enjoying the mild air. When he reached the shack, he went in but left the light off. He didn't want to draw attention, didn't want the caretaker returning and wondering if he'd forgotten to flick the switch when he closed up for the night.

He tested himself as he walked on blades across the wooden floor and out onto the path that led to the rink. First time on skates this season. He stepped onto the ice without hesitation and began his long, even strides around the oval. He might not see as well as he used to, but he hadn't forgotten how to skate. Round and round, a dozen times. He had plenty of strength in his ankles, his calves, his thighs. He opened his jacket so he wouldn't become overheated and saw, when he looked toward the opposite end of the rink, a still, dark figure. The figure moved. He pulled up short, wondering what his eyes were telling him now. He was certain he was out here alone. He skated to the end, turned, skated back down the middle. He turned again and did a lap around the edges. The dark figure emerged again. He recognized his nephew, let out a low whistle.

"You gave me a start," he said. "Where did you disappear to?"

"I didn't mean to startle you. I move about pretty easily in the dark. When you came round again, I saw that it was you."

Kenan was wearing boots, not skates. Am saw that he was inspecting his territory, an extension of his backyard, really. Out walking on the bay on this balmy night, almost thaw conditions but not quite. Too early for that. An unusual December night, that was all.

"I wondered if you'd be coming by the tower later," said Am. "And then I decided to come out myself. I'll skate around a few more times. Why don't you come back with me? We'll have a drink." He looked away. "I have a flask from my brother. My Christmas present from your father-in-law." He laughed.

"I generally walk the other direction from here," said Kenan. "You could come along. There's a good trail."

"I reckon there is by now. All right, I'll come. I'll take the skates off first, in the shack."

"Leave them at our side door," said Kenan. "Pick them up on your way home."

"Good enough."

Am went into the darkened shack and pulled off his skates. The stove still radiated warmth; the air was close, almost damp because of the temperature outside. Kenan stayed by the door and kept it ajar. He glanced out nervously several times while Am tied his skate laces together and got into his boots. Am hoisted himself up from the bench and followed, allowing Kenan—head down, sure-footed—to lead the way. The skates were dropped off beside the step of Kenan's house and the two men carried on. Kenan turned right at the boardwalk. A man walking on the other side of the street gave a nod and raised his hand in greeting. He was headed in the opposite direction, toward the newspaper office. Kenan ignored him, but Am returned the wave. Calhoun, the editor of the *Post*. His wife was expecting a baby any day now. To be sure, Calhoun would make the announcement in the *Post* when he became a father for the first time.

Kenan reached the end of the boardwalk, leading with quick strides. Without a pause, he stepped down into the frozen ruts of the road. Am was more cautious leaving the boardwalk. The shadowy changes in depth were the ones that tricked him the most. He'd be doing just fine on level board and then, without warning, he'd step down unexpectedly and hard, feeling the thump through his entire body because of the shallow drop.

When they reached the eastern edge of town and moved onto the path in the woods, Am used the white of the snow on either side to guide him. He didn't want to stray from the trail, though he was only five or six feet behind his nephew, whose moving figure he kept before him. The path followed the edge of the bay, the inlet, and then swerved away from the old pier. Am hadn't walked here for a long time. Up a rise, then to the right, past a couple of small farms. Kenan didn't look back, not once. He moved with ease and stealth through the night and turned up a low slope that led to the rotting barn on Zel's property. Am was surprised. He glanced up at the sagging roof of the old barn. If he had misgivings, he said nothing. Kenan squeezed between a couple of loose boards and Am followed. He knew enough to duck to get through.

"So this is where you come." Am's eyes had not yet adjusted to the blackened space and he inched forward, testing before he planted his weight, concerned that his feet might disappear down a hole. He could smell, however. He reeled from familiar scents and odours such as those he had known both on his parents' farm when he was a boy and on his own farm after marrying Mags. A faint trace of kerosene. His mother had always been fussy about what she used in her lamps because bad oil had an unpleasant odour. The scent of hay and oats, of stored apples, of pig shit, of cow shit swept over him. He could have sunk to his knees and wept.

But he couldn't see. He stood still, knowing Kenan was beside him. He heard a sound, smelled whisky. Kenan reached and drank, then placed a bottle directly into Am's right hand.

"I don't know who it belongs to," said Kenan. "It was just here. Somebody stashed it; somebody must come here. Besides me. Old Mr. Leary, maybe. He and his wife board at Zel's.

Tress said they're away for a few months. Or maybe the liquor belonged to the salesman and he forgot to take it with him. That's a more likely possibility. Anyway, it's here for the taking. Or the drinking."

His nephew was full of surprises. Not only could he see in the dark with one eye, he also drank another man's whisky. Am liked the feel of the raw liquor against his throat. He liked the old barn. His eyes were adjusting to the shadows. He understood why Kenan would be comfortable here, even if it was to stand in the dark. The place would make sense to Kenan. He could be out of his house, but he also had a place where he could retreat.

Kenan was looking through an opening in the boards. Smoke was coming from the chimney of the main house and from the smaller building next to it. The smaller building was in darkness. He cleared his throat, said he had something to ask.

"What is it?" said Am.

"I wondered—I'll give you the money for it—if you would pick up Tress's Christmas present for me. At the jeweller's. I want to buy her one of those new bracelet watches."

"I will," said Am. "I'll go tomorrow at lunchtime and get one."

"The one that was described in the ad in the *Post*," said Kenan. "That's all."

"Don't worry about it. I'll buy the watch tomorrow and drop it off at your house while she's at work."

Am looked through the opening in the boards and saw a light come on in the small building next to Zel's house. The door opened and a woman hurried out. She was not wearing a coat. She moved along the short path to the door of the main house and let herself into the boarding-house kitchen.

Moments later, the light went out again in the small building. A man dressed in a dark jacket, his head bare, a scarf around his neck, left the workroom and shut the door behind him. He walked quickly toward the road and down the slope, passing close to the abandoned barn as he did so.

Neither Kenan nor Am moved. From the crack between the loose boards where he stood, Am strained to see the man's face as he passed.

Lukas, the piano player, the music director.

The woman who had hurried through the doorway and into Zel's house—he would never mistake the lines of her body; he would never mistake the way she moved. The woman was Mags.

DESERONTO POST, December 1919

Local Items

In this year of "Peace at last," your editor and his staff at the *Post* wish all of our loyal readers a very Merry Christmas!

> *Have yourself a merry day*
> *With family, friend and child at play.*
> *Enjoy the peace of happy nests*
> *And all of those you love the best.*

The Women's Patriotic League has been raising money to contribute to the War Memorial Fund. Dig into your hearts and your pocketbooks during this season of giving, and remember our fallen heroes who made the supreme sacrifice in the World's Great Struggle, so recently brought to a close.

The entire town awaits Naylor's New Year's Eve concert. What can be in store for us?

Assuredly, we know that the singers and musicians have been working hard. Members of many of our town families are involved in this production, and they are certain to be rewarded by the appreciation of ticket holders. The concert is sold out!

The successful businessman is the man who stays with his business and does his outside work by telephone.

Chapter Twenty-One

MAGGIE LAY AWAKE HALF THE NIGHT. ALL night. Part, all, she didn't know how long she'd been awake and how long she'd slept. *Do you remember how we used to have hope?* she wanted to say to Am. He had returned to the apartment late, long after she had gone to bed, and had lain motionless beside her. She did not speak when he came to bed. There was whisky on his breath and the smell of whisky in the room.

So much hope, she wanted to say. *For anything, for everything. We were so young. We wouldn't have known what to call it then. Our energies worked toward loving each other, even though we didn't say that in so many words. We needed no confirmation of love; it was just there, moment by moment, day by day.*

How did we allow that part of us to drain away? she wanted to ask.

But she could not and would not ask. Because what she was this morning, this moment, was a woman who loved another man so dangerously, so recklessly, there was no turning back. What was done could not be undone. Every action she took would be swallowed by the town. Everything would come to light. After that, regardless of the consequences, whatever happened would be covered over in darkness, the way things always were.

She reached for the chain that hung around her neck, beneath her nightgown. Smoothed her fingers over the gold locket inscribed with the letter *H*. Luc had given it to her. It had belonged to his grandmother, he said, and after that, to his mother, Hanna, who had died in her thirties. He wanted Maggie to have it as a Christmas gift. He wanted her to have the locket because it had been in his family and it was precious to him. He'd fastened it around her neck while she was dressing in the dark, preparing to leave and go home.

WHEN SHE HAD SLIPPED INTO THE WORKROOM, HE HAD turned the key in the lock after she closed the door behind her. She did not object, but had a fleeting thought that it was probably the first time the door had been locked since the former owner, the salesman, had kept his supplies in the building, long before Zel had purchased the place.

Luc was glad to see her, happy that she'd returned, that she had come back to him. She had visited Zel first, stayed for a while, exchanged gifts, left her coat in Zel's kitchen and then went on to the workroom to take Luc's scarf to him. Luc was at the long table when she arrived. He returned to his chair after locking the door. They spoke for a while and then he turned out the light and led her to the back of the room, the part that was curtained off. She followed, to his bed. She had lain naked beside a man who was not her husband. She had allowed herself to love, to be made love to by a man who was not Am.

She went over every detail in her mind. She had turned on her side, stretched the length of the mattress, scrunched her pillow. Luc's fingertips had traced the prominences of her spine, one by one, soothingly, tenderly.

"When we find caring, when we know there is love," he told her, "we hold on. We hold on as long as we can." The sadness in his voice, always the sadness. But even as she heard the words, Maggie knew that other words had been choked off, remained unspoken.

Once again, she thought of what Nellie Melba had said to her in the diner. About men and women using love—the state of love, even the word "love"—to excuse the way they behaved. Melba had loved other men and her marriage had come to an end. The world knew all about that; Melba was a public figure.

Maggie tried to push aside what others might think of her own behaviour. She was not ashamed of loving Luc. She did not want her friendship with him to be an excuse for anything. But she had known Am a long time, since childhood. It was impossible to sort out her feelings.

"What are you thinking that makes you so serious?" Luc asked.

"I once met Nellie Melba," she said. "I was thinking of something she said to me during that meeting."

He pulled back in the bed, surprised by her answer. The two of them laughed together. *How long?* she thought, in the midst of releasing laughter. *How long since I have laughed like this with a man?*

"It's strange to think of her now, I know," said Maggie. "She and I had breakfast together one morning during the war. An accidental meeting in Toronto. She said things to me then that I thought of now."

"What things?"

"About how love can distort, how love can excuse our actions. I suppose she was saying that we can excuse anything."

"We need not excuse or distort anything," said Luc. "We need no excuses to love each other. It is this moment that is important. For both of us."

There was nothing Maggie could say to explain herself. She had placed herself close to a fault line that was shifting.

"I never met Melba," Luc went on. "But I heard her sing. She is a passionate woman onstage. Passionate, controlled. I saw her in London. I heard Madame Albani, too. Her final perform-ance at the Royal Albert Hall in 1911. Such a privilege to hear both Melba and Albani during my lifetime."

"Do you miss . . . ?" Maggie wasn't certain how to finish. "England? Europe? What those places offer to someone like you?"

"What does Europe matter? Parts of Europe are destroyed. People have been destroyed. Vanished." His arm swept out and his hand collided with the wall in the cramped space. "Someone like me is from anywhere, Magreet. From everywhere. I am like you, no different. I am here now. That matters. We are here together."

He said nothing about Am. Nor did she. And what she saw in that moment was that no matter how intimate she and Luc had been or would be, they were responsible for their actions. Each had made a decision. Alone and together, they had decided. To ward off longing, to seek what each could give the other, to find again what they had once had.

WHEN MAGGIE WOKE AGAIN, SHE COULD TELL BY THE light coming in around the curtains that it was mid-morning. She hadn't slept so late in years. She was startled for a moment, because she thought she felt movement at the end of the bed. There was no one in the room. Nor was Am in bed beside her. She had not heard him get up. She could hear no footsteps in the apartment. He must be working on one of the floors below. He must have boiled the water for his tea, poured too much milk into his cup, prepared his own breakfast. She looked at the wind-up clock. It was after ten. She was almost certain someone had been in the room with her. Who? What? Her heart was beating rapidly, but she lay still and forced herself to remain calm. *Don't allow the past*, she warned herself. *Don't allow it in.*

She spoke aloud, into the room.

"Get up, get washed, get dressed. It's Monday. Knit from a pattern. Sew. Deal with ripped seams, loose buttons, elastic waists. Walk over to the hotel and visit Agnes. Find out what she wants you to contribute to the family meal on Christmas Day. Ask, even though you know she'll have every detail in hand. Go out into the air and talk to someone about anything, about the overcast day, about decorations in store windows, about whether to buy potatoes by the bushel or the peck, or whether one family will cook goose for Christmas dinner and another will cook turkey . . . it doesn't matter. Just go out."

She must start her day as if it were an ordinary day.

But it was not. Her entire body knew there was nothing ordinary about this day.

She stayed there, thinking about getting up and having tea with toasted bread and jelly, and she remembered the luscious wild grapes that had grown on the farm and probably still did. She'd loved the deep blue clusters as they ripened each year. One time, she had made her own raisins, but that had been too much bother. For three days, the grapes had to be spread out under the sun on framed wire—covered, to keep off the flies. There were flies aplenty on the farm. Every night she carried the frame into the house so the grapes would stay warm, and every morning she carried them out again, in and out for three days, until the tiny raisins were finally dry enough to bring inside for storage.

Grape jelly was less trouble. She made this after the first frost, straining the juices from the fruit mash through cheese-cloth slung between two chairbacks at one end of the kitchen. The juice dripped all night through the sagging cloth and into a bucket on the floor. All she needed were grapes, sugar, an orange if one was available. The results were worth every bit of effort when she saw the gleam of light that shone on the wine-coloured jars lined up in rows on her pantry shelf. Every December, she and Am opened the prize, the first jar of fall jelly for their breakfast Christmas morning.

She stretched and made herself get up, sat on the side of the bed. She thought of Kenan and how he spent his days indoors. She was almost certain he would venture out in daylight some-time soon. He'd been coming to the tower to visit Am more and more frequently, still after dark. He'd been out on his new skates several times—always after the rink closed at ten. Changes had taken place slowly since his return from the war, but now he seemed to be moving forward at a rapid pace. Not too rapid, Maggie hoped. A misstep could throw him into confusion again. She knew how fine a line both he and Tress were walking right now.

During the last decades, it had been easy to love Dermot and Agnes's four children: two boys, two girls. Red-haired Grania, finding her strengths, learning to embrace life. Tress, the beautiful older sister with the dark hair, longing to have a baby, forced to learn strengths she didn't know she had. But as much as Maggie had always loved her nieces and nephews, loved them as children and now as adults, the love had been at a distance because they had never been hers.

She thought of Luc again. She could not stop thinking of Luc. She knew Zel would be leaving early the next day for Belleville, which meant that Maggie could not go back to the rooming house after tonight, not until her friend returned. Her dear friend, who asked no questions, who neither judged nor interfered, who somehow seemed to understand.

Luc had told her the night before that Andrew had invited him to spend Christmas afternoon and evening with his family. Maggie was glad that Luc would not be alone. She could hardly invite him to join the family dinner at Dermot's hotel—not now. Though he would probably be welcomed by his former boarding house on Fourth Street. The owner and roomers there would want to have him join their Christmas celebrations, she was certain of that. With all the talk in the town about the upcoming concert, they would consider it an honour to include him.

She would go to him again, today, tonight. She had already decided. She had decided even before waking, before getting up.

Chapter Twenty-Two

MAGS LEFT SHORTLY AFTER SEVEN AND HE DID not try to stop her. He could have. He could have stopped her with a word. She left with her music in hand, the last evening she would be able to practise, she told him, because Zel was to leave the next morning for Belleville. After Christmas would be too late—with only one rehearsal remaining.

Am paced the floors of the apartment, took a pink pill, climbed the ladder, brooded in the tower, looked out through the clock. The temperature had been dropping all afternoon and evening. Wind was blowing in off the bay, and passersby were bundled in thick clothes. The surface of the bay glistened with cold. The ice would be thick and deep and reliable, on the rink and far out across the bay. It would stay frozen like that for months; he had *ice out* dates carved into the beam as past proof. He wished he still owned a horse he could take out onto the bay, race around the ice in the cold air with a sleigh hitched behind. He thought of how Mags had always been good with horses.

She had a way of approaching them. She could take charge but put them at ease; they trusted her.

He wasn't certain what to do. The past was inching forward and he could no longer ward it off. Neither he nor Mags was able to handle, to live with what they'd left smouldering behind. They'd done their best, but their best had not been good enough.

He wanted to go out into the cold; he didn't care if his face froze or his fingers or his feet. He'd take his skates and skate hard around the rink until he was fatigued, until the pain was gone. He would talk to Mags. He would say something, but he was not sure what. He would put his thoughts together when the occasion arose. After Christmas, perhaps. Get Christmas out of the way, and after that, her concert, and then . . . he couldn't think this through. Everything he had known and counted on was zigzagging like a crack in the ice, its sudden angles altering a surface over which he was forced to step.

When he saw the lights go out on the rink, he grabbed up his skates and left the apartment. There had been few people skating because of the cold, but he was used to raw nights. He'd walked in worse and he'd skated in worse.

He left his boots inside the shack and got himself onto the rink and let the wind push him around. He had to face the bite of it every time he turned to do a half-lap. The wall of snow was still there, on one side of the rink, slight and diminished but there. He thought of the way he'd battered at it with the shovel. But only days earlier, someone else in town had done the same.

He skated through the dark and the wind, bent over when he had to, the skin on his face needled with cold. He saw

Kenan's figure rise up before him, emerging from the shadows but this time on skates. Am wasn't alarmed. He'd half expected Kenan to show up, an apparition in the night. They didn't speak immediately, but when Am stopped, Kenan stopped too, and skated near. Am saw that Kenan's dead hand was tucked deep down inside his jacket pocket. The two of them were facing what remained of the buildup of snow. They looked at each other and, with a shock of recognition, decided at the same moment. They made their way to the shack and grabbed for the shovels. Their blades crunched and cut through the path as they reached the far side of the rink, and then they demolished the rest of the wall, once and for all. The satisfaction was enormous. Am was astonished at the one-armed effort of his nephew. Kenan wielded the shovel as if a hidden rage had boiled to the surface with the first swing. As for himself, Am didn't know what to do with the energy he still had left to release.

"Come back to the tower," he said to Kenan. "We're both damn near frozen. We've done what had to be done, and let the town be damned if they don't like it. That heap of snow has never been needed there anyway."

AM DID NOT LIGHT THE LANTERN. NOR DID HE FLICK THE electric switch. Shadows shifted around them from lights in the street below. The two men were winded from the cold air and the skating and from breaking up the snow, and they sat there in the dark surrounded by clocks. Am pulled out the flask and they drank from the shot glasses he had carried up.

With a half-grimace, he stood to look through the front clock. He came back and sat on the stool again and glanced over at the younger man.

"I grew up around silent men," he said, and nodded into the shadows. "Father, grandfather, uncles, men on nearby farms. Speak when spoken to. That was the message."

Kenan nodded, too, but said nothing. He'd been raised by one of those silent men. Kenan helped himself to another whisky and poured to Am's glass as well. Knowing that Maggie was out, he glanced at Am's face and then quickly away. He should say something to take the older man's mind off his marriage. But what was to come could not be deflected. Am's sorrow was bursting all around him in the dark.

"I'll soon be fifty years old," said Am. "I loved her so much. I've loved her all my life. She was eighteen and I was twenty-four when we married, but this happened later. You'd have been four years old. What I have to tell, it's her story, too—goes back to the terrible winter of ninety-eight."

There was a long pause, and Kenan understood that Am had decided not to continue. But another noise erupted beside him.

"Mags and I," Am blurted out. He wasn't looking Kenan's way now; he was looking at the lower hand of the front-facing clock. "We've been living two sets of lives in the same life. One on the farm, the other after we moved to town—when I took the job of looking after this."

He motioned to the tower around them, to the building beneath their feet.

"In our first lives, Mags and I had children. The reason you never knew was because our loss wasn't talked about. The women were in this as much as the men. No one allowed it. Mags wouldn't allow it. It was unmentionable."

Kenan looked at the older man as if seeing him for the first time. Throughout their lives, Maggie and Am had loved and indulged their nieces and nephews—Bernard, Tress, Patrick, especially Grania. Kenan himself had been a childhood friend right alongside Dermot and Agnes's children. He had grown up and married Tress and joined the family, and there had never been any mention of Uncle Am and Aunt Maggie having children of their own.

How was it possible for an entire community to maintain silence? Others in town would have known. Tress's parents. His own uncle Oak—he had been silent, too. The community had created a grim kind of solidarity. And as Kenan began to understand, he saw that he was as much a part of this as any other. He'd been brought up in the same town. Ranks closed around certain of life's events. He'd been adopted but had no idea who his birth parents were. Someone had to know. But there had been no discussion about that, either. Yes, ranks had closed.

And hadn't the same thing happened when he'd come home from the war? No one was pushing him to behave in any particular way. He'd chosen to stay—had been left to stay—in his house until he was ready to leave. His condition had, in some ways, become unspeakable. Still, it was almost impossible to believe that no one had ever spoken about Am and Maggie's children.

As if reading his thoughts, Am said, "To speak was not possible. Mags forbade it. She forbade the mention of our own babies. We had to behave as if they hadn't existed. After you've bottled up the words long enough, they get sealed off so tightly you don't say them anymore. I bit down hard on the jealousy that twisted inside me when I saw other fathers with their children, leaning down to tell them something, or to listen. Even if they shouted at them in anger."

He spoke loudly and with anger, himself, now.

"It was the diphtheria that took them. Donal, two years and one month. Annie, four months and three days. Our beautiful children. If you could have seen them.

"So much snow fell that winter, the drifts on Boundary Road were higher than the horses and sleighs that drove between them. It was the same all over the county. Most of the time, I couldn't get to town. Even with the big sleigh and the strong team I had. For weeks, it was impossible to buy supplies. Sometimes a couple of neighbouring farmers would make it through the snow as far as our farm on a Wednesday night after chores. We couldn't go anywhere. We'd pull out a pack of cards and play Forty-Five, or Five Fingers. The rules were the same no matter what we called it. We were filling in time in winter."

Am paused. "And then, the deep cold set in. And the illness."

Kenan had stopped hearing. He was beginning to see death. The faces of friends and the faces of enemies. He was seeing Bill's face, and now Hugh's. Hugh was farther along, at the other end of the trench, but Kenan knew he was there. Bill was directly beside Kenan when the first explosion came.

Kenan bent forward at the waist, his good hand pressed to the side of his head. *How do we learn to love and hate? How do we learn to grieve and mourn?*

Am looked at the younger man and realized he shouldn't be speaking like this. Kenan's body was leaning toward the nearest clock, and Am reached out with a hand as if to stem his own words. How could his pain compare with Kenan's pain from the war, the wounds in Kenan's mind? He shouldn't have told him about the babies. Mags was right to keep the silence.

But pain was pain. One person's and the next person's and the next. One kind of pain was no more weighty than another, surely. Where the pain took place, the map of it, made not a speck of difference.

He went on, unable to stop. "Donal had a hernia, a rupture in his little groin." His voice softened as this new memory burst. "The lump showed itself soon after he was born. But right away, Mags knew what to do." He was smiling to himself now. "She told me to bring her a silver dollar and she washed it off and wrapped it in a piece of foil. She moulded the foil around the coin. She did this with so much love. The foil came from a package of tea, Salada tea." He laughed out loud, harsh tears trapped in the creases beneath his eyes. "She sewed a tiny pouch out of cotton and slid the silver dollar inside the pouch, then closed it with a safety pin and stitched it onto a band of flannel that we wrapped around Donal's groin. It was a simple matter to take out the coin when the pouch was soiled—both the band and the pouch could be washed easily enough. Well, that bit of extra weight from the silver dollar, that's what kept his little hernia from popping out. And then, Mags lifted him into her arms. If you could have seen the rush of pleasure on her face when she picked up our babe."

More and more. He couldn't stop. "Donal had his second birthday a month before the illness. We had no birthday candles at the farm, so Mags stuck two long wooden matches into the icing on the cake, and I lit them and they flared up. Donal blew them out and laughed and clapped his hands.

"When he and Annie got sick within days of each other, Mags and I took turns sleeping in the kitchen beside them. We brought both cot and cradle to the kitchen because the stove was there and we knew there'd be no icy draft in the room. There was a long narrow couch, tobacco-coloured, at one end of the kitchen. I was used to having a quick nap after lunch before I went back out to the field or the orchard. I slept less than an hour in the middle of each day, but I liked that quick nap.

"After the babies came down with the diphtheria, Mags and I took turns sleeping on the brown couch all night so we'd be beside them and hear every sound. If I dropped off to sleep I dreamed of Donal's face, his shout of glee when the candles flared on his birthday cake. And then I'd wake up and put a hand to his forehead, and to Annie's, and their skin was so hot, so hot. We couldn't cool their bodies, no matter what we did. Mags tried cool cloths and willow bark. The doctor came—we got him there by horse and sleigh—but he had little else to offer. I can still hear them coughing. Their throats were swollen; they were strangling from the disease.

"After . . . after they were gone, Mags refused to have the brown couch in the kitchen. She refused to have it in the house, insisted on getting rid of it. Every time she slept on it when the babies were sick, she had nightmares."

Am's head bowed forward and he stared at the boards of the tower floor. "She told me to take it outside and burn it. I had to pound down the snow, flatten it with my boots and

the back of a shovel, to make a clearing before I could drag
the damned thing outside. I remember the smell of matches,
sulphur on winter air. Kneeling down, hunched over, pieces of
match-head flying off, trying three or four times. The couch
was hair-stuffed, went up in flames in a shot. Mags was at the
window watching; I didn't have to turn to know she was there.
I burned it good," he added fiercely.

Kenan was remembering a big grey house that had burned
at the top of Mill Street when he was a boy; he might have
been ten or eleven. Early evening, dead of winter. The whole
town turned out to help, though no act of heroism could save
the house. The most anyone could do was stand by helplessly
and watch. The entire house had burned to the ground. The
destruction didn't take long; nothing was left but a thick layer
of sparks and burned timber and glowing ruins. Nothing, that
is, but two clothesline poles in the backyard, and those survived
intact. On the line between the poles hung a pair of frozen long-
johns, icicles dangling from the sleeves. One sleeve had frozen
at an angle and appeared to be waving.

"I was glad to see the goddamn flames shoot out of it," said
Am, and Kenan realized he was still talking about the couch. "We
couldn't bury the babies until spring because the ground was frozen up tight. The snow came up past the window on the north
side of the house. We'd have made tunnels through the snowbanks if the children had been older—and healthy. For playing.
We'd have made tunnels and forts to crawl in and out of.

"Around the back, I had to scoop out a space about halfway
up, long and wide enough to hold both children. I made a little
shelf inside the snowbank. Mags dressed them and wrapped

them separately in thick baby blankets, and then she laid them beside each other inside one large bundle made from an adult blanket. She wanted the woollen blanket to keep them warm. She said it would keep the cold from penetrating.

"We went outside together. The sun shone that day; I'll never forget how cold and bright it was. I laid the bundle that held them on the shelf I'd carved out of the snow." He was sobbing hard. "And I sealed it up. I sealed the hole in the snowbank because Donal and Annie had to stay inside it until spring. I chose a snowbank we couldn't see from any window of the house, but it made no difference because we never stopped seeing. We never will. Not until the day we are laid in the cold ground ourselves.

"Every time I emptied the ashes and went out to the shed for a bucket of coal. Every time I picked up the poker to shake down the coals. Every time I lit a spill and held it to a candle or a piece of kindling, every time I watched a log burn or a blue flame, or felt a glow of heat spread through the kitchen, I thought of the babies out there in the snow. How could I get something like that out of my head? Mags and I were sheltered in the house while their little bodies were outside, rolled up, frozen inside a wall of snow. In spring, I was able to dig a proper grave—Dermot came up from town to help. We put the babies in coffins I built myself, and we buried them side by side in the ground. A special place we chose in the woods, their graves sheltered by trees. They're still there. No one has disturbed the site since."

Silence hung over the two men. The lower edge of the web that had kept Am's sorrow in place was flapping dangerously. In gale-force winds it had loosened.

"We stayed on the land for a while, but I'd had enough of the farm, and so had Mags. Eventually, we put out the word that our acreage was for sale. Dermot owned the hotel by then, and he was the one who heard about the job of caretaker in this building. I applied and got the job. The work kept me busy and still does. It may seem crazy to you but I get satisfaction from climbing up here, looking after the tower and the big clock. The clock is like an old friend now, ticking away up here. The hands could fall off and it would still go on ticking.

"After we moved to town, there were no more children for us. Mags did not become pregnant and we never spoke openly about our hopes of another child being born. Every family around us had riches, but ours were buried. We loved Dermot's children, but they weren't ours. Loving them was like watching over borrowed children from a careful distance. You, too. You were one of the children we loved and watched over because you grew up with our nieces and nephews and you were always together."

We are all caught in thick webs, every one of us, Kenan was thinking. Tress, too, because she is so desperate to have a child. But what he said was, "I thought I was going crazy. I didn't know who else could be bashing at the snow out there, breaking it up, spreading it over the ice."

He saw Bill's face again, laughing, chattering, and then, when the second explosion came, his mouth shaping the word *Help*. Bill reached for Kenan from the trench wall, his hand outstretched. If Kenan had been quicker, he could have dragged him out in time. But he hadn't been quick enough. There was a sudden wound in Bill's chest that Kenan could have put his fist inside—he saw it. There was so much confusion; the trench was exploding around them. They had to pull back, retreat. No one knew what the hell was going on. The noise, always the obscene, profane noise. And flashes of light, he remembered those, and Bill's face and the way, in an instant, it was covered with dirt and yellowish mud, his friend smothering, and Kenan couldn't reach him because already he had leaped for safety and the entire part of the trench where Bill had been only moments before had disappeared. Kenan was knocked back, all sound gone, his bones vibrating, his chest vibrating. Hugh was on the ground, too, his arms over his head, but he was farther along and couldn't see what was going on. And then, everyone was shouting, running—if they were alive, if they were able to run.

Kenan and Hugh remained safe that day. Their friend no longer existed. Wiped clean, the earth upon which humans had walked. The barren lands of war.

Am hadn't heard Kenan's remark about bashing the snow. "All this time," he said, "all these years, we've never uttered a word. It was Mags who demanded the silence. She said it would break her apart if anyone ever mentioned the babies. But the past few months, that's all I've wanted to speak about. I go to bed at night knowing that as soon as I pull up the covers, I'll think of nothing else. The sorrow pounces. I can't hold it in. When I see a snowbank, I can't bear to look. I want to kick it, smash it in, break it down. And Mags is remembering, too. I know she is. She senses them near. I can tell."

Kenan had seen arms and legs, body parts, hands and feet reaching through the walls of trenches, tunnels—entire bodies mired in mud. "I don't blame Tress," he said now, even though

Am wasn't hearing. "She had nothing to do with the war. She wants nothing more than to have me re-enter her world, but it would be just that: a re-entry into *her* world, not mine. The world I knew doesn't exist anymore. All I want now is to let out the dangerous words that are in my head. I can't say them, in or out of the house. I can't set things right. What happened over there. How could anything that comes from war ever be set right?"

Am looked over at Kenan. The two men stood. Awkwardly, the older man wrapped an arm around the shoulders of a lad who was half his age and who'd been a year old when Am's son was born. Donal would be twenty-four if he had lived. Maybe he'd have gone off to war; he probably would have. He might or might not have come back. But he'd have had some chance at life.

The two climbed down out of the tower and pulled on their jackets. Am waited while Kenan struggled with his dead arm in the sleeve. He did not offer to help.

They left by the side door and turned onto Main and crossed the street and walked back out along one of the paths to the bay. They didn't go near the rink. Instead, Kenan led Am out onto bay ice. Out and out, farther and farther, into the cutting wind. Neither spoke as they moved forward, hunched against the cold. Am followed blindly, walking into the wind, and they walked and walked, until nothing mattered anymore and they turned, finally, and headed back to shore.

Chapter Twenty-Three

S HE WAS CERTAIN SHE WAS BEING PURSUED. Through the darkness, she could hear chattering behind her. The wind, surely it was the wind. She tightened her scarf around her, increased her pace. Whoever was following was making no effort to be silent. Maggie turned several times as if to apprehend, but she saw no one. The chattering continued. When she reached the rooming house, she did not stop at Zel's but went directly to the workroom. She was out of breath, near panic. As she pushed at the door, she caught the heel of her boot on the ledge. Her music dropped to the floor. She hadn't knocked, and now she stood there, unable to move.

Luc, who had been at the piano, was beside her in an instant. He helped her with her coat, her boots. She attempted to hang her coat on a hook, but let it fall as she collapsed to the floor. She ended up in a seated position with her back propped against the wall. Luc was about to pull her up but, looking down at her, decided against. He sat on the floor next to her.

"What happened, Magreet? What has happened to you?"

"I thought . . . while I was walking . . . someone was behind me. It was not my imagination. I know it was not. But I couldn't see them," she said, and she began to weep.

"Come, sit with me at the table," said Luc.

But Maggie could not move. She was cold, she was shivering.

Luc went to the back room and brought a blanket, wrapped it around her shoulders. He checked the stove, turned out the light, returned to sit beside her again on the floor, and leaned into the wall, himself. The glow from the coals cast shadows into the room. He put both arms around her. She was trying to stop shivering.

"What could you not see?"

"The children," she said. "It's always the children. I used to see them everywhere. But now I've begun to hear them, too."

"Whose children?"

"Mine," she said. "My own."

Luc waited.

She pulled the blanket more tightly about her and stayed like that. Finally, she began to speak. Slowly at first, stumbling, unrehearsed. Words that had been forbidden began to tumble forth. Locked-in words that now refused to be held in.

"THERE IS MORE," SAID LUC. "THERE IS ALWAYS MORE. You have held in so much sorrow, Magreet. Too much sorrow. For too long."

His arms tightened around her. She felt his strength. She was soothed, freed in some way she had not experienced before.

What had encircled her for a long time was loosening its hold. At the same time, she experienced a wave of emptiness, a fear that she had deserted some essential part of herself.

"When something so terrible happens," she said. But there was a long moment when she added nothing. Tragedy had also happened to Luc, and she was aware of that. She tried again. "It is difficult to get through each day. Even to remember getting through each day. A part of you dies," she said. "That is what happened to me."

She waited again before continuing. She tried to take normal breaths, but what came out was a long, rattling sigh.

Luc kissed her temple, rubbed at her arm and shoulder, did not push her to speak, waited, waited.

"For weeks after our babies were laid in the snowbank, every night until the ground thawed, I lay in bed until Am was asleep—or feigning sleep—and then I went downstairs to the kitchen. On hands and knees, I began to scrub the stone floor by lantern light. I cleaned it section by section, moving backwards, sliding the lantern from one stone to the next so I could see. Lantern in front, bucket of water on my left. The stove burning low, the kitchen freezing, my hands and knees chapped and rough. They stayed that way the entire winter.

"Now," she said, "after these many years, I've begun to dream of the farm again—not the farm where I grew up, but the one where Am and I lived after we married. This started after I'd begun to dream about performing at the concert. That was a panic dream."

"And this?" said Luc.

"This begins in shadow," said Maggie. "From the exterior, I

see a silhouette of our farmhouse. I walk through the door and into the kitchen. There is never a choice; I'm forced to enter. Once I'm inside, the rooms open up to create a large space. The space is filled with echoes, voices. There are no walls, no dividers." She added, in a whisper, "But even inside the emptiness of the open space, a feeling of hope sometimes accompanies this dream. I hardly dare to feel it, but it lingers after I wake. I don't know what that means. And the other dream, the panic dream about singing, has stopped."

"Those are good things," said Luc. "The feeling of hope is a good thing."

Maggie continued. "About a month after our babies died, the priest came to visit. He came to comfort us, I know that. And when I say priest, I mean one of Am's Irish uncles. Of the ones who are still living, half are Protestant, half are Catholic. One of his uncles still rides the white horse every twelfth of July in the Orange Parade here in town. You'll see him doing that, next summer. Well, the priest who is Am's uncle arrived late in the afternoon and stayed for supper. I've been to his church only for weddings or funerals. When I first moved to town, I decided I would attend the Anglican church—St. Mark's—where you practised in the parish hall. It's an easy walk from the apartment, just up the hill. I was asked to sing in the choir and I agreed.

"I'm getting sidetracked. That night at our farm, Am's uncle, the priest, brought a bottle of whisky with him and pulled it out of his coat pocket and set it on the kitchen table. Am and I knew he was an awful drinker, so the bottle was no surprise. After the priest had eaten everything on his plate, and after dessert—I made up a quick gingerbread cake with hot sauce—he unscrewed the cap of the bottle, raised the lid of the stove and threw the cap into the flames. He said to Am, not to me, 'There now, we aren't going to let this go bad, are we?' And the two of them settled in to finish off the bottle. I wasn't happy about Am—he's never been much of a drinker—but I could tell that he wanted to join the priest. I said nothing, though I felt like drinking with them. Even though I don't like the taste of whisky.

"I cleared the dishes and lit a lamp and took it up to bed. I left the two of them at the kitchen table. I could hear their voices speaking low, but at first I couldn't make out the words. The more they drank, the louder they became. I couldn't sleep anyway, so I listened to what they were saying. Am was telling the priest about a tree he used to climb when he was a boy, a thick branch that hung over the quarry on his father's farm. The uncle knew the tree, of course. It had been on his brother's land. Am told how cleverly he'd been able to hide himself, how no one below could ever find him when he shinnied up the trunk. A burst of laughter followed and their voices lowered again. I thought, Oh, they're being foolish, the two of them. But I felt left out. I suppose I was jealous. I envied them their ability to laugh, even drunkenly. Our babies were out there in the snow-bank, and the two men were loading up with liquor.

"The priest-uncle finally left for home—a miracle he got there. Lucky for him, his horse knew the way. Drunk as Am was, he must have led the horse out of the stable and helped his uncle climb up into the sleigh. His uncle should have stayed over-night. He could have slept downstairs in the parlour, though we didn't heat that room in winter. He could have slept on the kitchen floor near the stove. Am could have made up a bed in one of the empty rooms upstairs. I half expected to find the man frozen outside the next morning, but there was no trace of him. The following Sunday—so I was told—he stood at the front of his church conducting Mass, no sign of wear or tear.

"But that night, after his uncle left, Am stumbled to bed and began to snore and he filled the room with his whisky breath. That's when the scrubbing started. I couldn't lie there and listen to the drunken snoring, so I went downstairs and lit the lantern. It was after midnight. I filled the bucket with soap and water, and got down on my hands and knees on the stone floor, and dipped the rag into the bucket. I was trying to cleanse myself of something terrible and wasteful. With all the remedies I'd learned and known, compresses, poultices, infusions, I had not been able to save my own children. Am had been told that a mare's breath on a sick child could heal, and we tried that, too, bringing the horse right up to the door of the house. I know it sounds preposterous now, but we'd have tried anything to keep them alive.

"So many times I've thought of those nights when I was downstairs, scrubbing the floor. It's as if I've been peering in through the kitchen window from the darkness outside. Watching myself move from stone to stone on hands and knees, trying to scrub away despair, trying to scrub away my babies' deaths. *Wash floor after dark, bring sorrow to your heart.*"

"Where did that come from?" said Luc.

"I heard it from my own mother. I don't know what it meant to her, but I know what it meant to me. I was keeping the sorrow and trying to rid myself of it at the same time. The sorrow stayed in my heart. I scrubbed every night because the physical act was something my body could do."

"What else?" said Luc.

"Am started to kill the house. The rest of the winter, until the ground thawed, he paced from room to room, looking to see what needed repairs: window sashes that stuck, floorboards that squeaked, marks on the walls that needed repainting, a cupboard door loose on its hinges. He banged and scraped and plastered. He knocked things around and scratched the surface of the hall settee. He took a hammer to the outside of the ice-box on the pretext of straightening a dent, and ended up putting a hole through the hardwood. He pried wainscotting off a bedroom wall with a crowbar. He broke everything he touched and he drove me out of the house. I wasn't able to listen to him hammer and bang at everything we owned. Most things he attempted to repair, I ended up having to nail together again. Sometimes I bundled up in a coat and scarf and went out to the drive shed and sat in the bobsleigh for hours. All I could think of was getting away. Straw was strewn across the bottom of the sleigh and I sat there and pulled the robe up over my feet and legs. We had an old buffalo robe that we kept year to year. I did nothing about my longing to escape except sit in that place. Until one day in late spring.

"The babies had been placed in proper graves by then, because the ground had thawed enough to dig. Each had a small coffin. The graves are in the woods, sheltered by trees. A sacred place, but there are no markers. Am wanted them buried on the land where they'd been born and died.

"I went from all of that. Being a mother, being their mother and having joy and happiness in my life. From that to a different kind of life. One that excluded the past, one that excluded my own children. I asked Am never to say their names again. I could not bear to hear their names spoken aloud, or even whispered."

"He respected that?" said Luc.

"Always. He knew how I felt. The two of us were undone by grief. I almost left him because of my own grief. In the spring, a few weeks after we'd given the babies a proper burial, I packed a small bag and came to town with a woman from a neighbouring farm. Clarice—she still lives in the area. She's married to a man so tall, so excruciatingly thin, everyone thinks he's consumptive. But he isn't. He just looks consumptive, always has. He's an auctioneer and in perfectly good health. Every bit of energy he has is coiled up inside him. From the side, his jaw looks as if it's been squared with a chisel. He travels round the countryside auctioning off farm property and equipment. He's still in the business, even yet.

"Clarice was often alone because of her husband being on the auction circuit, and she was in the habit of coming to our farm twice a year: once in spring to get a cut of fresh rhubarb, again in fall for a bushel of apples. We had crabapples, Snow apples, Spys. Well, when Clarice came by in her democrat to get her cut of rhubarb that day, she announced that she was continuing on to Deseronto. She always hitched up the democrat when she visited from farm to farm, and she had room for an extra passenger. I was alone at the farm and she asked if I'd like to come to town with her, so I agreed. When we reached Deseronto I asked her to drop me off at Dermot's hotel and told her I'd be staying overnight with Am's brother's family. I didn't have a plan, though I was trying to make one. I walked into the house beside the hotel, where the family lives, and had a visit with Dermot's mother-in-law. We all called her Mamo. I had a small bag with me and didn't say where I was going except that I was on my way through to Belleville. Am's sister-in-law, Agnes, was busy in the hotel kitchen. Agnes still does most of the cooking over there. She's known for it. I think you've taken meals there occasionally, have you not?"

Luc nodded, and stretched his legs. They both stretched their legs. But stayed where they were on the floor. Maggie pulled the blanket off her shoulders and spread it over the two of them.

"I stayed in the parlour with Mamo. I drank one cup of tea and then another, all the while trying to decide what to do. I loved Mamo as if she were part of my own family. She was Agnes's mother, came over on a ship from Ireland. She died in the terrible influenza epidemic, right at the end of the war— she's buried up on the hill in the town cemetery. I always felt as if she and I were related. Everyone who knew her loved her. You'd have loved her, too, if you'd had the chance to know her. And she'd have loved you back.

"Mamo could tell right away how troubled I was. Of course, she knew about the babies dying in the winter. She said to me, 'You've pulled away from what your heart can no longer with-stand, Maggie. You are moving toward what you are able to bear. But you must believe me. As deep as you might bury your sorrow now, it will burst free when it's least welcome and you'll have to be strong enough to meet it when it does.'

"After spending a quiet hour with her in the middle of the afternoon, I left feeling stronger. She could create calm, Mamo could, no matter what anyone was going through."

Maggie clasped her fingers around Luc's wrist as if checking that he was still there. She settled against him once more.

"I walked across the street from Dermot's hotel and boarded the train. I travelled to Belleville, but still had no plan. I sat outside the Belleville station, and it was there that I made up my mind to take the first train. Whether it was travelling east or west made no difference to me. I went inside and asked for a ticket for the next train. The man at the booth looked at me as if I were crazed, but I didn't care what he thought. I went back outside and stood beside the tracks and caught a train that happened to be on its way to Toronto. I'd have ended up in Ottawa if the train was heading east, but the first train was westbound. It was early evening by the time I was seated in a coach. I was caught up in a tunnel of sound, loud and muffled, near and far. I remember a pervasive odour, a contradictory mixture of must and freshly ironed linen. I stared out the window as dusk fell and thought about loosening my responsibilities. I wanted to let them fly behind me while the train carried me into the night.

"Am didn't know I'd left, but I knew he wouldn't panic. He's never been one to panic. In any case, he was visiting one of his uncles in Marysville that day and planned to stay overnight, so he didn't get back until the following day. When he found the house empty, he sent word to his brother, Dermot, to find out if I was in town. It was Mamo who sent a message back telling him I'd gone away for a few days. That was all she told him.

"I stayed in Toronto four days and scarcely remember what I did during that time. I booked myself into a small hotel. And then I walked. And walked some more. Up and down streets, in and out of parks and shops and along the waterfront. The dreams began when I came back to the farm, the dreams of baby fingers being drawn through my hair. My hair moved, I know it did. I felt it move as it was sifted through tiny fingers. My son used to do that when he was a toddler. He loved to climb up to my lap and play with my long hair."

"Say their names," said Luc. "Speak them aloud."

"Donal," she whispered. "Annie."

But she could say no more.

Chapter Twenty-Four

Deseronto: December 28, 1919

Dear Hugh

Happy New Year to you. Hopefully, you will be fully restored to health in 1920. You'll receive this after the new year, as it's already the twenty-eighth and there is no hope of it arriving before 1919 is out, but the wishes hold this year and into the next.

I have talked to Tress about you coming to visit and she would surely like to meet you. Maybe you could come to see us in the spring, when you've been discharged and are well and fit to travel. You must be cheered by the fact that you've been reclassified "up" one level—though in your case it means moving down one floor.

Once you're out of there permanently, we should think of working together. We could go into chick hatching (I'm joking) or start up some sort of business. We know how to be soldiers

but now we'll have to use our imaginations and reclassify our-
selves. I know about bookkeeping, storing and selling eggs, a
fair bit about banking. That's it for my skills. Oh, and I'll be
learning to adjust and do maintenance on the tower clock in my
home town—with one hand and arm. There are retraining
programmes, too. I've read plenty about them. I forgot to ask in
my last letter if you've joined the GWVA.

We had a fine Christmas celebration in our own small
home. Quiet and enjoyable, with just my uncle Oak visiting.
I told you about him. He's the one who taught me that "life
is treacherous," and I have to admit that to some extent he
wasn't far wrong. He wrote letters to me when we were "over
there." He adopted me when I was very young and raised me
here in the town.

At different times over Christmas, Tress's parents dropped
in. Also, her aunt and uncle. The town is decorated rather
finely, and I have wandered about at night to see the efforts
people have made to celebrate the season. Some evening, when
it's late and the streets are empty, I'll ask Tress to come with
me. I still don't venture out during daylight.

With extra money I earned from bookkeeping, I was able
to buy Tress a bracelet watch for Christmas and she is pretty
happy with it. Her uncle Am picked it up for me at the store.
My own uncle Oak wrapped up a gold-rimmed egg dish (with
lid), as well as a teapot and two cups and saucers, and that
was his gift to us. I was surprised to receive the "egg dish"
and will tell you about it when you come to visit. Part of my
family history goes with it, the few details I know. I suppose
that's the stuff we are made of, stories and journeys great or

small, complete or incomplete, whatever gets passed on to us down the line.

We've had brisk weather the past while, and skaters are out on the bay every day and evening. The town rink was erected on the ice just beyond my own backyard. I've been out skating a few times. It's good to be back on the ice, even after dark. Skating is an activity I loved when I was a boy. If you were here with me, we could go down to the bay together and stand there and shout curses into the night. There's still plenty to curse about in my mind, and probably in yours, too, and there will be for a long time, if not forever. We could curse about losing Bill, shout his name to the sky. Too many journeys ended sooner than they should have, and Bill's was one of them.

I didn't mention that Tress, knowing how much time I spend reading, gave me a set of Dickens's novels for Christmas, fifteen volumes, and I am now on the second. These might border between tragedy and comedy, but there's nothing like a good story that takes its time. With her aunt Maggie's help, Tress also knitted me a heavy sweater with deep pockets.

This isn't meant to be a long missive. I just want to send wishes from the two of us. Let me know what went on in the san on Christmas Day. I expect there were special treats to make up for the fact that you weren't with your families. Sometimes it ends up that the people around us become our families, whether we're related by blood or not.

My best to you, my friend,

Kenan

NEW YEAR'S EVE CONCERT

NAYLOR'S THEATRE, DESERONTO
WEDNESDAY EVENING, DECEMBER 31, 1919
MUSIC UNDER THE DIRECTION OF LUKAS SEBASTIAN

Recitation: "Poem for a New Year's Celebration"   T.S. MacIntosh

"A Wand'ring Gypsy, Sir, Am I"   Words by Dr. J. Wolcot
Maggie O'Neill, Soprano   Arr. Ludwig van Beethoven
Zel Jackson, Piano

"Clair de Lune" from *Suite bergamasque*   Claude Debussy
Lukas Sebastian, Piano

"Annabelle Lee" from the poem by Edgar Allan Poe   Henry Leslie
Andrew Newman, Tenor
Deseronto Choral Society

"Let All the World in Every Corner Sing"   Ralph Vaughan Williams
from *Five Mystical Songs*
Deseronto Choral Society
Zel Jackson, Piano

INTERMISSION

Tableau: "Peace for All Nations"   **Deseronto High School**
                                                    Theatrical Group

"The Sun Whose Rays Are All Ablaze" Gilbert and Sullivan
from *The Mikado*
Maggie O'Neill, Soprano
Lukas Sebastian, Piano

"Liebestraum" Franz Liszt
 Lukas Sebastian, Piano

V. "Peace, Gentle Peace" Sir Edward Elgar
VI. Finale: "Land of Hope and Glory"
from the *Coronation Ode*
Soloists: **Maggie O'Neill, Andrew Newman**
Zel Jackson, Corby Black & **Deseronto Choral Society**

"Auld Lang Syne" Robert Burns
Arr. Ludwig van Beethoven
Audience invited to join the Choral Society singers

GOD SAVE THE KING

Curtain rises at 8:15 p.m. Ladies Will Kindly Remove Their Hats

Admission: Adults 50c, Children 10c

Chapter Twenty-Five

L OOSEN UP," SAID ZEL. "BREATHE DEEPLY." SHE and Maggie were backstage with the others. Singers joined in as they arrived; the backstage area was becoming more and more crowded. There was chattering at first, and nervous laughter. After that: *Arms up and stretch. Two breaths in, six breaths out. Breathe, breathe.*

"What will happen if I can't force a sound out of my throat? What if nothing goes well?"

"You'll go to pieces," said Zel. "But that's all right. Some women are more experienced than others at going to pieces, and you'll make a damned good job of it. In fact, you'll be brilliant."

Maggie couldn't help laughing.

"You'll manage," said Zel, "because you sing wonderfully. Your dress is wonderful, too. You look completely beautiful, Maggie. Absolutely and completely. In every way."

"Thanks, Zel. You look wonderful yourself. I love your black dress." Maggie meant what she said. As one of the soloists, Zel wore a long dress, but with an oversized scarlet bow at her neck and long crystal beads that hung to her waist and sparkled with every turn toward light.

Maggie's floor-length dress was forest green, sewn from velvet. When she wore it, the green of her eyes darkened. She felt for her gold locket beneath the neckline, aware that it could not be seen.

"I might sing the moon verse first, Zel, instead of the sun. In the Gilbert and Sullivan. Without realizing. My brain might scramble."

"Of course it won't. Don't do this to yourself, Maggie."

"I don't think Am is here yet," said Maggie. "Have you seen him?"

"You mustn't think about anyone before the concert. This is not the time," said Zel.

"He knows," said Maggie. "I think he knows."

"This is not the time," Zel said again. "Not now."

"Is Calhoun in the front row? Pen and notepad in hand? I hope he isn't in a critical mood. Hyper-critical, I mean."

"He's in the reviewer's seat," said Zel. "Same as always. I peered around the edge of the curtain. His wife isn't with him. She's due any day, isn't she?"

"I don't know," said Maggie. "She's been covering herself with loose clothing for months, and I've lost track. I think their baby is due in January some time. I can't remember. I can't think about Mrs. Calhoun right now. It's all I can do to look after myself. And I'm worried."

"We have a full house out there, Maggie. People showed up, even through the winter fog. Did you fumble your way through the mist? Everything out there is damp; I had to hike up my skirts as I walked. Anyway, think of nothing but the beauty of the music we're about to perform. You and I are second up."

"I'm trying," said Maggie. She kissed Zel on the cheek. "You give me courage. When I hear your strong voice in the Elgar, or when you start up the notes on the piano, that helps to calm me."

Luc was suddenly beside her. She hadn't seen him arrive.

"Trust yourself," he told her quietly. He squeezed her hand. "Trust the preparation you've done. You're ready. You have to remember that the audience, every one of those people out there, wants you to succeed. They are on your side and they want you to do well." He moved off to speak to the others. She felt the touch of each of his fingertips on her skin. She dared not glance around to see what others had observed.

Lights flickered, the audience hushed. The poet strode out in front of the curtains and began to perform the opening recitation, "Poem for a New Year's Celebration." At the end of the last stanza, the audience clapped loudly. The festive mood had begun. Zel took her place. The red velvet curtains parted.

When Maggie walked out to centre stage, she stared down into the dark maw that was the audience, and heard applause. This took her by surprise, unnerving her. So far, she hadn't done anything. She found her position near the piano, where Zel was seated. With gaze lowered, head slightly bent, she collected her thoughts. Or tried to. When she was ready, she took a deep breath, kept her shoulders low and relaxed, raised her head, faced the audience and assumed her expression as it would be for the opening bars. One more slow breath and she fought off the conversations with herself that were competing for her mind's attention. Zel must have seen her raise her head, because she began to play. Maggie sang.

A wand'ring gypsy, Sir, am I
From Norwood, where we oft complain,
With many a tear, and many a sigh,
Of blustering winds, and rushing rain:

Her first notes were trembly and thin—long notes, especially—but she carried on, willing herself to continue. Her legs, too, had begun to tremble. She was singing into silence now, into the widening maw below. She chanced a quick glance over at Zel, who looked at her from the keyboard, raised her eyebrows, smiled. Zel's crystal beads flashed in the light.

No rooms so fine, and gay attire,
Amid our humble huts appear;

Get past the fussy part, the humble huts, the huts that threw me off during early rehearsals. Don't think about anything but the song, Maggie told herself, even while she was singing. And the crescendo was happening naturally, her voice went up in pitch, her volume increased, and then the startling thing was that she began to hear herself inside the theatre. She was hearing her voice in the same large room she'd been inside hundreds of times, but now she was hearing it from the stage. At first, the sound came back to her as if someone else was singing in her place. But it was her own sound she was hearing. The sound of her own soprano voice.

> *Nor beds of down, or blazing fire,*
> *At night our shivering limbs to cheer.*

She understood that she was reaching the audience, the men and women and children who had bought up every ticket and every seat, and who were sending encouragement in her direction in a way that she could feel, physically, in her muscles and bones, in her heart and lungs.

Her legs became stronger. In the instant of realizing that she was listening to her own sound, she also realized that she had begun to sing with confidence. She allowed her nervousness to drop away.

> *Alas! No friends come near our cot,*
> *The red-breasts only find the way;*
> *Who give their all, a simple note,*
> *At peep of dawn or parting day.*
> *But fortunes here I come to tell,*
> *Then yield me, gentle Sir, your hand;*
> *Amid those lines what thousands dwell,*
> *And bless me! What a heap of land!*

She wondered, during the applause and while she and Zel took their bows, hand in hand, if her own mother had sung the songs that Beethoven had put his quill to, the Irish and Scottish songs he'd set to music. She walked off to the left, passing a smiling Luc, who was about to take his place at the piano to play the Debussy.

"Brilliant!" Zel whispered as they moved to the side. "A wonderful start. Calhoun will have plenty to say in the *Post*. Just wait until he hears the next."

But Calhoun had gone. Called away because of an emergency. His wife was in labour. His front-row seat was empty.

Andrew's solo, with the choral group backing him, followed Luc's performance. The singers filed onto the stage, Maggie and Zel among them, and took their prearranged places. Even while they positioned themselves in two arced rows with Andrew at the front near the piano, students from the high school theatre group were tiptoeing in the wings, preparing to set up their tableau after intermission. The chorus was to remain onstage for the Vaughan Williams, and Zel would be back at the piano for that, while Luc would take his place in front of the singers, his wonderful, expressive hands and body leading them into the rousing opening of "Let All the World in Every Corner Sing."

From where Maggie stood as part of the backup to "Annabelle Lee," she peered down into the dimmed theatre at the third row centre, where Am should be. But his seat, like Calhoun's, was empty. He must, then. He must know.

DURING INTERMISSION, THE SIDE DOOR WAS OPENED AND pushed back. From backstage the singers were remarking on the thick and unusual winter fog. A few stood about outside;

some peered through the doorway. The high school thespians were setting up their "Peace for All Nations" tableau and had donned costumes: uniformed soldiers; diplomats carrying portfolios of documents; men of the cloth; representatives from multiple nations; men and women wearing the robes of kings and queens, others wearing Ottoman fez and Arab headdress. At one side of the stage, a woman and her children depicted the family at the hearth, the mother standing in strength and looking off in the distance as if defying the world, daring it to make war again. Several arbitrators of peace, wearing suits and top hats, were hunched around maps spread out over a round table. Others held a banner across the back of the stage declaring: THIS MUST NEVER HAPPEN AGAIN!

Before the second half of the programme began, Maggie went through the Gilbert and Sullivan silently, in a corner, off by herself behind the curtains. She kept pushing thoughts of Am away. She had to focus. She had to tell the story of the song, put the text across, enunciate the consonants, remember where the stops should be, keep her air flowing. She talked to herself, reviewed the places where she should slow, knowing that Luc, on piano, would follow every nuance of expression she was about to deliver. She loved the lines. She loved to sing the words about "the sun and I."

But it was onstage, close to the end of the concert and during Elgar's "Peace, Gentle Peace," when she fully understood what was happening through her voice, through her singing, through all of the voices around her. Hope was expressed when the singers asked that peace "return and come." Hope was expressed with the tender drying of the "mourner's tears."

Yes, there was hope, and healing, too. Through Luc's playing of "Liebestraum," through every one of the selections offered. Each person in the audience was poised to join in with the rousing "Land of Hope and Glory." The anticipation could be felt by every singer. But only moments before that, the completion of "Peace, Gentle Peace," with its mood of calm and serenity, permitted a palpable hope that sifted out over the listeners, most of whose lives, in one way or another, had been affected by war. For those few moments the mood filled the space and encircled every man, woman and child. The soloists stood in strength, side by side, Andrew's tenor and Corby's bass, and Zel's dusky alto next to Maggie's soprano. The chorus sang behind them, all of the singers delivering what their art had taught them, what their music director had guided them to create, what their spirit allowed them to do.

Chapter Twenty-Six

EVERYONE WOULD BE AT NAYLOR'S. PEOPLE HE knew, people he was close to. Dermot and Agnes, Tress wearing her fancy new watch, friends and relatives from town and outlying farms. Maybe Oak would be there, too. It wouldn't be the first time Oak changed from overalls to proper trousers to go to the theatre; he loved the moving pictures and could be found at Naylor's on many a Saturday afternoon. Mags, in her green velvet dress, would be singing for a large audience, a big night for her. But Am would not be there to listen. He hadn't told her; he'd made the decision after she left. She'd said goodbye more than an hour ago, leaving early to warm up with the other singers. She'd left his ticket on the kitchen table, third row centre, where he liked to sit for any performance.

He didn't feel well enough to go. He had taken a pink pill, and that was helping. Maybe the pain really was in his mind. Maybe Dr. Clark had been right when he'd told Am he was as strong as a bull. Later, after the concert, after Mags returned, Am would tell her he'd been suffering from something, but he didn't know what. If she cared to know. As if she didn't already know. Maybe he would confront her. What he couldn't do was sit in an audience and watch her onstage with the music director—the two of them performing together.

He wasn't going to think about that now. He climbed up to the tower and pulled the flask of whisky out from behind the beam. There was plenty left; he and Kenan would finish it off. He knew Kenan would be outside once the streets were clear of theatre-goers. He would watch for the boy's inimitable stride, even through the fog. He would intercept.

Am poured his first drink, gulped it back and kept a steady watch through the clock. By the time he spotted Kenan, he had two drinks under his belt. He went down to the street without a coat and called out. Kenan was surprised to see Am at home and came up the ladder behind him, hoisting himself with his good arm. Both men knew there would be a hubbub later, the street filled with revellers. Neither wanted to be part of the din. Am wanted more to drink, and now he had company. He was cheered by the younger man's presence.

He poured a whisky for Kenan and another for himself. The two clinked glasses and swallowed it back. Am hadn't asked his brother where he'd obtained the whisky. He didn't care if it came from a blind pig or from a speakeasy farther along the shores of Lake Ontario. Dermot was now calling himself a wine merchant in an attempt to get around the authorities. No matter what the changes in the laws were, Dermot found a way around them.

Am drank a fourth and Kenan a second glass of whisky. When that was gone, Am urged his nephew to split the rest with him. Am's pain had completely disappeared.

He peered out between the numerals of the clock. The winter fog was taking serious hold of Main Street. Most people would be inside the theatre, where he should be. Where Mags believed he'd be.

Kenan had removed his jacket and was sitting comfortably on a crossbeam. He looked over at Am, who hunched back down on the stool in front of the south-facing clock.

"When you learn that someone is lying to you," said Am, staring at the floor, "you start to lose your bearings. That's what's happening under my own roof. This roof. Mags and I were devastated by what happened to our family, and we made the mistake of living with the sorrow pushed under like a deadhead, a hidden threat under water. We did that instead of dragging it up into view so we could talk about it, try to make ourselves better."

A long silence followed and neither man spoke.

"We might have been afraid of what would happen if we did talk," Am finally went on. "There was plenty of anger, too. I was angry that there was nothing anyone could do to stop those two utterly useless deaths. There was nothing *I* could do."

How many layers of anger? he wondered. How many layers had he erected between himself and his own feelings during the intervening years? Now Mags wanted a different kind of life, that was clear. Well, he didn't like the way things were either, but he didn't know how to get to a different kind of life.

"There must be things that can't be fixed, things that have to be smoothed over," said Kenan. "Between every man and his wife." He drank the last of his whisky. He wasn't sure of his ground here. He was thinking of his own marriage and what needed fixing. He was thinking that things were somewhat better around his place right now.

Am thought they'd sat there long enough, so he walked over to the opening in the floor, certain that the tower was swaying. He gripped an overhead beam until the tower stopped moving, and he stepped onto the top rung of the ladder. He felt Kenan's hand on his arm, steadying. He descended without a word and missed the bottom rung, but corrected his balance in time. Even so, his foot hit the floor with a thump. Kenan was right behind. They left the hatch open above. Am backed into the cupboard of sand that hid the pendulum cables, and banged his right shoulder hard against its door. He and Kenan laughed as if something hilarious had just happened. They laughed even harder when they put on their boots. But Am sobered suddenly as he remembered that he had a duty to perform. It was New Year's Eve; the bell was supposed to be connected to the workings of the clock so that it could ring in the new year at the stroke of twelve. Back up to the tower they went, leaving their boots on as they climbed. Am fiddled with shaft and gears and connections. The clapper was set to strike the giant bell in the centre of the tower. His familiarity with the mechanism allowed him some clarity, and when he was satisfied, or at least half satisfied, he went back down the ladder. He took the side stairs from the apartment down to the street, glad to have Kenan with him.

The hell with Mags, he thought. The hell with the concert. The hell with the music director. Who did he think he was? The hell with Calhoun, the editor of the *Post*, who had tried to make life difficult—and public—because of a little snow scattered around the rink.

The hell with New Year's Eve.

He started laughing again, and now he let Kenan take the lead, thinking the younger man would head toward the rink or the skaters' shack or maybe the widow's barn. But Kenan surprised him. He took to the centre of the road and walked into the night and the fog, toward the opposite end of town. Because it was New Year's Eve, the rink had to be avoided. There would be skaters and revellers out there until after midnight. The skaters' shack would be kept open; the fire would stay lit in the stove. A faint glow from a light on the pole at one end of the rink, a dim glow like an aura, signalled inside the fog as the two men turned away.

Am wondered if Kenan was becoming used to the idea of being outside, with people moving around. Or the *risk* of people moving around. There was still no one in sight along the road. He didn't know if Kenan spoke to anyone when he went out on his night walks. That wasn't the kind of thing Kenan talked about in the tower, or in the back veranda of his house when Am was visiting.

The air was damp, and Am didn't speak any of these thoughts aloud. He figured that if he did, he would start laughing again. Laughing at nothing. What did he have to laugh about? He rubbed at his shoulder where he'd bumped into the pendulum cupboard. He was beginning to be more concerned about paying attention to his feet, because each step was now demanding his attention. The distance between the soles of his boots and the surface of the road was not measuring up the way it should. With some steps, his feet came down heavily; with others, the road rose up to meet them. He needed to stay upright, didn't want to end up with a broken leg because of hidden ice on the road.

As usual, Kenan had his hood pulled up, his face partly covered. It didn't bother Am to look at Kenan's face; he was used to him. The scars had never bothered him anyway, once he'd paid his first visit. This was Kenan, who had grown up in the town and gone off to war. The same boy he always was, as far as Am was concerned. Even if Kenan himself was aware of having changed. Suffered. Yes, that was the word. The boy had suffered, and the memories of the war had not let go of his mind.

They passed the hotel and Am peered through the windows, wondering who was looking after the place. If Dermot and Agnes were at Naylor's listening to Mags sing, then their oldest son, Bernard, must be in charge. Bernard pretty well managed most things at the hotel now, which gave Dermot a break to spend his time whatever way he wanted. Crowing about his automobile, for one.

He thought of the concert, which would soon be over. No one expected Kenan to sit in the middle of a crowded theatre, but Am would be missed. Everyone in town would expect him to be there to hear Mags sing. Didn't matter. It was too late now.

Kenan was walking past the corner of Main and Mill and he continued in a westerly direction. The night was darker, the fog thicker, once they left the lights of town behind. Am's feet were becoming less and less reliable, but he was doing his best to keep up. The boy walked with such uncanny confidence, he could probably see with his good eye closed. Am wondered how many shots of whisky they had downed in the tower, but the thought vanished before he could calculate the answer. His arms and legs felt as if they were flailing now, and he told Kenan they'd better head back. He *thought* he told Kenan; he wasn't sure he'd spoken the words aloud. He must have, because Kenan did a brisk about-turn, as if he were in uniform again. Am stumbled to try to keep up.

They had retraced their steps and were passing Dermot's hotel for the second time when Am weaved in front of Kenan and led him around to the drive sheds behind house and hotel. Dermot loved his horses, but he also loved his Dodge Brothers Touring Car. He was as proud of his auto as he was of any of his mares.

The car was where it always was, under a wooden overhang specially erected to protect it from wind and blowing snow.

Am walked to the car and threw back the big tarp that had been spread over the top. He put his hands on the door and pulled it open and squeezed himself in behind the wheel, holding himself sideways and upright as long as he could before he collapsed, laughing, down onto the seat. There was so little room, the only way he could get himself in was by bending double. He decided that he'd drive the damned car up and down the street to celebrate the new year. And why not? The year coming in couldn't be any worse than the one on the way out. His brother wouldn't be happy, but he'd get over it. If he didn't want anyone to steal his car, why didn't he secure it better? From the tower, Am had seen Dermot drive it up the street only the day before. In any case, Dermot and Agnes were at the concert and wouldn't know. Am would steer it back under the

overhang and cover it over before Dermot had a chance to leave
the theatre. Am had no idea how much time had elapsed since
he and Kenan had finished off the whisky. The clock faces on
the tower couldn't be seen through the fog, not from this far.
Otherwise, he'd have glanced up to check.

"Do you know how to start this thing?" Kenan was standing
directly in front of the car, staring at him through the fog with
his one eye. He had pushed the hood of his jacket back and his
head was bare. He was grinning.

"Of course I do. Do you?"

"I can turn the crank with one hand. Do you have the key?"

"Of course I have the key. Damned fool leaves it right here
for anyone to grab."

Kenan was in a half-crouch in front of the Dodge. He was
muttering and laughing to himself. He peered up at Am, who
was flicking switches, pushing and pulling at knobs. Kenan
turned the crank: up, back to the side, up and back. It seemed
to take forever, but the car suddenly sputtered and Am gave a
shout. Kenan raced around to the passenger side and yanked at
the door and half fell into his seat. They were laughing like crazy
now, and couldn't stop. Not while the car jerked and spluttered
and jerked again, and started to move. Am barely managed to
get it out from behind the hotel without bumping into the side
of the building, and finally, they were out on the street.

Am turned left. Silver arrows of light exploded like fire-
works before his eyes as he tried to get his bearings on the road.
He felt that icicles were being hurled at him from every direction. He blinked and blinked again. He ducked. Tried to clear
his vision. He bent a bit lower and peered through the bottom

part of the windshield, but he could make out no more than the frozen ruts that rose up in front of the wheels.

He stopped the car in the middle of nowhere, anywhere, though the vehicle took its time shuddering to a halt. He was aware that he was laughing like a fool again.

"Get out there and be my beacon," he said to Kenan between gasps. "I need you to give direction. Get out there and climb up onto the hood and straddle it and pray that it holds your weight. Dermot will take after the two of us if we put so much as a scratch on this car. Use your good eye to see what it can see and point your good hand so I can follow the direction you're pointing."

Kenan doubled up to get out of the car, and he climbed onto the hood, his long legs dangling. His body was rocking with laughter that couldn't be controlled. It kept rising up, hiccupping out of him. He was hearing the voice of his friend Hugh: *"I plan to come out laughing, and you will too, Kenan. Even if it's the laughter of madmen."*

"That's exactly what we are," Kenan said aloud, to the fog. His drunken thoughts whirled through his brain. "We are madmen. Raising war, raising hell, trying to raise peace. Dying along the way, or surviving—to do what? To kick up our heels, to try to love our wives, to find decent work, to drink whisky in a tower and steal a man's auto . . ." His thoughts gave out. He almost fell off the hood.

The two of them bumped and rattled along, splitting their sides. They could have walked as fast as the car was moving. Am steered blindly from inside. Kenan was in front of Am, but on the outside, one-eyed, pointing this way and that with his good arm and steering the course for both. He was trying to lead the way down the middle of Main Street, but a sudden memory of planes flying freely above the trenches of grimy mired men made him stretch his arm out horizontally. His torso swayed, weaving back and forth as if he were flying.

He heard a shout from behind the opening in the windshield.

"What the hell kind of direction is that? Do you want . . . fly . . . right up off . . . road?"

Am was having trouble with his speech. The words were bumping into one another, skewing his thoughts. He should have carried the big flask down with him, but it was probably empty. Was it? Had they finished it off?

Kenan was still trying to fly on the hood. Am heard him give out a whoop of laughter and he tried to stop the car, but again, the effort took some doing. They both felt a large thump. When the vehicle came to a halt, it was halfway up the boardwalk, directly opposite the theatre. There was no starting it up again.

The doors of the theatre opened. People, young and old, spilled out of the foyer and down the steps on either side of the entrance. They collected on the street, some still singing "Auld Lang Syne," which they'd begun inside. Others were peering through the fog and up toward the clocks, waiting for the reconnected bell to reverberate in the tower and send its echoes out over the streets as it chimed in an untarnished new year.

Dermot was one of the first people out of the theatre, Agnes right behind him. He saw his own car through the fog, saw his laughing brother playing the fool, saw his son-in-law collapsed in laughter on top of the hood. He came striding across the street and left Agnes to walk home along the boardwalk, following the crowd.

Tress was still inside, waiting to congratulate her aunt. People from the town were trying to decide if that was Kenan Oak sliding off the hood of Dermot's car across the street. The tower clock struck twelve and the bell began to ring. All eyes looked up to the tower. Am stared up, too, as if he were new to the town, glad to be present while a bell chimed in the new year. And then he realized it was his clock, his tower, his bell, and he said aloud, to no one—as no one was listening—"At least I got one goddamn thing right."

Maggie was spared the sight. She and Zel and Luc and Andrew and Corby and the entire choral society had begun to celebrate on the open stage. They were hugging and laughing and shaking hands, heady with the elation that accompanied their success. Luc was already beginning to plan, talking about a more ambitious choral work for a spring concert.

It was only when Maggie was home again, only when she removed her green velvet gown, that she realized she had lost her locket. It must have become unfastened. Or the chain had broken. It must have slipped from her neck.

She retraced her steps in the apartment, put on her coat, went back down the stairs, opened the side door. Am still wasn't home; he would have gone back to the hotel with Dermot and the limping auto. She didn't know where Kenan was. He might be with Am and Dermot, but she suspected that her nephew was at home with Tress. Maggie had been told about the commotion outside the theatre, about Dermot taking charge of his auto, but she had remained onstage, where, for this one evening, she felt she belonged. She had stayed and celebrated with her friends.

Now she checked the snow-cleared path leading away from the door of the building. She took a few steps farther out into the street. The locket was in none of those places. She would have to return to the theatre tomorrow. She would have to look there.

She put her hand to her throat, and wept.

DESERONTO POST, January 1920

Local Items

Your editor and his wife announce, with great delight, the arrival of their baby girl, Breeda Calhoun, born January 1, only moments after the bell in the clock tower rang in the new year.

Special note: Immediately after the esteemed T.S. MacIntosh gave his excellent recitation, which opened the New Year's concert at Naylor's, I was called away from my reviewer's seat because of my wife's condition. Therefore, and to my regret, I am unable to report on the evening's entertainment. If someone with nib in hand cares to step forward to write up the grand occasion, I shall be happy to meet with said person. The performers, singers, soloists, musicians, as well as the high school students who created the tableau, deserve to have their efforts lauded. Also, those citizens who were unable to attend deserve to read an account of the evening. Drop in at the office of the *Post* and let me know if you would like to write a review.

An ice boat recently made the distance from Trenton to Belleville in one hour.

The town's annual masquerade party will be held on the rink on the bay in late January. That event is only a few weeks away, so start planning your costumes. People are expected from near and far to join the celebrations. As happens every year at this time, bodies will be whirling hither and thither in all directions, by means of the skate.

Found on Main Street: A woman's gold locket upon which the letter *H* is inscribed. The finder has conferred a favour on the owner by leaving it under lock and key at the office of the *Post*. The owner of the locket may present herself to the editor in order to identify and claim said item.

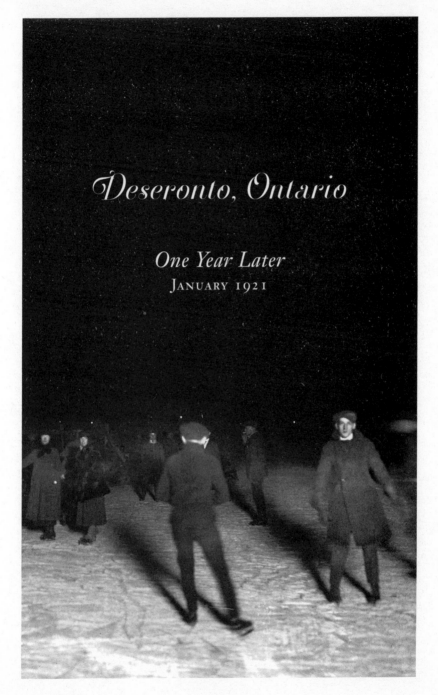

Deseronto, Ontario

One Year Later
JANUARY 1921

Chapter Twenty-Seven

Deseronto: January 1, 1921

Dear Maggie,

You asked me not to write until I heard from you. So you will understand how relieved I was to receive your letter when the post office reopened after Christmas.

It is New Year's Day. How could I not think of you today? I think of you every day, my dear friend.

So much has happened during the past year, so many decisions were made, and yet, at this moment, I am thinking of how you sang onstage exactly one year ago. All of those beautiful notes, well-rehearsed lines, all drifting out into the theatre air and vanishing. Those were moments of triumph. You captivated not only your audience but also the rest of us, your colleagues, who stood beside and behind you. No matter what else we do with our lives, Maggie, music will soothe and calm us. Music will last, and outlast, and cast its spell and enter our souls and connect us across time and distance. We must believe this, both of us, all of us.

Now, having thought of last year's concert, I must add what a shame it was that no one took up Calhoun's offer to review the concert for the Post. *A write-up would have endured in print. Or perhaps not. Even so, for years to come, people who were privileged to be in the audience will remember the wonderful soprano voice of Maggie O'Neill. (I'd have written the review myself if I hadn't been one of the singers!)*

But the news you await is Hanora's news, of course. I visit as often as I can, not only to send a report, but because she creates so much happiness around her. She is healthy and plump-cheeked and beautiful, just as she was in Toronto in November. It goes without saying that she brings her new parents more joy than they have known since Kenan came home from the war. Tress has stopped working for the time being, though she visits her parents at the hotel every couple of days. Agnes and Dermot, with two grandchildren to love, have embraced their new roles without partiality. They bestowed new carriages upon the offspring, and for a few short weeks before snow fell, the town was treated to occasional glimpses of two young cousins being wheeled about, side by side—the elder of the two crowing with delight, the younger, little Hanora—it seems almost certain that her eyes will be green—staring up at all who stopped to greet her. Grania gets to town frequently, as her new home is not so far away.

I visit Tress and Kenan at their home, which is where I see Hanora. No one discusses what so few of us know. You wondered, in your letter, about the rest of the town. Not a person, I believe, has made the connection to you. Especially as it's generally known that you moved to Oswego so early last spring, to be close to your sister's family. Hanora has been accepted as any other child is accepted. Nothing is known except that the adoption took place "away," in the city. When I think of that day, I believe we live in the Dark Ages. Of one thing, I am certain: everyone involved is capable of closing around this secret.

My concern is for you, Maggie, and I will be more than happy to see you when we meet again—perhaps in Oswego, perhaps in Toronto when steamer traffic resumes. I do want you to know that Lukas was able to hold Hanora in his arms before he moved away in the fall. He adores and loves the child, as he does you. As difficult as this has been for both of you, I believe he understands your decision.

I, too, am trying to understand, now that I know the entire story. I try to understand what you are going through, knowing that Am was unable to accept the child as his own. You tell me that you stay with him because of what you both had, because of what you were together in the past, because of what you both lost. Tragedy, it seems, is measured out in unequal parts among us. I know that your heart must be broken yet again.

If, whenever you travel to Toronto, you meet with Lukas, I will probably never know. Perhaps your life in Oswego has settled into a bearable pattern, with your sister near and with Am having found work. You must create something new for yourself, Maggie, and I hope you will continue to sing. I hope that you will find a way to carry on, and that music and song will always be included in your life.

I will continue to see Hanora as often as I can. I have passed on the locket to Tress, and she understands that it is to be given to the baby when she is older. She understands that she is to tell Hanora the locket arrived with her at birth, a gift from her birth mother. Someday, who knows, Hanora may own her life story.

Tress and Kenan will send their own news. I know you will destroy this and all of my letters as they arrive, as we agreed. I wish I were there to help support you, Maggie. But we will meet soon. My house and the workroom are completely filled with boarders, and I shall have some income to spare for travel.

Several of us have worked at keeping the choral society going, now that Lukas has moved away. And though we had no New Year's concert last evening, we hope to prepare a spring performance. A new music director will eventually be found.

I'll end this letter now, and will go directly to the piano, which has found its way back to my dining room. I will play something peaceful and beautiful by Chopin, and I will think of you.

Write again soon, my friend.

With love,

Zel

ACKNOWLEDGMENTS

The following important books (among many) contributed to my knowledge of the period: *Winning the Second Battle: Canadian Veterans and the Return to Civilian Life, 1915–1930* by Desmond Morton and Glenn Wright; *Paris 1919: Six Months That Changed the World* by Margaret MacMillan; *Letters of a Canadian Stretcher Bearer* edited by Anna Chapin Ray; *Testament of Experience* by Vera Brittain; *Melodies and Memories* by Nellie Melba; *A History of Music in Canada, 1534–1914* by Helmut Kallmann. I'm grateful to have had access to the few surviving issues of the 1919 *Deseronto Post*, as well as an issue of *The Napanee Express*. CBC audio recordings of First World War soldiers were helpful (at Library and Archives Canada).

The epigraph is from a poem by Helen Humphreys: "For Jackie, Who Will Never Read This" in *Anthem*, published by Brick Books, 1999, used with permission.

The four lines from the poem about "War and Love" are cited from a yearbook in the Deseronto Archives and date to

1858, perhaps earlier. The choral adaptation of "Annabelle Lee" is based on Edgar Allan Poe's poem "Annabel Lee."

The great Australian diva Nellie Melba sang for the Heliconian Club, founded in Toronto in 1909, but not at the present Heliconian Hall, which was purchased by the club in 1923 and renovated. The club met elsewhere until acquiring the present building, a former church in Yorkville.

The sausage story (about Enrico Caruso and Nellie Melba) is recorded in several places, including on the website of the Victoria and Albert Museum: www.vam.ac.uk/content/articles/e/ enrico-caruso/.

THANKS TO: Jackie Kaiser, always supportive friend and agent; my good friend Phyllis Bruce, who listened to my ideas about this story and encouraged me from its beginnings; Jennifer Lambert at HarperCollins, for her enthusiasm, editorial suggestions and follow-up; managing editor, the truly professional Noelle Zitzer, who never lets me down; art director Alan Jones; copy editor Janice Weaver; the informed, innovative and exemplary Amanda Hill at Deseronto Archives, for professional help with historical references, and for responding in detail to my questions about 1919 Deseronto; Norman Takeuchi; Marion Takeuchi; Cathie Vick; Howie Wheatley; Ann Moore; Yehudi Wyner; Terry Flynn; Jack Granatstein, for pointing me in the direction of post-war books; Margaret McCoy (Soprano) and Mary Gordon (Alto), for agreeing to meet with me to discuss their love of singing; Matthew Larkin; Jordan de Souza; the Ottawa Choral Society, for permitting me to sit in on rehearsals; Barbara Clubb, for making arrangements for me to visit the Bytown Voices. A huge thanks to Eric Friesen, for meeting me in a café off Highway 401 and helping to plan the concert. Thanks to the late Barbara Adams, born 1913, who recounted stories of her early life on PEI's north shore; also to her son, Don Adams, of Sea View. The first sanatorium in PEI was at Emyvale, built in 1915 and closed 1922 (http://www.lung.ca/tb/tbhistory/people/dalton.html).

Tuberculosis, a major problem for returning soldiers across Canada, during and at the end of the Great War, remained an issue well into the 1960s, when I worked at a sanatorium in Sainte-Agathe-des-Monts, Québec. The incidence of tuberculosis decreased for a time, but it has again become a global concern.

Love and thanks to: my daughter, Samantha Leiko Itani, for proofing; my son, Russell Satoshi Itani, Flautist, for advice about music; Aileen Jane Itani, Soprano—who sang in my office, sang in my dining room, sang to me over the phone, and responded to my barrage of questions about "voice" while I created Maggie; Dorothy Mitts; Joel Oliver, for jumping on the ice on the Bay of Quinte with me, and for skating photos and prints found in antique stores and flea markets; Larry Scanlan, my shadow-skater, who gets out there every week on Kingston winter ice and has the words to describe. I must also acknowledge here extended family members who have discussed with me the sad facts of infant and child mortality in our own early pioneer families—proof of which becomes all too real when one visits old graveyards across this country.

Finally, I thank Sally Hawks, who insisted.